CRY FOR HELP

Also by Steve Mosby

The Third Person
The Cutting Crew
The 50/50 Killer

CRY FOR HELP

Steve Mosby

First published in Great Britain in 2008 by Orion Books,
an imprint of The Orion Publishing Group Ltd
Orion House, 5 Upper Saint Martin's Lane
London WC2H 9EA

An Hachette Livre UK Company

1 3 5 7 9 10 8 6 4 2

A CIP catalogue record for this book
is available from the British Library.

ISBN (Hardback) 978 0 7528 7414 2
ISBN (Trade Paperback) 978 0 7528 7415 9

Typeset at The Spartan Press Ltd,
Lymington, Hants

Printed in Great Britain at Mackays of Chatham plc,
Chatham, Kent

The Orion Publishing Group's policy is to use papers that
are natural, renewable and recyclable products and
made from wood grown in sustainable forests. The logging
and manufacturing processes are expected to conform to
the environmental regulations of the country of origin.

www.orionbooks.co.uk

For Lynn

Acknowledgements

Huge thanks to my agent, Carolyn Whitaker, and to everyone at Orion who helped with this book and the others, especially Jon Wood, Genevieve Pegg and Jade Chandler, who all have infinite patience. More personal thanks go to the usual people: Ang, J, Keleigh, Rich, Neil, Helen, Gillian, Roger, Ben, Megan, Cass and Mark. To Mum, Dad, John and Roy. Extra thanks this time to Becki and Rainy, and extra special thanks to Emma Lindley. Most of all, thanks to Lynn, for putting up with me during the long work on this one, and for being wonderful.

Prologue

'Get out of the way!'

Roger Ellis didn't stop running as he collided with the group of drunk kids. His shoulder caught the nearest, knocking him into his friends. One of them shouted something, but Roger was away by then, already dodging around the next bunch.

It was chucking-out time in the city and the pavements were crammed with people. Girls in tiny dresses were shivering and stumbling, hugging themselves as they tapped awkwardly along; lads were remonstrating with bouncers, or each other, or else leaning into taxis and haggling over prices. The ground was painted in cast-off, primary-coloured neon from the club overhangs, and the subdued thump of music from inside was punctuated by regular bellowing and cat-calls from across the street.

Roger had been a part of all this until a few minutes ago. Now it was all simply an obstacle.

He angled between another two groups as he rounded a corner – then smacked head first into a young guy in a white T-shirt, sending him sprawling against a railing. Roger stopped for a second, dazed, and saw a girl wide-eyed with shock—

'Hey!'

—and then he was running again, avoiding the man's friends as they stepped towards him from one side, and slipping past the outstretched paw of a bouncer who tried to grab him. Feet began pounding after him. But Roger was always going to be faster, and the sounds of the pursuit quickly faded away behind, until all he could hear was the sound of his own shoes, slapping hard against the pavement.

Ten years ago, at the age of nineteen, Roger had been one of the top young decathletes in the country. He didn't compete anymore, but he trained teenagers who did. Nobody was going to catch him – especially not someone reeling with drink.

He sped up: his legs stretched out and the streets flashed past, the night air roaring in his ears above the steady thump of his heartbeat. At this time of night it was quicker to run than fight his way to a taxi that would, in turn, have to fight its way out through the streets.

But as fast as Roger could run, it wasn't fast enough. He didn't know what was wrong, but he knew it was something, and he had a terrible feeling he was already too late.

He took another corner, heading away from the centre, and ran out into the criss-cross of junctions where the ring road scarred the edge of the city. Headlights blinded him; he heard tyres screech, a horn blaring. Someone shouted. Roger ignored it, concentrating on the street bobbing up and down towards him. Left into the industrial estate. The footpath at the end was a fairly dubious shortcut in the dark, but he took it anyway.

The whole time, his mind kept coming back to something Karli had said a couple of weeks ago.

You never really talk to anyone on the phone.

And the conversation had actually been about her – his ex-girlfriend, Alison. Roger had mentioned he hadn't spoken to her for a while, trying to make Karli jealous for some petty reason he now couldn't recall. But she hadn't taken the bait. Instead, she'd told him that: *you never really talk to anyone on the phone, anyway.* At first, Roger had thought she meant him specifically – criticising his manners – but she meant in general.

It sounds like them, she explained. *But it isn't. It's just a computer interpreting information and doing an impression of their voice.*

She'd sounded disappointed – as though reflecting that you didn't even get a real person lying to you and letting you down. So perhaps she'd taken the bait after all, and was just more intelligent than him. Whatever her reasoning, Roger had shut up about Alison.

Now, running down the footpath, he thought again about the phone call he'd just received. The number that appeared on the display had been Alison's home number, and when he'd answered it he'd heard an approximation of her voice. But it wasn't her. The person he remembered was full of enthusiasm and laughter and hope; the voice on the phone had been flat and lifeless. *Help me.* There wasn't any fear there. It sounded like she was huddled up in the corner of an empty room, whispering the words to keep ghosts away, but knowing there was nobody in the world who could hear her anymore.

Help me.

Then a pause, filled with a sound like rushing wind.

Help me.

No matter what he said, she simply kept repeating it. A few seconds later, Roger had hung up and started running.

At 3.15 a.m., he jogged to a stop outside Alison's house, then leaned down on his knees and took deep, professional breaths.

Like all the buildings on the street, hers was dark and silent. This was a quiet residential area, just outside the centre. Nobody was up at this time. Cars in shadowed driveways had been draped with dark cloth for the night, and the houses behind slept along with their owners. The only sound was the lonely hum of the streetlights. After he'd caught his breath, Roger looked up to see a solitary moth fluttering soundlessly against the nearest. It felt like the only other living thing for miles.

He walked up the short path to her house and was about to knock, but hesitated. Suddenly he felt unsure about being here. Thinking back, he could no longer explain the effect the phone call had on him, beyond that it had made his hairs stand on end. It reminded him of those tapes of static you heard on ghost documentaries, where the random, scratchy noise suddenly created an old man's laugh. *Help me*, she'd told him, but from her tone of voice it was already too late.

A breeze picked up. Behind him, hedges rustled.

Roger shivered. Then knocked.

The door moved away from his knuckles. Open a notch, it creaked back now to reveal a sliver of night-time kitchen. He listened.

Heard . . .

Something.

Roger pushed the door wider and stepped inside, and the sound resolved itself. It was the buzz of flies, moving through the kitchen, whining towards him and then away. He flicked on the light and saw what they were interested in. The room was filthy. A few old plates rested on the counter, pasta sauce dried and cracked on them like old skin, and small white dots of mould peppering the creases. Another plate edged out of the full sink like a pale fin. There was a web of mist on the water around it.

Jesus, the smell . . .

'Alison?'

The dark house soaked up the sound and gave nothing back.

He went through to the living room and searched quickly for the light switch. The dark felt too ominous, as though someone might be standing in a corner, watching him. The lounge, at least, was empty. And cleaner than the kitchen, too.

But too cold, he realised. Like the heating hadn't been on in days.

The wooden staircase was built into the edge of the living room, and he moved up it cautiously, keeping an eye on the gloomy landing above. Shivering slightly, he recognised the same adrenalin that he used to get before races. Again, he was sure that something was wrong. Alison had called him from here, but you could tell an empty house when you walked into one, and this place seemed more than empty. It felt abandoned.

On the landing, the smell hit him properly. He pushed her bedroom door open.

Roger stared at the bed in shock, his mind refusing to accept what he was seeing. It couldn't be. The thing that was lying there . . . it *looked* like Alison – but that was impossible because . . .

His mobile started ringing.

For a few numb seconds, he let it. Then he took it out of his

4

jacket pocket, the screen glowing a soft green in the bedroom. Finally, he glanced down.

The Caller ID on the screen said:

[Alison Mobile]

Shaking now, Roger pressed the button and then held the phone to his ear, staring firmly at the object on the bed, which he knew deep down was his ex-girlfriend. For a moment, all he could hear through the phone was the rushing sound.

And then, in that same flat voice, Alison said, 'Help me.'

Part One

Chapter One
Sunday 7th August

I met Tori by magic two years ago.

It was on an otherwise average night at Edward's Bar in the city centre. It was one of those places where they don't serve pints, only bottles, shots or cocktails, all at prices that make you feel you should be somewhere better. There was bar space for about five people, assuming they hunched their shoulders. If you actually wanted to sit with your drink, you had the choice of perching on stools with supermodel legs, or else hunkering down on fat leather settees round shin-high coffee tables. That was if you got in early. Otherwise you had to stand, and ignore the sensation of your shoes slowly sticking to the tiles.

Everything was a misfire. When he had started the place, the manager – who was called George, not Edward, which is exactly what I mean – had hoped for a slightly better-groomed clientele. The customers liked to think they were posh and trendy, but if anyone genuinely well-heeled had ventured inside they'd probably have been robbed in the toilets by someone who would have gone back and finished their drink afterwards.

George persevered. A friend introduced him to me and Rob, and George decided that a couple of roving amateur magicians might add a touch of class. Not a bad idea in itself. Unfortunately, it was another slight misfire, because he got us.

Rob and I would work the room separately. Rob did a fairly impressive mentalism routine, whereas I concentrated more on sleight-of-hand: close-up stuff, most of the time with cards. We weren't classy, not by any stretch of the imagination: the best you could say was we started off well. By the end of the evening, I was usually more drunk than the punters, telling them secrets that the Magic Circle would have frowned upon, while Rob would be staring into some girl's eyes, attempting to guess a phone number off her.

We made beer money. And, one night, I met Tori.

The secret to handling a group of drunken strangers is picking out the leaders and winning them over. So I didn't notice her straight away. I targeted a couple of her friends instead, as they seemed to be the ones holding court at the table.

The most vocal, a guy called Choc, was a small black man in his late thirties, wearing an unironed shirt, cheap suit trousers and old, white trainers. His hair and beard were bobbled to the same short length, and from both his manner and his breath I guessed he'd been drinking for a while: possibly several days. Sitting beside him, Cardo was taller, rangier and in his early twenties, dressed in baggy sports gear and a baseball cap that hid most of his face. In contrast to Choc, he was slouched and uncommunicative: more interested in his mobile than the people beside him. But I did a trick – bare hands, sleeves rolled up, coin produced from behind his ear – and he broke into a sheepish grin, like a teenager whose cool had slipped.

Aside from those two, the rest of the table was a weird mixture. It felt like a gathering of strangers who'd all, if they were honest, probably rather be somewhere else. As I worked through my routines, I slowly figured out the glue between them all was the girl on one end.

I perched on the arm of the settee across from her.

'Hi there. What's your name?'

'Tori.'

'Nice to meet you, Tori. I'm Dave.'

She was small and self-contained, wearing her long brown hair tied back, and dressed in a flimsy, pale-blue shirt. The top two buttons were undone, revealing a silver cross on a necklace that I would later learn belonged to her sister, who'd died four years ago. Her face was pretty without being beautiful, but there was something about her that caught my attention as soon as I sat down there. Throughout the earlier part of my routine she'd been quiet, mostly just sitting back and smiling to herself, as though content to enjoy the evening from a distance, comfortable in her own thoughts.

I didn't know it properly then, but this was the truth about Tori. Most people, by their mid twenties have usually been messed around with, and they've hardened themselves up as a result. They take longer to trust someone: to relax the protective shell they've formed. Tori wasn't like that; she offered everything about herself without any kind of guard. That's a rare thing.

'Okay,' I said. 'I want you to tell me when to stop.'

I held a pack of cards face-down, then riffled slowly down the edge.

'Stop.'

I did: not quite halfway down. I cut the deck at that point and, turning my head away, held it up for everyone at the table to see.

'That's the card you cut to. I have no idea what it is, but I want you to remember it.'

'Okay.'

I put the deck back together, then handed it to her.

'Have a look through, and make sure the cards are all different, so you know I'm not cheating.'

I watched her fan them out towards her. Her hands were very delicate and precise.

'That's good. Now you might think I know where in the pack your card is, so I want you to shuffle them as much as you like.'

She did, her actions methodical and unhurried.

Then I went through a few more things she should do. By the time we were finished, the cards were shuffled, cut, back inside the packet again, and she'd chosen a bemused man standing nearby to hold the resealed deck for us.

I looked into her eyes.

'Okay. I can't see him. He's not making any sounds or giving me any clues. Right?'

'Right.'

We'd both leaned forwards a little now, and she was looking back at me, amused and unintimidated. I realised that although her face was pretty, her eyes – big and brown – were fully beautiful. For a moment, the trick almost got away from me.

'Okay.' I breathed deeply, apparently making a real effort, then said to one side: 'Sir? Can you tell me – do you smoke?'

'Er, yeah.'

I nodded once, as though it mattered. 'I thought so. Tori, would you do me a favour and look under the ashtray, please?'

She lifted it up to reveal a single card lying face down.

'Is that the card you cut to?'

It bowed in the middle as she fumbled slightly, and then a smile broke across her face when she turned it.

'Yeah.' She looked across at the guy holding the deck, then back at me, and it felt like my heart beat a little harder. Just once. 'Well, that's impressive.'

I smiled and stood up. 'Thank you.'

I'd noticed three couples in the group around the table, discounting Choc and Cardo, and then her. It was why I'd gone for that particular card: a small flourish that Rob swore – and occasionally boasted – by. I wasn't so good with the cheesy come-ons, but something about her had made me think: *why not?*

'Two of hearts. You know what that means? Maybe the man of your dreams is here tonight.' Whatever effect Rob managed with this, it sounded a lot less suave coming from me. 'But anyway – thanks for having me, and enjoy the rest of your evening.' I nodded around the table. 'All of you.'

I got a small round of applause, Choc clapping like he was smacking something hard, over and over, one step from fucking wolf-whistling, and I acknowledged it all gratefully before moving on to the next table. And later on, when I was done for the night and a few drinks down, I tentatively went back.

It's at this point that I'd like to be able to tell you it was perfect. But it wasn't. It turned out that Tori and I had very little in common. She didn't drink, for example; I did. Her CD collection consisted mostly of women playing acoustic guitars or pianos very quietly. I liked heavier stuff, but never dared put any on in case it bruised her. I watched crap, whereas she knew a lot about obscure foreign arthouse films, and for some reason wanted to see more of them. And she was ludicrously well read: an English graduate with shelves full of poetry and proper literature, which she was actually capable of *discussing*. When we were together, I found I was always editing myself in a bid to keep us together, and a relationship like that is never going to last.

Ours lasted for two and a half months. I spent most of it feeling very confused with myself, and I could tell that she did too. We both liked each other a lot, but for some reason it wasn't enough. There was destined to be no happy ending. But at least there was an ending. The night it finished, we were lying in bed together in her house: on our backs, arms touching. We both knew it was over.

'This is probably where it should stop, isn't it?' Tori said.

I forced myself not to disagree. Something told me not to ruin this the way I might have ruined other things in the past.

'I think so,' I said. 'It's not what I wanted to happen.'

'Me neither. I'm sorry it's not worked out. I really am.'

'Can we be friends?'

'Of course.' She turned on her side to face me, and I did the same. Huddled up together, she smiled and touched my face. 'Always.'

I looked at her and, even though I knew it was right, I felt about as sad as I could remember. I'd never been in a relationship that had ended up this way. There'd always been cheating, or screaming, or just growing indifference; whereas with Tori, I felt none of those things. Whatever would or wouldn't work between us, something about her mattered to me more than I could explain, and I wanted her to be part of my life.

'If you ever need me,' I said, 'I'll be there for you. No matter what.'

She smiled at me again. 'The same.'

And then, perhaps stupidly, we made love for the last time. It felt different from all the times before. There was an emotional connection that had always been missing in the past, perhaps because we'd admitted now that we were nothing more than friends, and that, at least, was something we didn't have to pretend.

Over time, Tori moved slowly but surely into the periphery of my existence, but she was never far from my thoughts, and I never stopped caring about her. Because what else is there? If someone's important to you then you make an effort to keep them.

So I never forgot what I said to her that night: if she ever needed me, I'd be there. No matter what.

And, two years later, I found out exactly what that meant.

It's a rare thing to know you've just had the worst day of your life, but this was mine. At the time it was true, but I didn't know how bad things would get afterwards. Later on, it would just be the day when everything began to fall apart.

I woke up at eight o'clock, and was up by five past. It's usually the way for me – ever since I was little, my body has felt programmed to burn the candle at one end as a default setting, whatever happens at the other.

As it happened, the other end had been burning too, but not by choice. My mind had kept me awake last night. It had been exploring, and whenever I started to drift off, it picked that moment to nudge me awake again and show me whatever it had just found. Stuff about Emma, mostly. None of it was helpful, but it kept dredging all this shit up anyway: turning good and bad memories round and blowing the dust off them, maybe hoping that one piece or another might turn out to be gold.

Emma had been my girlfriend for the last year. I hadn't met her by magic – I'd met her on the internet – and things had been good to begin with, to the point that she'd actually moved into my small, rented flat only two and a half months after we met. We liked the same music, films, books. Things had been *great* for a while. What my subconscious had been busy searching for was the single moment when great turned into okay, or when okay had turned into indifferent. Maybe it would have settled for the shift from indifferent to suddenly miserable, but that had probably been last Monday, when Emma had told me it was over between us and moved out. Later on today, she would be calling round to collect the last boxes of her things from the lounge. The jury was still out on how that was going to feel.

Regardless, I had work to do.

I drank some coffee, ate some toast, and then took another coffee through to the study. It was really just the spare room: barely large enough to fit a couple of bookcases along one wall, a desk in the corner, and a 'second bedroom' into the estate agent's lies. As with the rest of the flat, nothing in here matched. I'd been renting the place for nearly three years, but generally bought furniture on a whim rather than as part of any overall plan. When I ran out of shelf space, for example, I bought a new bookcase, then searched for a wall where it would fit.

I sat down in a leather executive chair that still had the price tag on the lever, booted up the computer and thought about the day in front of me.

Work-wise, I had an article to write for *Anonymous Skeptic*. That was the monthly magazine Rob and I produced. We ran some magic reviews in there, but mostly we were dedicated to debunking a wide variety of New Age claims. Ghosts, psychics, UFOs, alternative therapies, crystals, anyone who uses the word 'energy' without knowing what it means – we're onto them. The piece I had to do that day was about astrology, and it was paint by numbers stuff – just a couple of pages I would have been able to write in my sleep, if I'd managed to get any.

Twenty minutes later, I was about halfway through the article when my mobile phone rang, jittering on its back on the desk. I paused, my fingers hovering over the keyboard.

[Withheld number]

I picked it up.

'Hello?'

'Dave!' I recognised Tori's voice, but already something about it sounded wrong. 'It's so good to hear you.'

'You too. Sorry – it's been ages, hasn't it?'

I realised I hadn't spoken to her properly for at least four or five months; I'd barely even emailed or texted. It was mostly because of how things had been deteriorating with Emma, who'd never been pleased I was still friends with an ex at the best of times. So I hadn't wanted to exacerbate any problems. But now, the way things had turned out, that didn't seem like much of an excuse, and I felt a twinge of guilt over the lack of contact.

'How are you doing?' I said.

'Not great. Although I've been sitting out in the sun this morning, and that's been nice. There are leaves everywhere.'

The warning bells sounded louder now.

'Where are you?'

'I'm in Staunton. I've been here a couple of days. They sectioned me.'

'What happened?'

'It was Eddie.'

Without thinking, I picked a coin off the computer table and began palming it. It was a repetitive motion to keep myself on a level: I used my middle finger to slide it down my thumb and into position, held it for a second, then dropped it into my curled fingers and started again. Coin work has always been something to occupy my hands. To help me keep calm.

'Tell me.'

She did. Tori's latest boyfriend, Eddie Berries, was a skinny little guy with long brown hair. He played music, but seemed to think that getting a job while waiting to be discovered was beneath him. He did drugs, acted flaky and for some unknown reason thought he was very important – the sort of vaguely artistic type that feels the world owes them a living and then laughs at it behind its back. But Tori had always loved 'creative' guys. They were a weak spot for her.

If it was just that, I might have put my dislike down to jealousy, but something about Eddie had bothered me from the beginning. I'd only met him a couple of times and couldn't put my finger on what it was, but it started when I saw him drape his arm proprietorially around Tori – as though she was a possession that was his by rights. Right then, I'd figured he wasn't good for her. She looked too desperate to please him, and he seemed as though he liked that.

But he appeared to make her happy. Of course, I didn't know what she was telling me now – that Eddie had been losing it for quite some time. His drug use had escalated, and he'd unravelled and become increasingly unstable, exerting more and more control over her life. Tori took medication daily, but – in his wisdom – Eddie had decided that was bad. It was a weakness, he said, to rely on pills, and he'd eventually persuaded her to abandon lithium and battle through her illness 'naturally'. Since then, there'd also been arguments and intimidation. Eddie kept putting her down: letting her know all the things that were wrong with her, all the ways she didn't measure up to being with him. How lucky she was to have him. As a result of all this, having her self-image knocked from side to side like a mouse between a cat's paws, Tori had descended into mania.

Their life together had come to a head last Wednesday, when Eddie had lost it completely and beaten her up. Tori had been taken to hospital for an overnight stay. The next day, she was sectioned for her own safety and taken to Staunton.

Despite occasional detours and distractions, the story came out simply and quickly. By the time she finished, I was still palming the coin and my face felt like it was made of iron.

'Are you okay?' I said. 'Physically, I mean.'

'My face is purple.' She laughed. I didn't.

'What about the police?'

'They're looking for him. He's disappeared off somewhere.'

I put the coin down. 'How long do you think you'll be in hospital?'

'I don't know. Until they decide I can go. At least a week.'

'Right.'

'I can have visitors, though. If you fancied coming to see me? It's so boring here.'

The computer screen had gone to screen-saver. The half-finished article was only a key-press away, but it wouldn't take long. Aside from that, there was Emma to think about. But she still had a key, and maybe it would be easier for both of us if I wasn't here when she picked up her stuff. I'd probably only make some misguided attempt to cling on to her – the relationship equivalent of throwing yourself onto a coffin.

'What time?' I said.

'Between two and five. You don't have to stay all that time. It would just be . . . nice to see someone.'

'Okay. I'll be there.'

'That's so brilliant! Thank you.'

I tried to smile. 'No problem.'

'You're such a good friend, Dave. Honestly.'

I wished that was true. I didn't feel like a good friend.

'I've got to finish something off,' I said. 'I'll see you soon.'

Chapter Two
Sunday 7th August

It was his son's birthday and Sam Currie was on his way across town to see him. Which meant that when his mobile rang, there was no way he was going to answer it.

No work. Not today.

Even so, he kept one eye on the road and picked up the mobile, just to check who was calling. When he saw it was James Swann, he immediately wished he'd left the damn thing on the seat. Swann wouldn't be phoning unless something had come up at the office, and Currie knew he should take the call. Whatever it was, it would be important.

His mind threw up unwanted snapshots of his son's childhood birthday parties. Neil, in a conical hat with a string round his chin, blowing out candles. Dressed as a cowboy, playing on the lawn – or with that tooth missing, posed on his red bicycle.

In the earlier photographs his son was always smiling, but as he hit his teenage years, he began to glower more. The only real constant over the years of photos was Sam Currie's absence from them. Work had always come first, and that had been a mistake – but you couldn't change the past, no matter how much you might want to. There was only this. Neil was twenty-one years old today, and Currie had booked the day off, and he was going to share a drink with his boy. It was what his father had done with him at that age, and it was one thing he could say with absolute certainty he'd been looking forward to since Linda had fallen pregnant, accidentally, all those years before.

He cancelled the call, then replaced the phone on the passenger seat, next to the bottle of Scotch.

Work was work. But a promise was a promise.

And yet . . . as he turned the steering wheel gently and eased the car up Bellerby Grove, Currie found he was already beginning to make the familiar compromises. Deep down, he knew he had to return the call, but if he could delay it a while, at least he'd have time to say 'happy birthday' and have a quick drink with Neil. His son was old enough to understand that now. In fact, he'd probably expect it.

Why didn't I switch the thing off?

The weather had turned out nice, anyway, even if everything else now felt a little darker. Currie squinted overhead through the windscreen. It had been grey and overcast earlier on, but now, coming up on midday, the clouds were gone and the sky was bright and clear. A good, clean day. The sun was beating down; skewed yellow squares rolled along his brawny forearms as he drove. The houses here had long front gardens, and he could hear the *swish-swishing* of lawn sprinklers and the buzz of strimmers as he passed, breathing in the aroma of cut grass that wafted in through the open window. It was tranquil, and he was glad. Over the years, Neil had made his home in far worse neighbourhoods than this.

Currie parked up just inside the gate. When he killed the engine, the world outside was quiet, broken only by birds and the peaceful rush of distant traffic, like water in the pipes.

The car beeped twice as he locked it. Then, bottle in hand, he began the long walk up the drive. The breeze rolled warm air against his face. It hit the trees to one side a second later, and they rustled quietly together, then became silent again. When he reached the top of the steep hill, he was out of breath. *Nearly forty-five now*, he reminded himself ruefully. Time got away from you. He'd put some gym work in store in his teens and twenties, but that had all gone out of date by now. The promises to get back to it . . . well, he never seemed to find the time. And anyway, at this point it was all catch-up, wasn't it? He'd broken the back of life, and it was all downhill from here.

This week, he thought. Some time.

A few paces away from the path, he found his son.

Currie stepped carefully around.

The stone was arched and plain. The inscription, simple: Neil S. Donald – his wife's maiden name – and two dates that book-ended a shade over nineteen years of life. There was a spread of fresh flowers on the grave, no doubt left by his wife and her brother earlier in the day. It was what they'd agreed, but it still bit him slightly that Linda had got here first.

A few brief words were carved into the stone.

Beloved son.

At last you are at peace.

Stay safe.

Other snapshots occurred to Currie as he read that, but he put them out of his mind. None of that mattered now, because the only truth that mattered was in those words. At last, you are at peace.

His phone went again. This time he answered it, watching the grass waver slightly in the breeze.

'Currie,' he said.

'Sam? It's James. I'm sorry to phone, but we've got a major incident here and I thought you'd want to know.'

'Who?'

'A female in her twenties.' Swann paused. 'It looks like she's been tied up and left to die.'

That pulled him up slightly. He hadn't been expecting that.

'Like the one in May?'

'Yeah.' *And the one last year.*

'Give me the address.'

Swann did.

Currie resisted the urge to ask the usual questions. Swann had been his partner for over ten years now, and he'd already have the scene contained, everyone moving.

'Give me half an hour.'

'Sam – I'm sorry.'

'Don't be. I'll see you soon.'

Currie hung up, then turned the cap around on the bottle of whiskey: click, click, click. The smell rose in the air and he took a long swig, allowing the liquor to burn into his tongue and the sides of his mouth, branding them with the silky taste before he finally swallowed. Immediately, his throat burned bright, followed by his chest.

'Happy birthday, Neil.'

He left the bottle closed and almost full, resting out of sight behind the headstone. Someone might take it, of course – either a groundsman or a derelict – but that was all right. In fact, it was probably what Neil would have wanted.

Half an hour later, Detective Sam Currie was standing in the doorway of a hot bedroom to the south of the city centre, looking at the body of Alison Wilcox.

She had been found by her ex-boyfriend, Roger Ellis, earlier that morning. Ellis was back at the department now, awaiting further questions, and Currie imagined the man would probably be suffering from what he'd experienced. He'd attended two scenes like this himself in the last year and a half, and the sight of the bodies still shocked him. Police work had brought him into contact with a great deal of violent death, but in this case it wasn't the assault that appalled him so much as the indignity and inhumanity of what had been done. And perhaps what hadn't.

Alison Wilcox's body looked thin and wasted, her skin slack and yellow. Her hands and feet were bound to the bedposts by thick coils of leather – and the hands in particular were dreadful: bent at the wrist and frozen into waxy claws. But if the case was like the others, they would find little actual violence had been done to her once the attacker had subdued his victim. The bindings had been all that was necessary to kill her.

Behind him, scene-of-crime officers were moving slowly through the house while, in front, the pathologist, Chris Dale, was squatting on his haunches beside the bed, tilting his head as he examined the body. A bluebottle landed on her thigh and Dale brushed it away. It settled a moment later on the side of her face, and began rotating slowly.

Standing beside him, James Swann popped a piece of chewing gum into his mouth and then offered Currie the packet.

He took one. 'Thanks.'

'No problem.'

'Looks the same as the others. You were right to call me.'

Swann didn't reply for a second, then said: 'Sad to think of her, isn't it? Alone like that.'

Currie nodded. Other detectives might have frowned on such an emotional statement, even delivered in such a controlled way, but it was one of the reasons he and Swann had lasted so long as partners. And it *was* sad. Assuming they were dealing with the same killer, Alison Wilcox had been tied up and left here to die slowly of thirst.

There was some controversy within the medical field about what that was actually like. Some said the body produced pain-numbing chemicals after the first day or so, while others maintained it was a hellish way to die. What wasn't in doubt were the physical consequences and processes. As Alison Wilcox's body dehydrated, she would have lost the ability to sweat, and her body would have heated up intolerably. Her mouth, tongue and throat would have become agonisingly dry; her skin would have cracked like parchment. Any urine she managed to pass would have been increasingly concentrated, becoming so hot it burned her. At some point, as her brain cells dried, she would have grown feverish and confused. Eventually she would have fallen totally unconscious. It could have taken her anywhere between a few days and two weeks for her organs to shut down – blinking out like lights – and for her body finally to die.

And throughout that time, nobody came.

Because of the anniversary, Currie thought about Neil again. When he'd stood outside his son's house on the day he found him, he'd noticed the building seemed darker and more potent than those around it. The sun beat down on the neighbours' houses, while Neil's was in shadow, and everything had been too still. As he'd opened the gate and walked through the litter-strewn garden, a part of him had already known what he was going to find inside.

Now, he wondered whether anyone had felt something similar as they walked down the street outside this house. How could they not? It seemed impossible. There was a pocket of sadness around the whole scene. Her death was nothing short of an accusation.

Swann's mobile went then, breaking his thoughts, and his partner moved back down the landing to answer it, muscles bunching beneath his pale-blue shirt sleeves.

Dale, the pathologist, stood up.

'It's certainly consistent with what we've seen before,' he said. 'Difficult, in these circumstances, to determine the actual cause of death.'

'Dehydration?'

'Yes. It's likely to be organ failure, but it's possible her throat was so swollen that she was unable to breathe any longer.'

Currie chewed the gum slowly. His own mouth felt dry.

'There are no obvious indications of sexual violence, and no apparent injuries, aside from the bruising to the wrists and ankles.'

She'd fought against them, of course.

Currie said. 'And she was kept here?'

'It looks that way. The state of the bedclothes would indicate that, although it's impossible to know for sure right now.'

The state of the bedclothes. Currie's gaze flicked across the soiled, crusted sheet beneath the body. He wondered if she'd been embarrassed at first, before she stopped caring: before embarrassment gave way to panic, maybe even madness.

'Ideally we should get her back as soon as possible,' Dale said. 'I'll be able to be more exact then.'

'No. We need her in place for a while.'

It went against his instincts to leave her body in situ. Currie stared at her and imagined time passing, uncaring, around her. His thoughts produced a stop-motion video of Alison: fighting at first, and then spasming as muscles cramped; her head moving from one side to the other, like a dreamer in a nightmare. The days and nights brightening and darkening the room as she died by increments.

The video uncurled in Currie's mind, and he felt sorrow for each lonely moment that nobody had come to find her or check she was okay. So he wanted to get her out of here – finally – but they were too late for that to make any difference anymore. The only thing they could do for her now was catch the man responsible.

'We can't afford to miss anything on scene.'

'Of course.' Dale nodded slowly, then puffed up his cheeks and blew out. 'I've got a few calls to make. I'll be back.'

'Okay. Thanks, Chris.'

Currie moved aside so the pathologist could leave. A moment later Swann rejoined him, clicking his mobile shut then running his hand through his close-cropped hair.

'We've got traces on the phone calls,' he said. 'The first one was made from the phone downstairs. The second, the one using Alison's mobile, was sent from the street outside.'

Currie put that together.

'He watched Ellis come in, then played him the recording again.'

'Looks that way. They're going through Wilcox's phone accounts now to look at activity over the past couple of weeks.'

Currie was sure what they were going to find – that the killer had sent his usual holding messages to Wilcox's family and friends – doing just enough to convince them she was alive and well. It was frightening how easy it was to assume someone else's identity, he thought. How reliant society had become on communication that was ultimately impersonal. Emails, texts, Facebook profiles. People never stopped anymore. Just flitted around each other's lives obliviously, like butterflies.

Swann indicated his mobile.

'That was Collins, by the way.'

'Yeah? What did he want?'

'The domestic last week. You remember it?'

Currie raised an eyebrow.

He remembered it, although 'domestic' made the assault sound somehow more palatable, as though it had just been some petty disagreement. In reality, the girl, Tori Edmonds, had been badly beaten by her boyfriend. Even so, as unpleasant as that was, it wasn't the kind of disturbance that would normally have registered for very long. A couple of elements had lifted it out of the ordinary.

The first was the girl herself. Something about Tori Edmonds had struck Currie when they visited her in the hospital. She seemed . . . not innocent, exactly, but more open and vulnerable than he was used to. From the moment he'd seen her, he'd felt protective. Perhaps it was as simple as that. The reaction had made him even angrier with her errant boyfriend, a man called Eddie Berries. When faced with something valuable, Currie divided people into two groups. There were those who treasured it, and those who couldn't bear it. Some people, for some reason, always felt an urge to bring others down to their level.

Tori Edmonds seemed like a good kid – intelligent, sharp and clean. The more they learned about her boyfriend, Edward Berries, the more he seemed a strange fit for her: a low-level dealer and addict by some accounts; a general waste of space by many others. No criminal record, but hardly a catch. They certainly seemed an incongruous couple. But then, Edmonds was also known to consort with Charlie Drake – Choc to his friends – and Drake was a far more dangerous proposition on every level. Apparently they'd met while organising club nights when Edmonds had been a teenager. These days, Choc was known to run a large portion of the city's cannabis trade, practically single-handedly.

It was an ungodly mixture, and it meant that Berries needed to be found quickly, not least for his own protection. After what he'd done to the girl, of course, most police probably wouldn't sleep too badly if someone got hold of him first. Many would even feel he deserved whatever was coming to him. Currie wavered on that one, but if his son's death had taught him anything it was that you didn't abandon people. No man left behind. Whatever you might think of him. Especially when someone like Drake was involved.

'So where are we up to on that?' he said.

'There was a disturbance reported earlier this morning on Campdown Road: a guy was pulled out of a squat and bundled into the boot of a car. The description matches that of our friend Eddie.'

'Small, ugly and worthless?'

'That's almost word for word. And the address looks right for his place on Campdown.'

Idiot doesn't know when to lay low, Currie thought. But then, they were all like that, weren't they? A self-destructive spiral wasn't the most obvious place for someone to start acting clever.

Currie chewed the gum thoughtfully.

'What about the bundlers?'

'They were black.'

'That's a start. Car?'

'Also black. Four wheels. You know the area. Nobody wants to talk.'

Currie grunted. There were certain people's business in the city that you didn't want to get involved in, and everyone knew it. Drake was somewhere near the top of that list.

'Nothing doing for now,' Swann said. 'Not round there.'

'We'll see.'

'We will. But we have bigger things to deal with now.'

Currie looked down at the dead girl again, her head turned slightly to one side. On one level, he didn't like what his partner's words implied. *Priorities*. The idea that Berries didn't matter; that they could simply let him go in favour of someone more important. But at the same time, he knew Swann was right. Somewhere in the city, Alison Wilcox's killer was moving on. Someone else would be lying there soon. Waiting. Forgotten.

Suddenly, Currie felt very weary.

Swann said, 'Head back and talk to Roger Ellis?'

'Yeah.' He sighed. 'Let's do that.'

Chapter Three
Sunday 7th August

Tori had explained she suffered from manic depression the first week we were together.

We'd been out that evening at the travelling fairground that parked on the moor once a year, and we'd spent the evening breathing hot-dog fumes in the freezing air, sticking candyfloss to our faces and leaning into each other on the waltzers, traffic lights and fruit-machine noise whirling around us. Later, back at my flat, Tori had been sitting cross-legged on my bed, rolling a joint on a magazine balanced over her slim thighs. The whole time she told me about her illness, she stared intently at the construction, not looking up once.

She'd been sectioned twice before, but thankfully not for a few years. Nevertheless, it remained a condition she lived with every day, and if I was going to be involved with her, I had to know what it could mean. Even though she took both medication and great care – she said, with a wry smile at the joint – it could still affect her at any point in the future. When she was finished she looked up at me, and I didn't see the faintest trace of self-pity. *This is who I am.*

Despite her expression, I think that deep down she worried how I would react: that I might not want to be with her anymore, and that this, in turn, might shake some foundation she'd fought hard to get level. It didn't change anything for me, of course, and I told her so. But in her face, just for a moment, I saw someone who'd had her sense of identity and self-worth swept away, and then had to stand in the eye of that tornado while the pieces of everything she'd believed about herself whirled around in the air. She had gathered them back together and clung on tightly.

If anything, as patronising at it might have been, the challenges she'd faced, and the way she faced the world afterwards, made her even more important to me. I told her, 'You're the sanest girl I've ever been out with,' and I meant it.

Two years later, as I drove to Staunton, I felt guilt and anger spreading through me. It wasn't my job to check up on Tori, but she was still my friend, and maybe I could have done something to help if I'd only taken the time.

That's what happens. People slip if you let them.

I arrived just after two.

The hospital was built on the side of a gently sloping hill: a series of pale, single-storey buildings spreading out and down, some connected, some not. There were tall hedges along the roadside, with a single entrance to the car park, manned by a guard. The gravel beyond was white and carefully levelled off, while the fields around the wards were neat and luscious: bright green in the sunshine, with the lollipop trees nodding gently in a calm breeze. The car park was half full, but when I got out of the car everything was incredibly quiet. The hospital and its grounds were designed to be as tranquil as possible.

I walked down the path to the main entrance, smelling cut grass in the fresh air. Once inside, the main corridor was quite busy, and I glanced into some of the other wards as I passed them, seeing nothing to differentiate them from those in a normal hospital. By contrast, when I reached Eight, I was faced with a set of blue double doors, magnetically sealed, with a touch-key pad on the wall beside them. That brought it home – the fact that my friend was confined here. It was for her own good, but it was still strange and sad to think we couldn't walk out of here together if we wanted.

I buzzed the intercom and the door was opened a minute later by a young, unshaven man in casual clothes: jeans and jumper. The name tag attached to his belt told me his name was Robert Till, and that he was a care assistant.

I said, 'Hi. I'm here to see Tori Edmonds.'

'Right.' He let me in. 'Tori's outside on the patio. It's at the end. You need to sign in and then I'll walk you down.'

'Thanks.'

Ward Eight was basically a long, wide corridor with doors branching off it. There were bedrooms off to the left, some open, some closed. None appeared to have locks on, but there were white boxes painted on the floor around doorways, clearly indicating 'exclusion zones' for guests. The air smelled of a combination of cleaning products and unidentifiable school dinners.

'I feel awkward asking,' I said, 'but what should I expect?'

'Have you ever seen her during a manic episode?'

'No.'

'Well, she's getting better. She's sedated a little, but just talk to her the way you would anybody else. How do you know her?'

'We went out together a couple of years back.'

'Oh, okay. Are you the magician?'

'Kind of. Journalist, really.'

'She's talked about you a lot. She'll be pleased you came. Even if she doesn't really show it.'

Towards the end of the corridor there were large rooms to either side. We went right, into an area filled with comfortable seats and tables with magazines fanned out on them. Groups of people were dotted around, and it was difficult at first glance to distinguish who might be a resident or a visitor. The atmosphere appeared quiet and relaxed, somewhere between a hospital ward and prison visiting hours, but much closer to the former. These people were patients, after all, and so the security was subtle and unobtrusive, designed to disappear unless you looked for it. Locks on the windows; assistants casually mingling. But aside from the patio doors in here, the keypad at the entrance appeared to be the only way in or out. As Robert led me across, I noticed the large security bars here as well.

Outside in the sun, light-brown paving stones ran the length of the hospital building, the walkway expanding into small squares at the external doors of every ward. There were semi-circles of wooden seats at each, linked by tables, and cylindrical bins topped with sand for extinguishing cigarettes. People were sitting or standing all the way along, smoking, talking carefully, or just squinting against the sun and enjoying the fresh air.

Tori had her back to me, but her hair was tied up to reveal the star tattooed on the back of her neck and I recognised her immediately. She was sitting with a bunch of people. One was painfully thin, her skin almost yellow, and I presumed she was another patient. There was an older couple next to this girl, who I guessed were her parents.

Sitting opposite were Choc and Cardo, looking at me.

I nodded hello. Choc returned the gesture, but Cardo just slouched down a little more and stared off to one side. His foot started tapping.

'Hey there.' I wanted to put my hand on Tori's shoulder, but I didn't know if that was allowed so I leaned around instead. 'I made it.'

She looked up at me, saluting against the sun.

'Hello. Come and sit down.'

I rummaged in the bag I'd brought: 'Some cigarettes.'

'Thank you.'

'Let's have a look, then.'

She turned her head for me to see, and I held back a wince. Sunlight brought out the colours in the side of her face, which was a swirl of purples, yellows and blacks. Her left eye was pink and bloodshot, like she was wearing a contact lens for a part in a horror movie. I felt another sharp jolt of anger at Eddie Berries for what he'd done, and myself for what I hadn't.

'Very pretty.'

'I think so, yes.' She said it decisively. 'Purple's always been my favourite colour.' She turned to the anorexic girl beside her. 'This is Amy and some of her family.'

'Nice to meet you.'

We all smiled at each other a little awkwardly, and then Tori started talking to Amy as though I wasn't there. 'You must remind me to send it to you when we're out of here,' she said. 'I think it's one of his best.'

I lit up a cigarette and for a few minutes the rest of us sat in silence. When the assistant had told me Tori was sedated, I'd half-expected to find her subdued or sleepy – but it was more that she seemed easily distracted: flitting between topics, beginning and ending new conversations almost at random. Without the drugs, she'd probably have been bouncing off the walls. With them, the manic side was still there, but came through in a kind of grey-scale, like a dance tune with the volume turned down.

Eventually I turned to Choc. 'How are you doing?'

He shrugged, lit up a cigarette of his own. 'This and that, you know. We're doing all right.'

'That's good.'

He gestured across at Tori. 'She tell you what happened?'

'Most of it.' I shook my head, hesitating, and then said: 'I wish I'd done something.'

Everything dropped out of his expression, leaving it flat and blank. He nodded slowly, then said quietly: 'Tell me about it.'

I'd only met them a couple of times since that first night at Edward's. On both occasions they'd been pleasant enough company, and it had been easy to forget what they did for a living. But of course, once I knew, it was always there. *They're very protective of me*, Tori had said once, and I supposed that was one of the reasons I'd never taken against them. There was something about her that attracted all kinds of people; how those people behaved towards her had become a sort of barometer for me. If Choc cared about her and looked out for her, then he couldn't be so bad. Whereas Eddie was equally drawn in, but could somehow bring himself to hurt her.

'I'm glad you came, anyway,' Choc said. 'She's not stopped talking about you.'

'I wanted to. I felt like I should, you know?'

He exhaled smoke and nodded thoughtfully, staring off into space, considering something. I let the silence pan out. When he was done with the cigarette he put it under his shoe rather than in the bin.

'What you got planned after this?' he said.

'After this?'

'Yeah, yeah. You got some free time?'

I opened my mouth but he interrupted me to clarify.

'We're gonna have a word with someone. Thought you might like to come along.'

Tori turned around. 'Dave, you need some sun-cream, or else you'll burn.'

'Er, right.'

I looked around a little cluelessly, as though sun-cream might magically appear, but then Tori produced a bottle from beside her. She squeezed some out on my left arm and began rubbing it in. There was nothing sexual about it, and yet for some reason it felt totally inappropriate. But I let her.

As I did, Choc leaned back in his chair, watching me, and I knew our conversation wasn't over yet. I also knew exactly what he was talking about. A word with Eddie. As much as I hated him right now – and would happily have beaten the living shit out of him if I'd been there at the time – I wasn't sure I wanted to go down that particular route. Well, I did. And then I didn't.

But I could feel him watching me, and the weight of his gaze intensified everything I was feeling inside.

Tori was diligent and slow, making sure all of the sun-cream was rubbed in before I leaned around so she could do the same to my other arm. I watched her concentrating, the bruise on her face visible once again. Her legs were tucked under her, her shoulders narrowed from hunching over my arm, and she looked smaller than ever.

I could have picked her up with one hand, and she seemed so slow and steady that I might have managed it before she even realised.

As Tori finished, she looked at me and frowned. And then something occurred to her and she grabbed my wrist—

'Come on. I'll show you around.'

—as though she could physically move me away from the guilt she sensed in me. And perhaps away from Choc as well.

First of all, she showed me her bedroom.

'My diary. My books. I hang my clothes up in here.'

Tori moved quickly from item to item while I carefully observed the exclusion zone. Her room smelled of the perfume I associated with her. It came in a tall, thin bottle and had a flower inside.

Sometimes, even now, I'd smell it while I was walking along and I'd turn around, expecting or hoping to see her.

'This is where I can get washed.'

She worked her way around the room, concentrating hard. And I knew it was all for my benefit: an attempt to distract me from how she could tell I was feeling. She probably wouldn't have been able to articulate it that way, but even now, at angles with the world, she was thinking of other people: sending me a radio message of reassurance from behind the static.

She came back out into the corridor.

'And how is Emma?'

'Emma?' I didn't know what to say. 'Things aren't great right now.'

'I'm sorry to hear that.' She tilted her head. 'But if it doesn't work out with her, there's always me.'

I felt that solidly, like a punch, and immediately told myself not to take it seriously.

'Ooh,' she grabbed my wrist again, eyes wide. 'Come on. I know what else to show you.'

She took me through to the second lounge, the one I'd not been into yet. It was almost identical to the other: comfortable chairs, tables, newspapers. But there weren't any people in here. Tori led me across to the far side of the room. She sat down at an upright piano, her back to me, and after hooking a stray hair behind her ear her fingers moved nimbly above the keys, expectant and ready.

'What shall I play?'

And seeing her like that, perched in front of a musical instrument I'd seen her play before, in better times, took everything up another notch.

'I don't know,' I managed to say. 'Do you know any Nine Inch Nails?'

'No, silly. You know this one.'

She started playing *The Heart Asks Pleasure First*, the one classical piece she knew I could bear to listen to.

But she couldn't quite do it. She missed notes and occasionally pressed two keys at once, and the more she went on, the more it faltered. As her fingers let her down, she frowned, then added her

34

voice as well: gently singing along, eyes closed, supplementing the melody. But again, slightly off.

I listened to the fractured music. Even confined in this place, she was guileless and uninhibited, but I saw the frustration on her face as she noticed her mistakes. A piece of beautiful music, reduced to stops and starts.

Eddie did this, I reminded myself. *It's not your fault.*

But as she stopped playing, her expression full of bemused disappointment, I felt a knot in my throat tighten with anger until I could hardly breathe. Until – rightly or wrongly – I knew exactly what I was going to do.

Chapter Four

Sunday 7th August

When she had finished on the computer, she opened the internet browser's history menu and began erasing the pages one by one. Even though her flatmate was away, the deletions were a necessary part of the ritual. First you externalised. Then you cleared up.

She removed the search engine items for extreme porn sites and chat rooms, and then the details of the sites themselves. Her anonymous email address. Chat transcripts from the sex forums where she'd allowed people to tell her the things they wanted to do to her. She deleted all the web pages she'd so diligently searched for and explored. All the things that had, in their own way, personified the self-disgust and hatred she felt for everything about herself.

When it was done, she walked back across the room to where she'd left her clothes, and knew that it wasn't even close to being enough.

Half an hour later, Mary was sitting on the settee with her legs tucked underneath her, watching the television. Whatever release she'd felt from the internet had retightened now, and she felt even worse than before. It was like lancing a boil. If you didn't get all the shit out in one go, all you did was make the infection worse.

The room was slowly darkening along with the day outside, and the light from the television flickered across her. Mary stared through the screen as images flashed up in front; news rendered meaningless in the silence. The only movement she allowed herself was to rub a single fingertip along one eyebrow, smoothing it down. One direction, over and over. Whenever she made a larger motion it shocked her body, as though someone had just shaken her suddenly and violently from a deep sleep.

No good.

It was astonishing really – how you could understand the emotions behind your actions and moods, and still remain in thrall to them. Mary knew from experience that in a few days' time, she'd look back on this and barely recognise herself. She'd see a stranger. A small, inadequate girl, curled on the settee, reduced to folding her arms and clenching her sleeves, and her skin along with them. Eventually, her mood would clear and the grip would lessen. But even though she knew this very clearly right now, it was no help whatsoever. Her depressions were like sinking into the blackest of dreams. No memory of the real world could help you.

A nightmare had prompted this latest attack.

As always, it had been drawn from her childhood, only for her mind to sketch over the top and elongate the details. Faces were stretched oval, so that teeth became fangs; fingers were popped double-length and formed into talons; an ordinary suburban kitchen was transformed into the scullery of a castle. Mary stood terrified as an enormous, dark-green vampire pressed the face of a peasant onto the top of a glowing red anvil. The man's fingers clawed desperately, but she couldn't even hear his screams over the angry barking of the monster holding him down.

Who sent you here? Who sent you?

Steam billowed up around a single, bright white eye, wide with panic, and Mary's mind flashed up images of burning meat, of charred carcasses hanging in the air around her, of blood running between the cobbles on the floor.

As frightened as she was, Mary was most concerned about the small, innocent boy standing behind her. She kept trying to block his view and protect him – but she couldn't, and it was making her cry. Every time she moved, his face slipped around her.

She'd woken up sobbing hysterically. That same feeling of helpless, terrified frustration had stayed with her for the past three days, building until now it felt like she would explode.

The silent television screen flickering before her, Mary leaned forwards and wrapped her forearms under her legs. Head to knees. Body shaking.

She turned on the light.

When she'd moved into the spare room of Katie's flat, Mary hadn't brought much stuff with her. There was hardly any room, but that was okay: her possessions amounted to little more than her clothes, a handful of books, her body, and a box full of more personal belongings that she always needed to have close by.

On her hands and knees in the bedroom, Mary rummaged inside the box until she found what she wanted, then went to the kitchen and selected a small bowl. She took the items back through to the lounge, moving slowly, as if sedated. Everything she saw in front of her was blurred by tears.

Thinking was almost impossible, but . . .

Close the curtains.

She could hear people on the main street outside, a storey below – laughing and joking – and she shut them all out and sat down on the settee. In the silence, she could hear herself crying.

Open the bag.

Once upon a time, as all stories begin, this had been her mother's sewing kit. When she was a little girl, she'd been fascinated by it: all those secret layers of fabric, slit open into hiding places for needles and packets of looped, multi-coloured thread. Her mother had left it behind when she finally moved away and, when Mary was a teenager, she'd discarded the sewing materials along with all the other things of her mother's she'd never look at again. From the very first foster home, she used the kit to carry tools she actually needed.

Mary took out the antiseptic liquid and poured some into the bowl. She selected a razorblade and immersed it, then produced cotton buds and antiseptic cream, placing them on the table beside the bowl for later.

Take deep breaths.

She did, but after a minute she was still shaking. Right there and then, she couldn't imagine anybody might feel more alone or completely without hope than she did. For the past few days, she'd resisted. But now, rather than fighting against it any longer, she allowed the feeling to fill her. It was like poison. The emotions poured out of her heart, forcing themselves in clotted lumps through her arteries and veins.

And then she finally began: rolling up her trouser leg, folding the material back on itself. There were a few scars there already – a criss-cross of old white lines amongst the fine, almost invisible hair – but still plenty of space.

Keep breathing.

She picked out the razor blade, shaking liquid off it.

When the first cut appeared, blood beading down the line, the sting of it felt like the first physical sensation she'd had all day.

Afterwards, Mary had exactly twenty new lines on the back of her calf, which was swollen, warm and felt like it was humming. The skin ached, but in a comfortable, pleasant way. She cleaned the wounds carefully with antiseptic before smothering her leg with cream. Blood still leaked out, forming red capillaries in the white, but she kept dabbing it gently with cotton pads. It didn't matter.

She was filled with euphoria.

Blood had gone everywhere, though. It had pooled around her ankle, and the smooth floor was messy with it. There were circles and stars from drips, and smeared curls where her bare foot had twitched across. The tissues she'd used were screwed up: blotched poppy-red, then discarded here and there. Even the mess was gratifying.

Sometimes, the only way to ease the feelings was to bring them out into the open, to create something physical that could be dealt with. Mary's calf had become a tapestry of all those unwanted emotions: the self-disgust and hatred; the regrets and frustrations. Each one was plain for her to see, and she could look after them now that they were visible.

Clean them carefully, and begin to heal.

She collected the tissues into a ball, wiped up the blood, and then took everything to the kitchen bin. When she walked back through to the front room, her leg was throbbing wonderfully, and it felt like she was walking on air.

Then she saw what was on the television screen.

It was only there for a second – a banner across the bottom of the screen that unfolded away, replaced by a different headline a moment later. But it was enough to make her weak. She collapsed on the settee.

It had said:

VICTIM 'TIED TO BED AND LEFT TO DIE'

Now, it said:

POLICE: POSSIBLE LINKS TO EARLIER KILLINGS

Breaking News.

Mary found the TV remote and turned off the mute option.

'—not in a position to comment on that at this time.'

It was showing a press conference: two policemen in suits were sitting behind a long table draped in white cloth. Microphones sprouted up in front of them.

'Can you confirm that the cause of death was dehydration?' a voice said.

'A full post-mortem is currently being carried out. We hope to know the answer to that question shortly.'

The man who was speaking was in his mid-thirties and impressive-looking. Neat and well-groomed and athletic: the kind of policeman a normal person would trust to solve a crime. But Mary's attention was caught by the other one. He was older – in his forties, Mary guessed – and his face managed to be both kind and unbearably sad at the same time. Whenever a camera flashed, he closed his eyes for too long.

'But you believe the victim was bound and left in her home for some time?'

The younger policeman considered that. 'It is one possibility we're looking into,' he said.

Mary was shaking. Despite everything she'd done, the pit inside had opened up again, and all those black emotions had returned.

The banner changed again:

VICTIM 'TIED TO BED AND LEFT TO DIE'

Something creaked upstairs.

Mary's heart leapt.

Nothing. It's nothing.

The doors and windows were locked. She lifted her feet up onto the settee, wrapped her arms carefully around her knees, and began rocking gently, trying to soothe herself. The words bore out of the television set and she understood exactly what they were intended to be.

A message, addressed directly to her.

You have to tell them.

A part of her wanted to, but at the same time she knew it wouldn't do any good. It never had done, had it? She'd learned enough through her own bitter experiences to know that the police did nothing. Nobody did. All you could rely on was yourself. And yet she was powerless here. The words on the screen had reduced her to nothing: she was a child again, cowering in a corner. Nobody would help her, but it was impossible to believe she could deal with this on her own. How could anyone expect that of her?

You don't know they won't listen, she told herself. *He has a kind face. He looks like he cares.*

That kind of hope was a dangerous thing. It was better not to reach out at all than have your hand ignored or slapped away.

But it's not just about you. What if he hurts someone else?

She could give no response to that. Who else was going to stop him? She had to tell the police, otherwise she would be at least partly responsible for the next girl he took, and the next.

Mary glanced at the phone on the table, but calling from here was out of the question. She'd worked too hard over the years to preserve her anonymity, and wasn't going to risk being discovered now. The jobs she took, when they weren't volunteer work, were all paid cash in hand, and her real name didn't appear on any utility bill, bank account or rental agreement in the city. Everything could be traced.

Somehow, though, she had to do this.

After thinking for a few moments, Mary snatched up her coat and made her way downstairs, glancing left and right up the street as she went outside. Cars whined past, shocking her. Everybody seemed to be looking.

He seemed to be everywhere.

He's not.

It took her half an hour to find a payphone a safe enough distance from home. Once there, ignoring the dull throbbing in her leg, she held the receiver up to her ear and dialled the number given on the screen just before she left.

As she waited, despite her surface intentions, she was aware of what she was feeling inside, along with the fear. It was that dangerous type of hope. Perhaps this time . . .

'Hello,' a woman said. 'Police special invest—'

Mary interrupted her. 'I know who killed those girls,' she said.

Chapter Five

Sunday 7th August

Outside the car, the sky was growing dull, the late-afternoon breeze now bringing the first traces of evening with it. But the residual heat from the day was enough to hold people out a while longer: as I drove past Hadden Park I saw groups sitting out on the grass, and students in bright shorts knocking a football around in the distance. Along the main streets, the benches outside pubs were full of people settling in for the evening, not ready or willing to move inside or go home yet.

At traffic lights, Choc and Cardo's car sat in front, red lights staring implacably back like the eyes of a rat in a tunnel. Each time we stopped, I felt an urge to flick on the indicator and turn off. But I didn't. Instead, as their car gunned off again, I released the handbrake and accelerated to keep up.

Choc hadn't told me where we were heading, but the place wasn't important. It was what would happen when we got there that mattered. I pictured it in my head like this: the three of us would knock on a door, Eddie would open it, and all the colour would drain from his face. That much I wanted to see. Then Choc was going to have a word with him. I knew that word wouldn't remain entirely verbal but, after seeing Tori at the piano, the thought didn't trouble me much. In fact, I was pretty sure I wanted to see that too – although I might draw the line at joining in.

And rationalising it like that, it wasn't too hard to stay behind them and ignore my common sense. Each turn-off, in fact, felt dark with my own guilt and failure, whereas following Choc and Cardo seemed like tracking the only ray of light I could imagine right now.

We crossed town and headed out to the east of the city, the main streets segueing into smaller, quieter country lanes. After twenty minutes their car indicated left, and I followed them up a thin, off-road track, driving slowly now, the tarmac switching to gravel that crackled beneath the tyres. We rounded a bend, and the track opened up into a parking area. Here, the gravel was piled up in several large mounds on the right, and a dense curl of trees stood in front and to the left.

A quarry, I guessed. Deserted on a Sunday.

One car was already sitting there, empty, and Choc pulled up alongside it. I drove in next to him and we sat for a moment, our engines idling.

The rational part of my brain was more worried now.

This isn't knocking on a door, is it? This is the middle of nowhere.

But we were here now. I cut the engine and heard nothing but birdsong, then the clunk of car doors as Choc and Cardo got out and started towards the woods. When they reached the edge they glanced back at me, impatient. I took a deep breath and then headed after them.

'If anyone asks,' Choc told me, 'you're in The Wheatfield right now. That cool?'

'Yeah,' I said uncertainly. 'Where are we going?'

'Not far.' They both moved off between the trees. 'Watch your step.'

We walked a little way in. There was no path here, just a tangle of roots and grass underfoot. Smaller branches had fallen from the trees and formed ribcage traps that snapped in the undergrowth. In the canopy above, the sunlight could hardly make its way through; it came down scattered into fragments, casting small patches of dappled brightness on the leaves and trees. This should have felt idyllic and peaceful; instead, it felt full of menace. But I couldn't turn around now.

A minute later we reached the occupants of the other car.

Three of them were little more than burly black shapes leaning against the trees, arms folded. More of Choc's crew. They looked like they'd been waiting around here a while, killing time. The fourth person was Eddie Berries. He was kneeling in the grass, his head bowed. Most of his long hair, ripped from that ponytail, now hung down to his thighs, and he was hugging himself and shaking.

I hesitated slightly, then took another couple of steps.

Choc and Cardo walked up to Eddie. I glanced to either side. It wasn't even a proper clearing here – just a large enough break between the trees to accommodate us. And far enough away from anything for us to be undisturbed, I realised.

What the fuck have you got yourself into here?

The quiet settled in my heart and set it humming, and I stared down at Eddie. Whatever he'd done to Tori, he was a pitiful sight right now: terrified and feeble.

'He didn't think we'd find him.' Choc sounded proud. 'But never overestimate a junkie, right? Get the fuck up.'

When Eddie didn't respond, Choc kicked him casually in the side of the face and knocked him over.

The electricity in my chest lurched up in a spike and stayed there.

'Get up, you piece of shit.'

After a second, Eddie climbed unsteadily to his feet. When he was as upright as he could manage, he wrapped his arms back around himself, head still bowed, body still trembling.

He said, 'I'm sorry—'

Choc palmed him in the forehead, knocking his head back.

'Look at me when you're talking. Act like a man.'

Eddie did as he was told and kept his head up. But his gaze wouldn't stay in one place. He was looking everywhere and nowhere: too frightened to meet anyone's eye. Choc began pacing back and forth in front of him, like a lion held back by imaginary bars.

'You know what you did, don't you?'

'I'm sorry. I don't know why—'

'What – you need a reason to be sorry or something?'

Eddie shook his head. He hadn't figured out that it didn't matter what he said: there weren't any magic words that were going to get him out of this.

You neither.

'I mean, I don't know why I did it.'

45

'You want me to give you a reason to be sorry?' Choc slapped him on the side of the head. 'Is that what you're saying?'

'I didn't mean to.'

'What, you just slipped?' Another slap. 'Like that?'

They weren't the kind of blows that would even leave a bruise, but the low-level violence was just as ugly as a proper beating. Choc was like a cat playing with a mouse.

'I've just been to see my friend in hospital. She'd never lay a hand on anyone, and yet you thought it was all right to hurt her.' Choc moved behind him now. 'You think you can hurt my friend and get away with it?'

Another bullying smack.

'You fucking piece of shit.'

And suddenly, he had a handful of Eddie's hair and was pulling him off-balance, his grip so tight the knuckles went white and the muscles in his skinny arm stood out. Eddie shrieked, but Choc hauled him over and pressed his face into the rough bark of a tree, leaning into him with all his weight, like he was trying to push him through it. Grinding slightly – four seconds, five, six – Choc's face contorting, concentrating on *hurting* . . .

My heart hitched, tumbled over itself once, then carried on.

Finally, he released him.

Eddie's face was mottled and blood-picked down one side, his expression frozen in pain, like a baby in the quiet, shocked second before it begins screaming. He reached up to his cheek in disbelief, but Choc knocked his hand away.

'Big man now, eh?' Choc sniffed, then glanced back at me, nodded at Eddie. 'Come on over and say hello.'

My legs felt shaky, but I did as I was told, standing in front of Eddie, breathing slowly, trying to keep calm. A string of mucus led from his nose to his mouth. For a moment, he couldn't look at me, but finally he glanced up, his eyes full of tears.

Please don't hurt me.

And honestly, I had no intention of it – not anymore. I hadn't worked out exactly what I was going to do, but there was no way I was going to be a part of this, and as long as I didn't hurt him I was only a bystander, not involved or culpable. Because this felt just as ugly in its own way as what he'd done to Tori in the first place.

But then his expression changed.

I can't describe what it was. Recognition, maybe. He saw me and knew who I was from those few times we'd met, and something shifted in the set of his face. I saw him thinking to himself: *who the hell do you think you are, acting on her behalf? You're nothing.* And right then, all the emotions gathered together and rose up.

I think the punch I threw took us both by surprise.

The trees tilted around me, my fist was solid – *crack* – then numb, and suddenly I was bent over, holding my hand, while Eddie sprawled down in the undergrowth. I watched, stunned, as he rolled slowly onto his back, a stick cracking beneath him, his hands cupping his face. No sound at all.

'Ha ha!' Choc rocked backwards and pointed. 'I think you broke his fucking jaw, man!'

What did you just do?

My voice, when it came, was barely audible.

'I broke my fucking hand.'

'No shit! Let's see.'

It was shaking as I held it out.

'You might have,' he agreed happily. 'You might. But you haven't broken your foot yet.'

I glanced down at Eddie. As I did, he slowly moved his hands away. His eyes were staring at me and, although there was still fear in them, he'd also summoned hatred from somewhere.

I felt disgusted with myself for what I'd done.

'I don't want anymore,' I said.

Choc looked like he was going to persuade me to carry on, but something in my expression must have told him it wasn't worth it. The enthusiasm and admiration on his face disappeared, replaced by a casual blankness. In that brief moment, I understood, I'd just gone from somebody to nobody.

I didn't care. I needed out of this. I needed to have never been here.

'That's cool. Wait back at the cars.'

I nodded, then turned and made my way through the trees, the pain in the back of my hand intensifying. There were flames build-ing there. Behind me I heard the *whump* of a kick, and glanced back to see Choc stepping away from Eddie, lifting his leg to stamp on him. Eddie wasn't looking at me anymore. I turned away.

Whatever happened now, it was nothing to do with me. All I'd done was throw one stupid punch, which was several less than he deserved. A lot less than he'd done to Tori.

I kept repeating that. From performing, I knew you could con-vince people of anything if you tried hard enough.

Back at the car park, I checked out my hand. The first two knuckles were burning badly, and when I touched the skin below them I winced at the purity of the pain. It felt like I'd rested a white-hot coin on the back of my hand.

Leaving everything else aside, if there's one thing you don't want to do as a magician, it's break your fucking hand. I flexed my fingers and my hand blazed. What had I done? I couldn't palm a coin right now, never mind trick-shuffle a deck.

I wanted a cigarette but didn't know if I'd even be able to hold one.

Then I heard it.

Just a single noise, coming from within the woods. I turned my head slowly in that direction. In the distance, above the trees, birds had scattered into the air.

And then it came again: a dull, flat *crack*.

The hairs on the back of my neck stood up, and I found I was breathing very slowly.

A lot of ideas flashed through my mind right then, each of them upping the fear inside me. But on the surface, all I was doing was staring at the implacable face of the woods.

Everything was quiet again.

It couldn't be what I was imagining. Even Choc wouldn't . . .

Get out of here.

A little way in, I heard the undergrowth crackling. Someone was coming back.

For a moment I was frozen in place – then, when I started to move, it felt like nothing on earth could have stopped me. Round the side of the car, fumbling for my keys, opening the door. Throwing myself in. The engine rolling, then churning into life.

Oh fuck.

The gravel crunched and spat up behind as I swung the car round too quickly, my broken hand trembling as I attempted to hold the wheel, checking my mirror as the woods rotated behind me. Nothing. Not yet.

I sped off down the dirt track anyway, car rolling with the terrain, and pulled out onto the street beyond without even checking it was clear.

They can't have fucking killed him.

Then I accelerated.

Heading anywhere, so long as it was away.

One inch of vodka and one inch of water knocked back in one. Not a particularly pleasant or sociable way to behave, I grant you, but it's enormously practical.

After driving around aimlessly for a while, trying not to panic, I went home, parked up, and walked into my quiet house. The entrance was street level, between two shops, with stairs leading up to the first level of my two-storey flat. Emma had posted her key back through the letterbox, and I found it lying on the carpet as I went inside. When I went upstairs, she'd left the front room light on, but all the boxes of her clothes and books were gone. That was that.

I turned the light off and went through to the kitchen.

There was a bottle of vodka in the fridge, and an ashtray on the side. My fingers shook too much to hold the cigarette with my right hand, so I smoked south-paw, and set about getting drunk as quickly and comprehensively as I could.

The fifth glass I sat with for a time, with the strange sensation of watching my hand trembling even though the alcohol had dulled the pain almost entirely. The first two knuckles looked black, and the bruise was already spreading down the back of my hand towards my wrist. I tried moving my thumb to my fingertips and was rewarded by the burning return of that white hot coin, cutting its way through the vodka.

I downed the drink and poured another.

49

Nothing had happened, I told myself. Those noises hadn't been gunshots. I'd thrown a punch, but that was all. Eddie had got himself beaten up – no more than was coming to him – and that was all.

I downed the drink and poured another.

Like I'd told Tori the first night I'd met her, magic is mostly about misdirection. You have to make someone suspend their disbelief and accept something they know deep down isn't true. Now, more than anything, I wanted to perform a similar trick on myself. I needed to convince myself that nothing had happened.

So I continued drinking, and I kept repeating the lie to myself, over and over, until the words sank into my subconscious like a blueprint. *Nothing happened. You went to The Wheatfield.* You need to practise a physical routine about three thousand times before your body will perform it instinctively, and I wanted a mental equivalent of that. My mind needed to know nothing had happened without me having to think about it.

Eventually, in the early hours of the morning, by which time I could hardly walk, I clambered carefully upstairs and collapsed into bed; at some vague point afterwards, in a trough between peaks of nausea and panic, I fell asleep.

I dreamed about my brother, Owen. He was standing in different woods, and there was gunshot that I'd never heard but *had* been real, and then there was the memory of a policeman, kneeling down beside me in my bedroom and talking to me gently, telling me that my brother was dead.

Chapter Six
Friday 19th August

The day two years before when Sam Currie had gone to his son's house in the Grindlea Estate had been a warm August day, much like this one. The slate-coloured sky had been free of clouds, the hazy sun like a coin dissolving behind blurred glass. Currie had been irritated as he drove into the estate. He was annoyed with Neil, and with his wife, Linda.

The last time he'd seen his son had been a fortnight earlier, when Neil had called by their house. It had been as strained and awkward a visit as always. Currie had barely been able to suppress his disgust at his son's appearance. Neil's addiction hung around him: an unwashed, animal smell. His body was weak and pale, like a thin string of gristle. Sometimes, Currie would look at the photographs of those childhood birthday parties – that happy, smiling kid – and try to imagine what had gone wrong. There would be days when he felt sad and guilty that his son had ended up living this dirty hand-to-mouth existence, and other times when he was simply angry. Neil slipped back and forth between victim and villain; Currie's opinion of himself shifted accordingly.

During that last visit they'd had nothing to say to each other. Currie looked into his son's eyes and recognised the distracted calculations of the addict. Nothing approximating love. But at least there had been some good news: Neil was off the streets at the moment, even if a flat in the Grindleas was less than ideal. He said he was off heroin too, but the lie stank on him, and when he left that day they found that money and jewellery had gone missing. Linda cried. Currie's heart, damaged repeatedly over the years, had set as scar tissue, but his wife's had always seemed to mend perfectly, ready and waiting to be broken again.

That night they had a difficult conversation about what to do, and the decision they reached was to cut Neil off. He was their son, and they loved him, but Currie convinced Linda it was the right thing to do. After only a week of non-contact, however, she'd started to worry. She went behind Currie's back and phoned Neil; there was no answer, and she asked her husband to go round and make sure he was all right. At first, he resisted – their son hadn't returned the calls, he told her, because she was of no use to him right now – and for a whole week he remained stalwart, stopping the subject dead when his wife brought it up. By the end, she was practically begging him to check on Neil. Finally, Currie relented.

He drove into the Grindleas that day seething at this waste of his time, parked halfway up the hill, then walked along the paths between council flats, searching out his son's address. But somewhere between the car and Neil's door, he developed a slight tickle at the back of his skull. Perhaps his imagination added that afterwards, but still, he remembered it clearly. Nothing had changed, and there was no way he could have known anything was wrong, but he felt it. When he arrived, he saw the outside of the house resting in shade, and his stomach fell away. The smell in the garden could have come from the bins, but he knew straight away that it didn't.

There was no answer when he knocked; Currie had to kick the door open. As it splintered inwards, a thousand flies buzzed into life as one – filling the front room with static – and a wave of warm air rolled out, sticking to his skin like grease, coating the hairs on his arms as they stood on end. Neil had been dead for nearly a week. Currie found his son's body slumped on the sofa, an electric fire glowing soft-red to one side.

In the days that followed, the clean-up crew would be forced to remove the settee, the carpet and ten of the floorboards. Men with masks and thick gloves would come and pick dozens of needles out from piles of rubbish. They would scrape faeces from the hallway. But to begin with, there was only Sam Currie. The implications of what had happened to his son were put to one side in the first instance, as his professional instincts took hold and began issuing orders. He walked calmly back out into the indifferent garden and closed the front door behind him. Somewhere inside himself, he understood that his marriage was over, his life crippled, but all he did for the moment was phone his partner, then lean against the outside wall.

He thought about nothing. Nothing at all.

A week was a long time for a man to lie undiscovered. When he allowed himself to drink, which was less often now than it had been, Currie thought a great deal about that week. In his mind, Neil was alive during that time: dead, obviously, but still somehow capable of being saved, waiting for a man who stubbornly refused to arrive. A man who had *priorities*, just as he always had. Every second of that refusal added to the sorrow Currie felt as he stared at whatever wall happened to be in front of him at the time.

He pictured his son as he'd been in the old photographs – a little boy – lost, alone and crying. Death did that. With precious few exceptions, it froze people as victims for ever. Question marks at the end of blank sentences they left you to fill in for yourself.

Now, two years later, Currie scanned the houses to the left as they drove into the estate. Neil's old flat was out of sight, but he still felt it there, or at least imagined he could.

Swann was driving. 'You okay?'

'Sure,' Currie said.

'Checking for an ambush?'

Currie smiled grimly.

There were poorer areas, but the Grindleas were notorious by name: a dirty little pocket of poverty and crime nestling between two affluent suburbs. Only one proper road in. Some police said that, if they wanted to, the residents could man a barricade at the bottom of the hill and keep them out for a good few days. There were probably fifty or sixty men living in this postcode who'd happily join it, many of them with guns. Charlie Drake made his home in here, as did most of his crew.

And a man named Frank Carroll.

'I'm just tired,' Currie said.

Swann raised his eyebrows. *Oh yes.*

The time since the discovery of Alison Wilcox's body had been full of both work and frustration. The forensics had given them little to go on, and the majority of Alison's friends and relatives had been able to tell them nothing.

Instead, a familiar picture was emerging. Alison had been a bright, attractive student – popular too, although recently she'd slipped from several radars in the way that people did. As far as anyone had known, she was okay, and so, without consciously thinking about it, they'd put her on 'standby' in their heads: *all fine; check again at some point soon, whenever I remember.* A few of her closer friends had texted or emailed over the past week. They'd all received replies, worded in exactly the same way. But the last time anyone had seen her in the flesh or spoken to her on the phone had been over a fortnight before her death.

The texts and emails offered a horrific insight into what had transpired in that time. They meant Alison's killer had gained access to her mobile phone – her accounts and passwords – and that while she lay slowly dying, he'd been pretending to be her: keeping in touch where necessary; allaying any concerns.

It was an awful thought for the people who'd received those messages to contemplate, but it was made even worse by what happened afterwards. Alison's death hadn't signalled the end of the contact. Six of her friends had received a message from her mobile phone on the morning the body was found. Each said simply: *You let her die.*

Of course, they'd all been traced. As with the previous murders, the killer had sent his emails from the victim's house, and his texts from anonymous, crowded streets, carefully avoiding any CCTV. He knew exactly what he was doing. For the third time, Currie suspected he was going to get away with it.

Swann approached the roundabout at the top of the hill. In front, there was a post office, an off-licence and a squat, vicious-looking pub called the Cockerel. Beyond the roundabout, the Plug: three tower blocks, with towels draped out of windows, and clothes strung on lines across the pockmark alcoves. Graffiti curled up from the base of the buildings like overgrown weeds. Swann took the car round, drove a little further, and then pulled in on the left.

When they got out, Currie could hear music drifting down from one of the open windows in the tower block behind them.

'So,' he said. 'Frank Carroll. Remind me again why we're here?'

'Because we're good cops who follow up every lead.'

'Oh yeah. That's it.'

Swann closed the car door.

'And desperate,' he said.

According to the Sex Offenders Register, Frank Carroll now lived in the house they were standing outside: a flat-roofed, single-storey council flat, with a mucky, overgrown garden. Someone had daubed the words *sick fuck kids bewear* in large white letters on the front door. Beneath it, earlier slogans appeared to have been rubbed off.

'Do you think it's the right place?' Currie said.

Swann shot him a wry smile as they opened the gate.

On the surface, this lead wasn't promising. Carroll's name had come in from an anonymous phone call the evening after Alison had been found, but the scant detail provided had kept the information away from their desk until yesterday. Having skimmed the basics of Carroll's file, Currie had been interested, but quietly unconvinced. They were good cops, though. And they were desperate.

At the front door, Currie could hear a loud television from within. It sounded like someone was being murdered: screams seeping out through the gaps in the bricks and panels.

They knocked, and the television immediately went silent.

And that was when Currie started to feel it. There was no sensible reason to be, but he was nervous. Not afraid, exactly, but not far off either. The speed with which the TV had gone quiet reminded him of a spider going still as a fly snagged on its web. He could almost imagine the man inside, equally motionless. Listening.

After a minute, the door opened. They were faced by a tall, thin man. He was wearing a white shirt too large for him, and old, rubbery tracksuit bottoms.

Currie didn't even recognise him at first. The photograph in the file had shown a man in his late thirties with a good-looking, symmetrical face. There had been a hint of cruelty in the strong angles at his jaw, but it was the eyes that gave him away: full of intelligence and hate. Twelve years ago, Frank Carroll – an ex-cop of only a few hours – had stared out at the world, looking like he understood a hundred ways to take you apart and was picturing them right then, enjoying each, one by one. By all accounts, he'd been a powerfully built man, equally as capable of carrying out those acts in the flesh as he was in his mind.

But prison clearly hadn't been kind to him. His skin was old and weathered, and his hair had gone grey and receded. He'd lost a great deal of weight, too. That solid, strong man now looked pigeon-chested and frail: hunched over slightly, like something in his back had gone. The old muscles hung down like slack, useless cords. His eyes still held that cruelty, but even there one of them seemed dislocated and wrong, as though it had been taken out and replaced at an odd angle.

Currie's unease intensified.

'Mr Carroll?' He held up his badge. 'Detective Currie, Detective Swann. We'd like to ask you a few questions.'

Frank Carroll stared at him.

Currie felt an absurd urge to scratch himself.

'Come in.'

He shot Swann a glance as they followed Carroll into his flat, closing the door behind them – then grimaced as the stench of the place hit him properly. It was like someone had dabbed ammonia under his nose. The small corridor reeked of old sweat.

In front of them, the man moved slowly and carefully into the lounge. The room was in a disgusting state. The carpet was covered with dust – *probably jumping with fleas too*, Currie thought – and the old wallpaper was stained yellow. There was an ashtray on a dirty table, full of cigarette butts, while piles of tattered newspapers and magazines lined the walls. The air felt hazy, grey.

Carroll sat down awkwardly on a two-seater settee, his bony knees poking up against the greasy tracksuit.

'I know why you're here,' he said.

'Oh yeah? Do tell.'

'You're here about those girls.' Carroll sniffed dismissively. 'I saw you on the television. Talking about them. I recognised you from there.'

'That's very observant. Once a cop always a cop, eh?'

'I'm not a policeman anymore.'

'Yeah, we know that.' He glanced around, taking in the details of the living room. *Not much of a decorator, either.* He looked back at the old man. 'Doesn't explain why you might be expecting to see us, though.'

Carroll just looked at him, the faintest trace of amusement flashing in his eyes. Currie flicked through a list of mental images to locate the one he was reminded of, found it quickly. The sly old man holding court; one who'd seen it all. *You don't impress me, son.*

'We were interested in your file. There are some peculiar similarities there. But then – you'll have realised that, won't you? Being so observant, and all.'

Carroll smiled, and his lips all but disappeared. 'Doesn't explain why you might be looking through my file, though. Get a phone call, did we?'

Swann moved over to one wall and nudged a stack of magazines with his foot. Carroll's gaze shot to him, quick as that spider Currie had imagined. Swann smiled.

'Anything we should know about in here, Frank?'

'Lots of *news*.' He rolled the word as though it might be unfamiliar to them.

'News is fascinating,' Swann agreed. 'The older the better. Are you planning on doing some papier mache, or something?'

'There's nothing illegal in there, if that's what you mean,' Carroll said. 'Why would there be?'

Currie said, 'Because you like little girls. Or at least, you did. Fifteen years, reduced to ten. I was quite appalled when I read the file. Your own daughter, Frank.'

He had seen a photograph of Mary Carroll in the file as well. She looked considerably younger than fifteen. When the picture had been taken, she was dressed in a white T-shirt, and her face was gaunt and hollow, with dark rings around haunted eyes. One of

57

them was swollen almost shut. Her straggly blond hair looked like it hadn't been washed or combed in a week.

'I don't have a daughter,' Carroll said.

'Unfortunately for her, you do,' Currie said. 'And a son as well. Although I doubt you get birthday cards from either of them. Does that happen often?'

'They're dead to me.'

'Well, we all know what you did to her.'

Carroll turned to him slowly. 'Lots of things.'

Currie made an effort to smile pleasantly. He'd become accustomed to dealing with that kind of filth, but sometimes it still shocked him. The things people did, and the way they managed to feel about it.

'We're thinking of one in particular,' he said. 'You used to tie her to the bed, didn't you? Leave her for days on end without food or water.'

'That's one of the less interesting ones.'

Swann nudged the magazine stack again, not even looking over. 'You were released two years ago, Frank. Coincidentally, some similar things started happening to girls just afterwards. We're *very* interested in those things, even if you're not.'

The whole time, Carroll just kept staring at Currie. The expression on the man's face was utterly blank.

'Did somebody call you?' he asked again.

'No,' Swann said. 'We have a computer that throws up names for us. And I do mean that literally . . .' The magazines spilled out across the floor. 'Whoops.'

Carroll glanced over, then shook his head and looked down at the floor in front of him. His hands twittered together – like birds with broken wings – and he steepled them before his face, bony elbows resting on bony knees.

'Do you know what they do to police in prison?' he said.

'I guess you can tell us,' Swann said.

'They break you,' Carroll said. 'My left eye is glass, and that side of my face is paralysed. I'm registered disabled. It takes me time just to walk across the room. And you think I could hurt someone?'

He had a point, Currie thought. The victims all appeared to have been subdued by hand, and Carroll looked as though he could barely lift his arms. So what was it? Nasty, broken old man, living out his days, or was there more to him than just the age and stench?

'I'm afraid you're going to have to come with us, Frank.'

Carroll shook his head again. Then he slowly reached down and hitched up the bottom of his jogging pants, revealing a pale, hairless stretch of leg. There was a black band wrapped around it. It took Currie a moment to realise what it was. And when Carroll glanced up at him, he looked intensely satisfied with himself.

An electronic tag, secured in place. GPS. The works.

'You can always check where I've been with this.'

Currie looked over at Swann, and his partner tilted his head: *your call*. Currie looked back at Frank Carroll and forced out another smile he didn't feel.

'We'll do that, Mr Carroll,' he said. 'In the meantime, and at your own speed, get your coat.'

Chapter Seven
Monday 22nd August

Two weeks after visiting Tori in hospital I drove across town, on my way somewhere I hadn't been in nearly a year.

The last fortnight had been a pack of hot, sweaty days, and today was the first real reminder that summer wasn't going to last for ever. The sun had spent the morning hidden behind a sky full of grey mist. It was still warm, but the air had a hint of winter to it now: the sense of cold and frost approaching steadily from the distance.

I liked it. It was a reminder that time moved on.

The last two weeks, I'd lived as much like a hermit as I could: holed up in my flat, expecting a knock at the door at any moment. I'd found it hard to sleep before, but for at least the first few days after my trip to the woods, it had been almost impossible. And yet nothing had happened. The police hadn't turned up and arrested me, and Choc hadn't called round either. I'd scanned the news, and as far as I could tell Eddie's body hadn't even been found.

The whole time, I'd kept repeating my mantra that nothing had happened. I wasn't sure it had worked, but for whatever reason – maybe just the passing of time – the guilt and fear had started to lessen, and I'd managed to shade things over in my head a little, and sometimes whole hours went by when I could kid myself I was a normal person with only normal things to worry about. Deep down, though, it still felt like I was living on borrowed time, and that might have had something to do with where I was going now.

I drove down into the Washmores and got the first thrill of

recognition. This was the area I'd grown up in. Everything here was familiar but subtly different, as though half the houses had received a paint job and an unidentifiable extension. Ahead of me the road finished at bollards, blocking off the bridge over the river, which I could hear rushing past in the distance. I drove right, down a thin, cobbled lane. The dry-stone wall to the side was hairy with moss, and halfway along there was the old streetlight. It had a glass box for a head, narrow arms sticking out sideways beneath the chin, and a thin, flaky green body below. I'd swung on that thing as a kid. Looking at it now, it was weird to think I could ever have been that small.

A minute later I approached a large Victorian house, set back and down from the road. The huge outside walls were soot-black with age, and a driveway curled away out of sight.

If I closed my eyes I could picture it.

Behind the building, a garden spread down over three tiers, most of it untended and overgrown now. Outside the front door, washing lines spanned the first level, and the memory associated with this was my mother stretching up to hang out wet clothes, spare pegs clipped to her sleeve. The second garden still had a bare patch of ground from the bonfires my father used to make for some reason known only to himself. I'd managed to reach the age of twenty-eight without needing to build a fire, but he was always burning something. And, at the bottom, a slope of long grass ended in the bushes and fence that marked the edge of my parents' property. Beyond them, the woods where Owen had been killed.

My brother was for ever frozen in my memory at the age of twelve. He'd gone out to play in the woods by himself, and my parents hadn't even realised there might be anything wrong until the police knocked on the door just before tea-time. Owen had been shot in the side by an air-rifle. Someone out walking had found him, curled up on the dusty ground like a caterpillar. Motorists reported seeing a group of older kids that afternoon, leaving the woods at the far end by the ring road, but they were never identified. Teenagers messing around. Over the years, I've wondered if they even realised what they'd done.

I parked up behind the *Domestic Goddess* van and made my way down the long tarmac drive. There were small trees on either side of the steps at the bottom, grown together overhead to create an arch. I paused underneath, peering up into the dark mass of branches above. I remembered climbing these as a kid – but now I could have reached at least halfway up on tiptoes and touched branches that would never support me again.

Time moves on.

My mother's old clothes-line still hung slackly across the top garden, running from a rusted hook in the house wall to a thick green tree by the fence, and the same grey slabs formed the path. It led to the front door, next to the set of sharp, rusty railings that edged the short drop to the second garden.

The front door was open. From inside, I could hear the sound of a vacuum cleaner.

It had been over three years since my mother's death, and a year since my father's, and in the intervening time I'd done absolutely nothing with the property beyond hire Linda – the Domestic Goddess – to come round and clean once a month. The house had been effectively held in stasis while I worked up the resolve to deal with it. The contents had to be boxed up and disposed of. Everything would need redecorating.

A big job, basically, and I could pretend that was the reason. In truth, it wasn't the size of the task that daunted me so much as the details. My memories of the first half of my childhood were good, but they were tarnished by the gulf that had developed in my family after Owen died. I wasn't entirely sure I was ready to deal with this place even now, but the events of the last few weeks had sharpened my intent a little.

If not now, when?

'Linda?'

I called out and knocked twice on the open door as I went in. She was expecting me – I heard a click, and then the whirr of the vacuum cleaner winding down.

Linda was in her early forties and pleasantly rounded: a lovely, amiable woman who turned up in old jeans and jumpers and seemed to get a kick out of cleaning. Which is a pretty enviable gene to have. She was standing just outside the kitchen now, wiping her forehead with the back of her arm. As I walked up, she smiled at me and blew hair out of her eyes.

'Nearly done.'

'Seems fine to me.' I looked dubiously at the carpet, worn down to a grey grid in the middle, and then at the cream woodchip wallpaper. 'I'll have to rip all this out anyway.'

Linda nodded.

'It'll be nice when it's done up. Are you going to sell it?'

'God, yes.'

For a terrible moment, I imagined moving in here.

'Well, it'll make someone a nice home,' she said.

'Here's hoping.'

Next to Linda, opposite the kitchen, was the closed door to my brother's old bedroom. It was the one area of the house I'd asked Linda not to touch. Nobody had been in there since the day Owen died. My parents never threw any of his things away, none of us went in, and the door remained closed. It was an unwritten rule. The room was sealed and buried, like a time capsule.

Occasionally I'd watch my mother in the kitchen, wrists foam-deep in the sink – and suddenly she'd look around, startled, as though she'd forgotten to do something very important. Then, she'd see that closed door and remember that Owen wasn't dead after all. He was just in his bedroom, out of sight, and it was all okay. Almost everything my parents did was built around a similar principle.

'It's fifty, isn't it?' I took the money out of my wallet.

Linda nodded and accepted it, then unplugged the vacuum cleaner. A touch of a button sent the cable clattering back inside.

Out on the path, she handed me the spare keys and looked up at the tall, looming face of the house with something close to regret.

'I'll miss working here.'

'You've done a great job.'

I meant it. Obviously, I'd paid her to clean, but there was more to it than that. When I first showed her around, for example, I hadn't known we'd be faced with more than fifty empty bottles of vodka secreted in the kitchen pantry. They were gone now, and Linda had never mentioned them to me, or done anything at all to underline the moment of complicated shame I'd felt when I saw them. *Why didn't you know how your father spent his last months?*

'It's just time I sorted the place out.'

'I understand. Take care, Dave. Best of luck.'

'You too.'

After she left, I locked up, and realised this was it: the responsibility for the house rested entirely with me again. Should I take a look around? I decided not to. I already knew about the scale of the job, and it felt like I'd done enough for the moment. One step at a time.

Back at the car, I turned on the radio and lit a cigarette. Halfway through, the local news came on: a lorry was jack-knifed southbound on the motorway; a local councillor had been caught forwarding a joke email about Asians; and the police were no closer to catching the killer of Alison Wilcox.

I put the cigarette out. As I did, my mobile vibrated in my pocket.

Hi there. Just checking we're still on for later? Hope so – looking forward to it. Tor xx

I smiled – she always signed off texts like that – and then sent a reply:

Definitely still on; looking forward to it too.

That was the one good thing that had happened recently. Tori had been signed off by the hospital at the end of last week, and we were going to meet up for a drink and a catch-up tonight.

If it doesn't work out with her, there's always me.

A stupid clump inside my heart twitched at the memory of that, and I reminded myself to forget it. Then I put my phone on the passenger seat and started the engine.

I met Tori at half past six inside the Sphere. It was an argumentatively-titled rectangular shopping precinct in the centre of town, comprised almost entirely of fashion shops, jewellers and a handful of expensive restaurants, none of which I'd ever felt the need to frequent. I was sitting on a bench on the ground floor. At this time of night the shops were either closed or closing up, but the walkways were still busy with people cutting through after work: suits and students. From one open storey above, beyond the escalators, I could hear the sounds of the cinema crowds and the chatter of slot machines. Nearby, a waitress stacked plates on her arm and carried them in from the terrace, while a lanky security guard meandered past.

'Hey there.'

Tori nudged me on the shoulder, and I turned around.

'Hey,' I said. 'I was expecting you from the other way in.'

She smiled. 'Keeping you on your toes.'

I stood up and we hugged. She turned her face against my chest and we held on for a few seconds – *it's so good to see you* – then I rubbed the back of her coat and we parted. I kept my hands on her upper arms for a moment and smiled back.

'Looking *fine*.'

'Oh, thanks, but I'm a mess and I know it.'

Well, maybe a little. Her skin was in bad shape, and the make-up she'd used to cover it was a bit patchy, but it didn't make any difference. Part of Tori's appeal to me had always been that she was pretty but didn't care too much about any flaws that made it through – as honest about herself as everything else.

'I think you look fine.' I held out my arm for her. 'Shall we?'

She took it decisively. 'Let's.'

We went to the Ivy, a posh wine bar on the edge of the complex. In a past life it had been an ornate hotel lobby, and it seemed slightly resentful of those better days, like an ancient, impeccably dressed butler reduced to waiting on a family of degenerates. The palm trees dotted around in enormous bulb vases were utterly incongruous. The tables and chairs were all sculpted from black wire, and about half of them were occupied with well-dressed couples, or businessmen impressing guests. I bought a Guinness for me and a Diet Coke for Tori – receiving scant change from a tenner – then we found a place to sit. A gold-plated fan hummed around overhead.

'Cheers,' I said as we clinked glasses. 'To your freedom.'

'Thanks. It's good to be out.'

'And are you okay now?'

She grimaced, as though she didn't know how to answer that question. I thought again of when she'd first told me about her illness, and tried to imagine what she was feeling right now.

'I'm on my way,' she said. 'I have someone calling in to see me, but it looks like I'm back on the straight and narrow.'

'That's good.'

'For now, anyway.'

'It was strange seeing you there. It wasn't what I was expecting.'

Tori looked at me, her head cocked a little quizzically.

'I didn't know you'd come. I appreciate it.'

'You don't remember?' Despite myself, I felt crestfallen. If she didn't remember my visit, then she didn't remember what she'd said. 'I was there when Choc was.'

'Choc was there a lot.' She frowned at that. 'How was I?'

I paused, considering the question, but deep down I was thinking: *If it doesn't work out with her, there's always me.*

A part of me had taken that seriously, and now I felt stupidly crushed.

'You were fine,' I said. 'I was sad that you were in there, but it was good to see you were doing okay.'

I smiled at her. All else aside, that much was true.

'It's always good to see you, in fact.'

She smiled back. 'You as well.'

After that, we chatted about nothing much over a couple of drinks. One of the problems back when we were a couple was that we didn't have a lot to say to each other, but weren't together long enough for those silences to be comfortable. In the intervening years, we'd become a lot more relaxed, and even when we were quiet, it was usually okay. Tonight, things felt different. I did my best, but it began to feel like I was wearing a mask with an un-convincing smile painted on it, and that any second she was going to notice. As the evening went on, I searched for any sign this might be more to her than a quiet drink with a friend. There was nothing. I'd been an idiot, and the events of the past month – everything from Emma leaving to what had happened with Eddie – suddenly all seemed present, correct and unbearably heavy.

By nine o'clock, she was yawning.

'Home time?' I said.

'Yeah. I'm sorry.'

'No worries. I'll walk you.'

We crossed the centre, arm in arm, and when we reached her stop the bus was already there, a queue of people boarding it slowly. She turned to me and gave me one of those big, affectionate hugs.

'Oh, it's been so good to see you. Thank you for everything.'

I rubbed her back gently. 'You too. Go on – you'll miss your bus.'

'Okay. Keep in touch, you.'

She got on and the doors hissed shut, and the pit in my stomach suddenly doubled in depth because I'd just realised something: I wasn't going to keep in touch with her. The realisation brought with it a profound sense of sadness, but I knew it was inevitable; it had to be. The mental weight I'd given this evening cast everything in a different light, bringing out sharp, complex angles on surfaces that had previously seemed so smooth and simple.

Tori waved to me from the aisle as the bus pulled away, and I waved back and thought, ridiculously: *I still love you. I don't think I ever stopped.*

So I don't think I can have you around anymore.

And a moment later, she was gone.

Chapter Eight

Tuesday 23rd August

As she walked along the pavement carrying two heavy shopping bags, so overloaded that the plastic was cutting into her palms, Mary remembered the night her childhood had ended.

In her mind, she saw two shivering children, struggling through the night. The girl was fifteen years old, walking barefoot in the snow, wearing only a T-shirt. With one hand she was pressing the garment tightly against her skin, trying to hug some heat into her body; with the other, she was clinging onto her brother's hand, pulling him along behind her. He was almost catatonic, and he walked placidly wherever she led him, apparently oblivious to the tears streaming down her face and the raw skin of her wrists.

The houses around them were all dark. The girl had no idea where they were going. All she knew was that nobody would help them, and they couldn't go back. And yet, somehow, she had to look after the little boy she pulled along behind her.

She was terrified.

Now, twelve years later, she turned the corner into her street, feeling something similar. The memory had been on her mind a great deal over the past two weeks. Since the Sunday she had made the call to the police, her whole life had felt like it was precariously balanced, ready to tumble in either direction at any moment. She wavered between panic and hope, aware deep down that both emotions were equally dangerous. She mustn't panic, because that would freeze her up when she had to keep moving forwards. And she mustn't hope, because nobody would help . . .

And then Mary saw him – standing outside her house, up ahead –

and felt the balance shift. She recognised him. It was the policeman from the news conference she'd seen on the television that day, and he was looking directly at her. Even as she tried to press it back down, hope flowered beneath her hands. Its petals twirled up through her fingers and she stopped attempting to control it:

They've found him.

Her heart could have been dancing.

They listened to you.

As she approached the house, Mary realised that they'd also found *her*, and that was less good – she was annoyed with herself for losing concentration and being spotted first. A lifetime spent looking over her shoulder ought to have prepared her better than that. She'd always been so careful in the past, even when there was no need. You were meticulous when you didn't have to be, so you'd be prepared when you did. And yet all that practice seemed to have failed her now, when it mattered more than ever. She couldn't afford to let her guard down like that.

What if it had been someone else?

The policeman stepped to one side. 'Mary Carroll?'

'Yes.'

Any other time she would have been aghast to hear her name being spoken out loud like that. She might have openly denied it, even to a policeman. But today she nodded, then gratefully put the bags down on the tarmac where they half-collapsed, like hot-air balloons crumpling on landing.

The policeman smiled.

'I thought I recognised you – from the picture in your file. I'm Detective Sam Currie. I wanted to talk to you about the phone call you made a couple of weeks ago.'

He has a kind voice, too.

'Oh yes?'

'Just a quick word, really. We followed up on the information you gave us, and I wanted to reassure you about your concerns.'

Concerns, she thought. *Reassure you.*

Suddenly, everything inside her felt dead.

Better to feel panic than this.

'You'd better come in,' she said.

Five minutes later, Mary brought two coffees through into the front room. She'd waited for the kettle to boil with her elbows on the kitchen counter and her face in her hands, hair brushing the crumbs of sugar around the base of her mug. Taking deep breaths and trying to gain some control over herself. How could she have been so stupid?

You have to convince him.

The thought took hold of her, but even as it did she knew it was just another burst of hope, destined to knock her down harder. What else could she do, though?

The policeman – Currie – was perched right at the front of the armchair, flicking through a book. He held it up as she walked in.

'The Knight Errant,' he said. 'I remember this. I used to read it to my son when he was little.'

She was annoyed with herself for leaving that out. It was only a kids' book, but she didn't like anyone getting such a personal insight into her childhood. Especially in circumstances like this.

'It was my favourite book when I was younger,' she said.

He swapped it for the coffee, then held the mug tightly between his hands, as though he'd been out in the cold for days.

Mary curled up at the far end of the settee, her legs beneath her.

'How did you know where I was living?'

'Your brother,' Currie said.

That startled her for a moment. Instead of the memory of the two of them in the snow, she thought now about the nightmare she'd had. Her brother, the small, innocent boy that she'd tried so desperately to shield from their father's violence.

'John,' she said. 'I've not seen him in a while. How is he?'

'He sounded fine.'

'You didn't meet him?'

Currie shook his head. 'He's living in Rawnsmouth. Our budget doesn't stretch to five-hundred-mile journeys.'

'Of course.'

'I spoke to him on the phone, though. He wasn't overly keen to talk about your father.'

'He's moved on with his life.'

'You don't have much contact?'

'Not for a long time.'

It made her sad to think about her brother. They'd been so close when they were young, and the years since had driven them further and further apart. Another legacy from their father. Another that broke her heart, and left her feeling almost unbearably guilty.

She said, 'I didn't know he even had this address.'

'He didn't. Just the phone number.'

Mary nodded to herself. So that was it. She was annoyed with him for giving away her privacy so easily: he should have known better. But she didn't want to talk about that with Currie.

'You said you followed up the information I gave?'

He nodded once, rolling the mug between his hands.

'Yes. We went round to see your father. After looking through the file, I can completely understand why you thought what you did.'

What did it say in there? she wondered.

Did he *completely understand* how it felt to be tied to a bed and deprived of food and water for two days? She imagined he didn't.

'But?'

'After thoroughly investigating the matter, we had to release your father. I'm sorry, but he's not responsible for these crimes.'

You have to try.

'You must have missed something.'

'I'm sorry.'

'He's sending a message to me. You don't realise it because you didn't . . . live through what I did. With him. You don't know what he's like.'

Currie frowned. 'Have you seen him since his release?'

Even the thought of it sent her pulse racing.

'Of *course* not.'

'Well, your father's a broken man, Mary. I'm not saying that means anything much, but he can barely cross the room without a walking stick. I've seen the picture of him when he was arrested, and he's changed a great deal. He isn't the man you remember.'

Could that be true?

No. He must have seen what her father wanted him to.

71

'People always underestimated him,' she said. 'My father could tear you to pieces if he wanted. If he looks weak and fragile now, then it's an act. Trying to . . . throw you off the scent. He's the one who's killing those girls.'

She paused, aware that she was on the verge of babbling. Currie was looking at her with sympathy now, and she didn't like that at all. She didn't care what he thought of her, but it was the face of a man searching for a way to let her down gently. She couldn't bear it.

'Please.'

'I shouldn't go into detail,' Currie said. 'But I will, if only to set your mind at rest. Your father is electronically tagged, Mary.'

'What?'

'It was a condition of his parole. He is not responsible for these murders. It simply isn't possible.'

No.

Mary blinked at him, her mind processing the information, and what it meant. Electronically tagged? She'd been prepared for the fact they didn't have enough evidence to charge him, or that he'd managed to dredge up a fake alibi from somewhere. But not this. *It simply isn't possible.*

'He's got around it somehow.'

'No. We have a complete record of his whereabouts.'

'Then he must have taken it off somehow. You don't know how clever he can be.' She thought of something, and desperately seized at it: 'Or maybe he's still got friends in the police. Someone faking it for him.'

'I'm sorry. I can see why you thought it might be him, but it's not the case.'

'It is.' She wanted to beat her fists against something until he believed her. 'I *know* it is.'

Currie shook his head and didn't reply. He was still trying to be kind, but he didn't understand. Mary wondered how she appeared to him right now. Just another damaged person, probably. Handle with care. But still, she couldn't stop.

'I wish you hadn't come here.'

He looked perplexed. 'Why?'

72

'Because he might have followed you.'

'Your father? I don't think you need to worry.'

Everything got the better of her then.

She said, 'You have no idea what I need.'

'Mary . . .' He struggled. 'People don't follow police around. They just don't. And anyway, it was last week when I saw your father.'

'You think he wouldn't do it? That's *nothing* to him. He'd follow you for a *year* if he thought it would help him find me. For the rest of his life. In his head, I'm all that matters.'

'I understand why you're concerned.' Currie looked awkward. 'But for your sake you have to keep a sense of perspective.'

'Do I?' Her throat was tight; she was going to cry. 'You don't know anything about my father or what he's capable of.'

'I know he was a dangerous man, but—'

'No, you don't know the half of it. It might say he was a policeman, but it won't say he was a criminal too. That he ran the whole neighbourhood.'

'Mary—'

She rested her elbows on her knees and pressed the palms of her hands into her eyes. Hard.

'When I was eleven,' she said, 'two men came to the house. They were drug dealers; I know that now. I guess they wanted to send a message to my father because he was moving too far into their turf. Expecting too much of a cut. They underestimated him. People always did that.'

The sound of her father's gun exploded briefly in her thoughts. At the time, she hadn't known what the sound was, just that it meant something bad was happening. But John, only eight at the time, had run through.

'He shot one of them in the kitchen. That man was already dead when I saw him. The other, my father just knocked him down. And then he turned on the stove.'

The tears came then. Two weeks of panic and fear welled up from inside her, and spilled out. While she could still speak, she said:

73

'That's one of my earliest memories. There are many more if you'd like to hear them.'

'I'm so sorry,' he said quietly. 'I can't imagine what it must have been like for you.'

She wanted to tell him everything else. About the policemen she would hear laughing downstairs in the lounge while she sat in the corner of her bedroom. The way people slapped her father on the back and sucked up to him, either because they were frightened of him or because they needed something. Those little words people had in the street about this or that, and the way he'd nod and say, 'Don't worry, I'll take care of it.' Good Officer Carroll. Hard yet fair. Nobody dared speak out about him and the things he did, *but they all knew.*

But what was the point? The hope she'd dared to feel when she saw Currie outside had been utterly crushed; it felt like she had a dead baby still inside her. She could tell him all those things, but what did it matter? People heard you but they didn't listen. You stood in front of them, screaming for help, and they stared right through—

'You won't believe it until he comes for me.'

'I'm sorry.'

'Just go. Please.'

He stood up. She heard the floor creak as he walked across the room. But not the stairs. She opened her eyes to see that he'd paused in the doorway.

'I've got to ask you something,' he said. 'I saw it when I came in.'

He gestured at the door handle.

'What?' she said.

'There's blood on it.'

What more did he want from her? She looked at him through her tears for a few seconds, considering it, and then reached down and pulled the leg of her jeans up. Showing him the scars on the back of her calf. They'd healed now, but they still showed up nicely in the light. She hoped he liked them.

'You did that?'

'Yes,' she said. 'It helps.'

Currie stared back at her for a second, and his expression seemed overburdened with sadness. But even so, she thought he understood. Maybe he didn't have scars of his own, but he had something. He nodded to himself.

'Thank you for your time, Mary. Take care.'

As she heard his footsteps on the stairs she allowed the material to fall back to her ankle. The front door opened, closed, and then – as she should have always known would happen – Mary was left entirely alone.

Part Two

Chapter Nine

Sunday 28th August

On a first date with someone, there are two questions I know I'm going to be asked. After getting through a thoroughly respectable pasta dish, most of a bottle of red wine and the whole 'isn't it weird meeting people off the internet?' conversation, a girl called Sarah Crowther asked me the first.

'Will you show me a magic trick?'

'It'll cost you,' I said. 'A guy's got to eat.'

She smiled. 'You've just eaten, remember?'

'And fine food it was too.'

'It was, but my point is, that excuse doesn't work.'

I'd brought her to Al Bacio, my favourite Italian restaurant. Even though it was in the city centre, it was nearly always dead, a well-kept secret that the Italian family who ran it would no doubt have preferred to be a little less secret. The waiter kept hanging outside the door, smoking, which probably didn't help, but the food was great and the kitchen was open-plan, so you could smell your dinner cooking well before it arrived. I came here a lot.

Sarah and I had a table for two over in one corner, with a single candle burning to one side that made her eyes sparkle. Although I knew a fair amount about her (twenty-three years old, social drinker, social smoker, atheist, currently two years into a Fine Art PhD) and had obviously looked at the photo on her profile, this was the first time I'd seen her in the flesh. That afternoon, Rob, who was always disdainful of my occasional forays into the internet dating thing, had counselled me to expect an enormously overweight social misfit with an ice pick in her handbag. Or possibly a man.

In reality, he would have been kicking himself. Sarah was smart and attractive, with dark blond, curly hair hanging around a friendly face. She was wearing a neat black shirt, and tight, dark jeans. In one of our flirtatious email exchanges I'd asked her to describe herself in two words, and she'd said 'giggles' and 'curls'. So far, the description was spot on, and I was having a lovely evening. There was still time for an ice pick to emerge, of course, but at the moment I'd die a happy man.

'Go on,' she said. 'I can tell you want to.'

'Okay. Take that ring off and pass it to me.'

She did. I placed it on the table and then smiled at her, allowing a moment of silence to pan out.

'More wine?' I asked.

She grinned. 'You're stalling. But yeah, go on.'

I shared the end of the bottle out between us, then cleared my throat, made a show of loosening my fingers. My right hand had healed better than I'd expected, but it still felt slightly strange.

'Pay close attention.'

I slid the ring towards me and picked it up in my right hand. Showed it to her briefly. Passed it to my left and closed that hand around it, then stared at my fist, both hands held out in plain sight. There was a look of concentration on my face: I'd seen it in the mirror a thousand times before. Somewhere around the five-hundred mark, it had started to get convincing.

'Nearly . . .'

I closed my eyes, grimaced and—

—then relaxed totally: it wasn't going to happen.

'I messed it up.'

I placed the ring back on the table. Sarah looked at me, amused.

'Sorry,' I said. 'It's been a while.'

'Well, I can't imagine why you stopped.'

'So it's to be sarcasm?'

I feigned annoyance, enjoying the easy flirtation between us. After that night out with Tori, I'd been unsure whether to take time away from the whole dating thing. Right now, I was glad I'd decided to dive straight back in.

'Okay, let me try again.'

I slid the ring towards me again and picked it up. Same as before: first in the right hand, then passed to the left. I stared at my fist for a few moments before closing my eyes, imagining the ring was burning me slightly as it disintegrated. Becoming more and more painful . . .

I'd like to thank the Academy . . .

. . . and then opened my eyes, pleased with myself.

'Gone.'

I uncurled the fingers of my left hand to show it was empty.

This time, Sarah looked impressed.

'Very good.' She tapped my right hand. 'So what about that one?'

I opened my right hand as well. Empty.

The expression on her face changed slightly. Now, she looked confused as well as pleased. I could imagine what she was thinking: she'd seen the ring in my right hand after I'd picked it up; both hands had stayed in full, open view, and my shirt sleeves were rolled up. Whatever I'd messed up the first time had been while I was holding the ring. So how on earth had I done it?

'That's very clever.' She frowned. 'So where is it?'

I sipped my wine innocently. 'It'll turn up.'

She looked like she was about to press it, but I was saved by the waiter.

'Everything all right with your meals?'

'Lovely, thanks.'

I put my napkin on the plate and he began clearing the table. Sarah narrowed her eyes. 'I'll get the truth out of you.'

'Is that a promise?'

'It's a *threat*.'

'I'll look forward to it.'

She sipped her wine. 'So how long have you been doing that?'

'What, anticipating threats?'

'No, magic.'

'Since I was twelve.'

'What, like a conjuror set for Christmas?'

I shook my head. 'It all started when my father tried to get me to bend a spoon.'

Sarah laughed. 'And did you?'

'Er, funnily enough – no. He'd seen someone on television do it, and I was too young to know any better. He was disappointed in me. So I learned how to do it just to show him it was a fraud.'

'How do you bend a spoon, then?'

'Lots of boring ways. That's the thing about magic – it's amazing what people won't see if they don't want to. My parents were convinced I'd done it for real. When they found out I hadn't, they still carried on believing in the TV guy anyway. Go figure.'

'People are strange.'

'They are.'

The story was basically true, although I'd softened it slightly. I hadn't told her about the vindictive way I'd done it – the fact that, at the time, I'd taken a cruel pleasure in trying to dispel my father's beliefs. It wasn't something I was proud of, but I was twelve.

After Owen died, my parents never met a New Age belief they didn't love, and had a particularly strong love affair with spiritualism. They became entirely different people. They went to mediums who told them everything they wanted to hear – that Owen still existed; that he was smiling at them; that he was happy now. Frauds and conmen, basically, who siphoned off their money and alchemised it into false hope. I was angry at them.

Of course, looking back as an adult, I could appreciate their behaviour for what it was – their way of dealing with the impossible grief of losing a child. At the same time, I could still sympathise with the way I'd reacted. Not only did I lose my older brother, but it felt as though I'd lost my parents too. Following his death, they were always far more preoccupied with his absence than my presence, and kicking back at them had been a thread that ran all the way through my life from that day to the present. I was older now and understood things better, but attitudes become ingrained over the years. Right up until my parents died, I couldn't think of them, my father especially, as anything other than combatants.

'So,' Sarah said, 'your skills are purely down to teenage rebellion.'

I smiled, but it faltered a little. 'You could say that, yeah.'

'And the magazine, too.'

I'd told her about my job in our email exchanges, mostly because it gave her a way of checking up on me and making sure I was legit. I was fairly sure the percentage of ice-pick-wielding men on the internet was higher than that of their female counterparts.

'The magazine started off as just a hobby. I never imagined I'd end up rebelling against my parents full time.'

I supposed that was the ultimate irony of the situation. When my mother died, most of the money went to my father, but she also left me a lump sum; then, after he died, it all came to me. Without it, I'd never have been able to afford to rent the flat I lived in now, or survive long off the pittance I earned from the magic or the magazine. It was my inheritance in every sense of the word.

'I think it sounds fun,' Sarah said. 'Investigating all that stuff, I mean.'

'Ghosts and ghouls and mediums? I used to enjoy it a lot more. It can be soul-destroying at times.'

'Soul-destroying?'

'Not that I believe in souls.' I put my glass down. 'It's just tough to see how manipulative it can all be. Like mediums, for example. They take advantage of people's grief; they milk it. I get annoyed at them more than anything.'

I stopped, knowing I was in danger of going off on one.

'Your mother's not a medium, is she?' I said.

Sarah raised an eyebrow. 'No, you're okay. And I see where you're coming from. To be honest, though, I have a weird attitude to these things.'

'Which is?'

'That I'm not sure the truth matters so much.' She shrugged. 'You know? People lie to themselves all the time. I mean, I do it. I bet you do, too. We all fool ourselves so we can feel better, don't we?'

I smiled. 'Yeah, I know that in my saner moments, honestly. Whatever gets you through the day.'

'Exactly. Or the night.' She raised her glass of wine, then immediately put it down. 'Not that I'm finding this traumatic, by the way. In fact, I'm pleasantly surprised. I'm already hoping we're going to do this again some time.'

'I'd like that. Next time, I promise not to get annoyed about anything.'

'Don't worry about that. I like it.' She sipped her wine and gave me a pointed look. 'A bit of passion is good.'

We both let that one hang for a moment, and then I checked my watch. It was coming up on nine. We'd met properly only two hours ago – which even a fruit-fly would class as early days – but it was obvious there was some kind of spark there. The conversation had come without a hitch. Sarah was attractive, articulate and intelligent. She'd made me laugh and – at the least – she'd been gracious enough to act as though I was funny as well. It all seemed very promising.

Early days, I reminded myself.

'We should head for a taxi, maybe?' I said.

'Sounds good.'

'I'll get the bill.'

I went across to the counter to pay. As Sarah headed towards the door, she called over to me.

'Oh yeah – can I have my ring back, by the way?'

'Of course.' I glanced over. There were two baskets of flowers on either side of the entrance. I gestured uncertainly at the one on the left. 'Check in there.'

I turned back to the counter and sorted out the money.

'Hey!'

'What?'

Sarah was standing, hands on hips, staring at me. Not only had I made the ring vanish, but I'd made it reappear again several metres away from where I'd been sitting, without moving a muscle. God-like genius.

That was when she asked me the second inevitable question.

'How did you do that?'

'You have no idea how much effort it took.'

I put fifty pounds down on the counter – the bill, plus the ten I'd agreed in advance for the waiter to deposit the ring in the flowerpot on his way out to smoke. He'd found it in my napkin, from when I'd brushed the ring into my lap the second time I 'picked it up'. Dull, really.

But it's good to maintain a slight air of mystique in the early stages; not so good to reveal the boring truth straight off, whether about a magic trick or anything else. I was no more going to tell her I bribed the staff than I was about to start belching words or leaving my pants scattered around. Those are third-date tasks at the earliest.

Sarah and I headed to the taxi rank down the road, her still pestering for the truth, me playfully resisting. The city centre streets were busy with people – couples and groups – but by this time most of them were just getting started, and there was no real taxi queue, just three cabs parked up, engines idling. Sarah slipped her arm into mine. It was the first solid physical contact we'd had, and it felt good. As we approached, she pulled back slightly, using the weight of her body to stop us both before we reached the taxis.

'Maybe we should get this out of the way first?'

She leaned in and kissed me, slipping her arm properly around me. I reached round and held her, marvelling at the sudden sensation of her lips and how slim she felt. Her personality had been so strong that it seemed there should be more to her than this, but I could feel her spine through her shirt. She was light as air. Then I smelled the faintest trace of it.

A flower in a bottle.

Tori's perfume.

But that was okay. In the week and a half since I'd seen her, I'd stuck to the decision I'd made. No texts, calls or emails. The association was still strong, of course, but I was determined. They had the same perfume – so what? Maybe it wouldn't be too long before I smelled it and thought of Sarah instead. I hoped so. And as she continued to kiss me, I hoped so more and more.

'Figured that would make things easier.' She smiled.

'It did. Thank you.'

'So . . . are you going to ring me, or shall I ring you?'

'Those are the options,' I said.

'Ah, but there's also that other option. The one where neither of us rings the other.'

I shook my head. 'Not going to happen.'

'Well, that's all right then. We can sort out the details later. I've had a lovely night, Dave. Thank you for dinner.' She held up the ring. 'And this.'

85

'Me too. We'll sort something out soon, I promise.'

'Cool.' She gave me another quick kiss and then headed for the taxi. 'See you, then.'

Definitely.

I took the second taxi in the queue, gave the driver my address, and we set off. The nightclubs and restaurants and bars began to flash past in the window, but I wasn't paying attention to anything apart from the feeling of excitement in my chest. It felt like a small sun was shining behind my ribs, warming my whole body with its energy. If I hadn't been strapped into the backseat – and if there hadn't been anyone around to see – I might actually have jumped up and down a bit. As it was, it felt like I wouldn't be getting to sleep any time soon – and for a good reason, this time.

Great, great night, I decided.

Bad morning, though.

I woke up with a dull ringing in my ears.

The ringing stopped. I groaned to myself and opened one eye to look at the clock on the bedside table. Quarter to eight. Why had I set the alarm for that time?

The ringing returned, and this time I recognised it for what it was. Someone was at the front door. I clambered out of bed and over to the bedroom window, and lifted it up. The sounds of traffic on the main road blew in on a blast of cold air.

Two floors below, a couple of men were waiting outside. One was in his mid-forties, the other slightly younger. Both were wearing identical long black overcoats.

'Hey,' I shouted.

They looked up. The older one called up at me.

'Dave Lewis? Police. Could you open the door, please.'

Shit. Eddie.

'Give me a minute.'

'Quick as you can.'

I hunted around for clean clothes to wear, feeling sick.

Just keep calm.

I managed to get dressed, then went to the bathroom and splashed water on my face, pausing to inspect myself in the mirror.

My expression bothered me. It was too nervous. I leaned on the sink, my shoulders hunched, and stared myself right in the eyes.

That afternoon, I thought, *nothing happened.*

You don't know anything.

Nothing happened.

Then I clicked off the light and went downstairs.

Chapter Ten

Monday 29th August

The weirdest part of not sleeping, in Currie's considerable experience, was when you looked back on yesterday morning and realised you'd actually been awake since then. It always felt like those things must have happened at least a week ago, and perhaps even to someone else. Just after midday, he walked down to the department's press room, finding it hard to believe that a hazy but continuous chain of events connected him to a breakfast he'd eaten nearly thirty hours earlier.

And one of those events seemed like a nightmare, even though he'd been awake at the time. Yesterday evening: standing in Julie Sadler's bedroom, looking down at her small, wasted body, while crime-scene cameras flashed around him.

The image of her lying there still haunted him, even more so than Alison Wilcox's body had. In the tilt of Julie Sadler's head, he saw an accusation; in her outstretched fingers – frozen in the act of straining – he sensed outrage. It was as though she'd screamed questions out as she lay there, slowly dying, and the ghosts of those words still hung in the air, a challenge to anyone that dared enter.

Why didn't you save me?

Why did nobody care enough to come?

The sorrow he'd felt in that tiny bedroom was so overwhelming it bordered on profound. It was the closest he'd ever come to tears while attending a crime scene, despite the absence of mutilation or even blood. What had been done to this girl – to all of them – was an affront.

Currie looked around the press room as he entered. It was

heaving today. The seats, split into two columns by a central aisle, were all taken, while more reporters were packed in at the back and down the sides by the arched windows. Television cameras were perched on wheeled tripods, or shoulders. The polished floor was a snaking mess of cables.

The scent of blood, he thought.

Swann was already sitting at the top table. Currie walked over, cutting through the solid heat of all these hostile people, and took a seat beside his partner, placing his notes down in front. Along with the official microphones, the table was strewn with small, rectangular handhelds, which appeared to have been thrown there almost as an afterthought. The desperate, haphazard sprawl of them symbolised everything he disliked about these press conferences.

'Good afternoon,' he said, not looking up. 'I'm Detective Sam Currie. Thank you all for coming. I'll be reading a short statement and after that there'll be time for a small number of questions.'

He heard the quick, swishing click of cameras, and a couple of lights flashed across him. The memory of Julie Sadler's house rose up again. Sweat prickled on his forehead. He looked up.

'At five p.m. yesterday evening,' he said, 'officers were called to an address in the Buxton area of the city. Upon entering the property, the body of a young woman was discovered inside. We are treating her death as suspicious. At this time, we will not be releasing or confirming the woman's name to the media.'

None of which, he thought, *will deter any of you bastards.*

'We are in the process of talking to the woman's friends and family, and the investigation is progressing along a number of different lines. We ask for the media's co-operation in this matter, and will make a further announcement as soon as possible. I'll now hand you over to my colleague, Detective James Swann.' He glanced sideways. 'James?'

Swann nodded and turned to the crowd.

'I'll take any questions you might have.'

There was a predictable flurry, both of hands and camera flashes, but Currie allowed himself to relax a little.

He had a certain amount of respect for the press, in that they could be useful, but after Alison Wilcox had been killed the media

89

had teased out the connection to the two earlier murders and Currie had found himself becoming increasingly tight-lipped. As he saw it, the dead girls were reduced to lurid details – morsels of gristle to keep the pages wet and the papers shifting – and he began to find the whole thing difficult to stomach.

Swann seemed more able to keep his cool in the face of it, so they'd agreed that he would handle the questions from now on. In truth, the press probably liked him more, anyway: thirty-five years old, muscled, photogenic. People generally wanted Swann to like them, and he had a knack for smiling without appearing flippant. When Currie saw himself on television, even *he* thought he needed to cheer up. He couldn't imagine what he looked like today. His face felt like old rock.

'Are you connecting this death with the earlier murders of Vicky Klein, Sharon Goodall and Alison Wilcox?'

'As mentioned, the investigation is proceeding down a number of lines.'

'And that is one of those lines?'

'It's one of the possibilities we're looking at, yes.'

'Was the victim tied up?'

'The victim was restrained. We can't go into detail on that for reasons I'm sure you'll appreciate.'

'Are you close to making an arrest?'

Currie thought about Frank Carroll: the amused look that had appeared in the man's eyes under questioning. The GPS tracking on his ankle bracelet put him entirely in the clear, and their IT tech had assured them the device hadn't been tampered with. It was a disappointment. Frank Carroll had never been near the girls' houses, or even the locations from which the texts had been sent.

Swann nodded. 'We're pursuing a number of leads. We're not prepared to discuss details of particular individuals.'

The reporter stared blankly, then made a note on his pad.

Scribble, scribble, Currie thought. The police know nothing.

On one level, he didn't care about media animosity. It had been inevitable that, eventually, the press would turn on them and start demanding results. He wanted those results himself. But in other ways, it angered him intensely. He and Swann – all the team, in fact

– had exhausted themselves on this case, and each of them cared deeply, both about the murdered girls and about finding their killer. All these people cared about was selling newspapers.

Another hand. 'Who found the body?'

'The body was found by a friend of the victim after they became concerned for her wellbeing.'

'Have any of her other friends received messages, as was the case in the previous murders?'

'Four individuals received mobile phone messages earlier this morning.' Swann nodded, then looked around the audience. 'We will not be disclosing the content of those, nor will we be discussing these in any further detail whatsoever.'

'Was this woman left to die of thirst?'

'The cause of death has yet to be established.'

The more the questions went on, Currie realised, the more oppressive the room was becoming. It was tiredness as much as anything, he knew, but the back of the room seemed to be receding one second and moving closer the next. Julie Sadler's indignant, unanswerable questions seemed to be hanging in the air.

Why did nobody come? Why—

'How many more girls are going to be allowed to die?'

Currie's gaze flicked to the reporter who'd spoken. Swann simply stared at him for a moment, but the man went on undaunted, shrugging the question out as though it was obvious and natural.

'You've been involved in this investigation for over a year now, detectives. How many more girls are going to be allowed to die?'

Swann stared for a second longer, then answered him as politely as ever. Currie looked down at the table in front of him and waited for this to end.

Half an hour later, the atmosphere from the press conference still trailing behind him, Currie walked into Interview Room Five.

It was deliberately designed to unnerve. Empty, it would have just about accommodated a double bed, but with the table, chairs and recording equipment in here, there was barely space to move. A single bulb illuminated the room, not quite reaching the edges, and the interviews were often punctuated by a judgemental *clank* of pipes from above. The air smelled damp. It was like coming down into a grave.

Dave Lewis was slouched in the moulded plastic chair on the other side, his face unreadable. Even with his stomach pressed up to the table, there was no room; if he leaned his head back it would touch the wall behind. Lewis was staring down at his hands beneath the table, and there was an intermittent *click* as he picked at his nails. His downcast face was frozen in place. In fact, he looked a lot like Currie imagined he'd done on camera just now.

He put a styrofoam cup of coffee down on the table, then offered his hand.

'Hello again, Dave. Sorry to keep you waiting.'

Lewis looked at him blankly for a second, then shook his hand. Currie nodded and sat down, putting the file on the table beside the coffee. He was quietly hopeful about this interview.

Julie Sadler's friends and family had been interviewed quickly, and Dave Lewis's name had come up over the course of them. He was only a short-term boyfriend of Julie's, and an old one at that, but Currie had recognised the name. He'd checked the files, and it wasn't on the system, but still . . . it was familiar, even if he wasn't sure from where. And when they'd arrived at his house, Lewis had come to the station without asking for an explanation. In fact, he didn't seem at all surprised to find the police on his doorstep. Currie wanted to know why.

'Okay, Dave.' He rested his elbows on the desk. 'I'd like to talk to you about Julie Sadler.'

For a second, the man looked confused.

'Okay,' he said. 'Why?'

'Julie was killed a couple of days ago.'

Lewis couldn't have looked more shocked if he'd reached across and slapped him. Currie, who liked to think he knew a liar when he saw one, was slightly disappointed: if the man was acting, he was doing it well.

'What? Why?'

'I won't be discussing those details with you just yet. And you'll be the one answering questions when I do. Okay?'

Lewis rubbed his forehead and stared at the table.

Currie took a casual sip of the hot coffee and then extracted a photograph from the file, slid it across the table to Lewis. It had been taken from the student notice board at the university.

'You remember her?'

Lewis nodded. 'Yeah, that's her.'

'I know it's her. I asked if you remembered her.'

'Of course I remember her.'

'When was the last time you saw her?'

Lewis thought about it. He looked to be still reeling – as though he'd been expecting a punch from the left and got one from the other side instead.

'I don't know. It's been over a year.'

'When she broke up with you, you mean?'

'No. We met for coffee a couple of times after that. I don't know when. A while ago.'

'Texts? Emails?'

'No.'

'No contact at all, then.' Currie folded his arms and leaned back in his chair. 'How long were you an item?'

'A month, maybe.'

'So you went out for about a month and you've not heard from her in about a year.' Currie smiled at him. 'You look pretty devastated to me, Dave. Why is that?'

'What?'

It had been an unfair question, but he didn't care. He was interested to see how Lewis would react to being prodded a little.

'Like I said, you barely knew her. What are you so upset about?'

Lewis seemed to wrestle with what to say.

'Because she's dead.'

A fair answer to an unfair question. Even so, Currie stared him out, and after a second the man looked down, shook his head once. Currie slid the photograph back and put it away again.

'Okay. Let's work through this a little. How did you meet her?'

'On a dating site.'

'Excuse me?'

'A dating website.'

Currie made a note to himself to follow that up. 'Why?'

93

'Lots of people meet online.'

'So you meet lots of people that way?'

'No. I just meant that lots of people do it these days.'

Currie frowned. Maybe he'd been baiting him a little with that question, but the truth was, Lewis did seem strangely upset. He wasn't even looking at him now. Currie had already grudgingly acknowledged to himself that Sadler's death was news to Dave Lewis – but he still had the feeling that something was wrong.

He settled back.

'What about Julie? Did she meet lots of people online? Guys?'

'I wouldn't know.'

'What about last year, then?'

'A few, I think. She was just out for fun, really.'

Currie smiled. 'Were you not fun enough for her, then?'

Lewis raised his head and looked at him.

'No,' he said. 'I guess not.'

'Is that why she broke up with you?'

'It wasn't like that. It was a mutual thing.'

'That's not what her friends told us.' Currie leaned forward and opened the file. 'They told us there was an incident. Is that right? You bumped into her while she was on a date with someone else?'

'It wasn't an incident.'

Some of the shock had gone: Lewis seemed distracted now. He was looking around the room curiously, as though suddenly it interested him far more than Currie did.

'What was it, then?'

'She met someone else from the web. We just had different attitudes to things. I thought we were in a proper relationship and she didn't.'

He wanted to click his fingers: get Lewis's attention back.

'That made you angry? You caused a scene?'

'When I saw them?' He shook his head, glanced over to the other side of the room. *What's he looking at?* 'I didn't even go over. But we talked about it the next day, and decided to break up.'

'Her friends said you pestered her afterwards.'

'No. It was fine.'

'She was bothered enough to mention it to them.'

94

Currie picked up the report and read over the notes inside. Julie Sadler had mentioned it to two of her friends, laughing a little, making light of the situation: *Oh God, you won't believe what happened* . . . They probably wouldn't have remembered it at all if they hadn't been searching for *something*. After a second, he turned the page to make the accusations within seem lengthier than they were. In reality, he had about half a paragraph to spin out.

'Apparently, there were emails and texts. You wouldn't leave her alone.'

'That's not true.'

'You even sent flowers to her lab. Is that right?'

Finally, Dave Lewis looked back at him, much calmer now than at the beginning of the interview. Currie felt this had slipped from him somehow, but he wasn't sure how.

'I did try to persuade her to give it another go, but we were just emailing, talking stuff over. The flowers were to let her know everything was okay. That there were no hard feelings. I even said that on the card.'

'So why do her friends see it differently?'

'I don't know.' Lewis leaned back and folded his arms. 'She was probably joking around. Maybe she made fun of me all the time.'

'Yeah,' Currie said. 'Maybe.'

'I like this room, by the way.'

'What?'

'The room.' Lewis nodded at the corner. 'The walls aren't at right angles, are they? Just slightly off. And the light, too. It's very clever.'

Currie stared at him.

'Dave—'

'I didn't kill her. You're wasting time with me when you should be out there finding the man who did it.'

'Calm down,' he said. 'We have to follow— '

'Okay. Why did we go out for coffee those times?'

'What? You're asking me?'

'If she was so scared of me. If I'd been harassing her. Why would she suggest meeting for lunch to catch up on things?'

There was no obvious answer to that. Currie knew he should end the interview now, because he was riled, but instead he shot back at random.

'So why didn't you keep in contact with her?'

And for some reason, that hit. He watched as the anger slipped from Dave Lewis's face and was replaced by something closer to the guilt he was feeling himself. But instead of triumph, it felt more like an own goal. He was stressed and annoyed with himself, and he knew he shouldn't be taking that out on someone else. It wasn't the way to do things.

Currie stood up, the chair squeaking, glanced up at the camera in the corner and then reached across to the digital recorder.

'One ten,' he said. 'Interview terminated.'

'That's it?'

'Yeah,' Currie said. 'That's it. A duty officer will be through in a moment to get you to sign some documents. After that, you're free to go. We'll be in touch.'

Currie closed the door behind him, then paced away down the corridor.

Swann was sipping coffee when Currie walked back in.

'That went well,' he said.

'Didn't it just.'

'Next time, can I do it? I hate it when you get the fun ones.'

'I messed up.' Currie sat down, leaned his head back and closed his eyes, trying to massage some life – and sense – back into his face.

'We happy?' Swann asked.

'I don't buy him for Julie Sadler.'

'I don't think he's for sale on that one.'

'But I buy him for something.'

'Yeah.' Swann drank some coffee. 'Maybe he's got a bag of dope in his flat. It doesn't really matter, Sam. We've got to keep our priorities straight here.'

That word again. Currie rubbed his hand over the side of his jaw. He needed to shave as well as sleep.

'Okay,' he said. 'You're right. I'm happy. So what have we got next?'

'Keith Dalton. A more recent ex.'

'Great, let's get him in there. Your turn to waste time while we "should be out there catching the killer".'

Swann smiled grimly and left the room; Currie settled down at the table and watched on the small television monitor as Lewis signed off the forms.

Priorities. His partner was right, of course. Even so, he filed Dave Lewis's name down in his head. The man had been expecting them. It might not have been to do with Julie Sadler, but there was definitely something going on with him. And not just a bag of dope, either.

Perhaps eventually, Currie thought, he'd find out what.

Chapter Eleven

Wednesday 31st August

'You know,' Sarah told me, 'this isn't quite the second date I had in mind.'

'Yeah, sorry about that.'

'Seriously, is this the way it's going to go? One nice meal out, and from then on you chain me to the sink?'

I smiled over at her. We were in my parents' old kitchen, where Sarah was sporting rubber gloves and working at a sink full of foamy water, leaning down hard as she scrubbed at the porcelain. I was on the other side of the room, a cardboard box at my feet, clearing out the pantry. Various items had become stuck to the shelves over time – old jars and bottles, a half-burnt candle, rusted keys – and I was busy peeling them off the tacky Formica.

'Hey,' I reminded her, 'you volunteered.'

'That's true. I'm only messing.'

I was still slightly bemused that she was here with me at all – bemused, but also about as happy as I'd managed to be in the last few days. With everything that had happened afterwards, my date with Sarah had slipped to the back of my mind. When she'd called last night, suggesting we could do something today, it had been a little like waking from a bad dream and remembering you had a winning lottery ticket on the nightstand. I said yes immediately – then realised I'd arranged to come here with Rob to make a start on the place. I'd called her back to apologise, but she'd taken it in her stride, surprising me.

'Plus,' I said, 'I'll cook for you later to say thank you.'

'That's just a cheap excuse to get me back to yours.'

'You turning me down?'

'I didn't say that, did I?' She smiled at me; my stomach fluttered a little. Then she turned back and grimaced at the sink. 'Just don't expect me to do the washing up, okay?'

'Not at all.'

Beneath the cleaning fluid, the whole house smelled of dust, even though we'd opened all the windows. Linda had done a good job of cleaning the basics, but once we'd delved below the surface and started moving stuff, it had been like unleashing a curse from an Egyptian tomb. A yellow skip waited at the bottom curve of the drive; we'd only been here a few hours, and we already had enough rubbish to half-fill it. Bin bags full of musty clothes lined the hallway all the way to the front room, from where I could hear Rob pulling books off shelves and dropping them into *clumping* piles.

The only room we'd not yet touched was Owen's. I was gearing myself up for that.

'Oh, this won't come off,' Sarah said.

'Don't worry. Here: I need to wash my hands.'

She stripped off the gloves, then moved aside to let me clean the tack from my fingers. As I rinsed them beneath the foam, she stared dubiously into the pantry.

'God. It's awful in here.'

'Awful, but empty. I'll give it a clean in a minute.'

I closed the pantry door over, and was about to take the cardboard box into the hallway when I saw what was on the door.

The husk of a drawing I'd done as a child. My mother had sello-taped it to the wood and left it there, the corners now stained and curled and crisp. Four scribbled figures stood on a green line at the bottom, next to a red house half their height. Blue was smeared across the top, in that universal way that children conceive of and draw the sky.

Sarah saw me looking and poked one of the corners back to get a better look.

'Is this one of your pieces?'

'I imagine it's my earliest surviving work.'

'It shows such promise. You should have been an artist.'

I smiled but it felt a little forced. I didn't know what made me uncomfortable about the picture. Was it that my mother must have looked at it every day, through all those strained years when we barely spoke? Or was it the scene I'd drawn – the four of us together? I peered closer at the figure on the right. Little more than a lopsided circle with a curved line for a smile, smudged dots of crayon for hair. No hands, either: just splayed fingers that started at the wrist, touching the line-fingers of the person beside him.

'Come with me a second,' I said.

'Intriguing.'

She followed me out into the hall and we stopped outside Owen's room.

If not now, I thought, *when?*

As far as I knew, nobody had been in here since the night we returned from the hospital, where my brother's body had been taken. With the door closed, it was almost possible to believe he was still in there. Sleeping, perhaps, or picking his guitar, or doing his hair in the mirror in that new way he'd started in the weeks before he died.

Deep breaths.

I opened the door, felt a *whump* of decompression, then reached in and turned on the light. The bedroom blinked into bright life in front of me.

And of course, it was empty.

'Wow,' Sarah said. 'This was your brother's room?'

I nodded.

It was like opening a door into another world: a silent, forgotten place. There was a quiet covering of soft, grey snow over everything. The bedclothes, the cupboards, the floor – all hidden by it. I glanced up. The corners of the ceiling were lost to cobwebs, and dust seemed to hang in the air.

My face felt blank.

'You okay?' Sarah said.

'Yeah. Just memories.'

She surprised me again: 'Come here, you.'

I did, and she gave me a hug, her hands tight against my back.

'Really,' I said. 'I'm good. That wasn't quite as bad as I expected.'

'Hey!'

Rob – calling through from the front room.

'Come and have a look at this!'

I stepped back from Sarah and she rolled her eyes at me. She'd got the measure of him already. I'd warned her about Rob in advance – that he could be incredibly charming, but was equally often abrasive and annoying, especially with girls I saw. And I'd warned him, too. So far, he'd been well behaved, and even nodded respectfully at me when Sarah wasn't looking, which seemed a good sign. From her, I was guessing it was closer to fifty-fifty, but for now she seemed more amused than annoyed.

'Hang on,' I called back.

'No, they've got Stanley's book here. I can't believe it.'

'Thom Stanley,' I explained to Sarah. 'He's the psychic I told you about on the phone. The one Rob and I are seeing tomorrow night.'

Stanley was a local man, and we'd had run-ins with him on paper before, each side firing shots at the other. We'd broken a story last year about his earnings, prompting a rather embarrassing investigation into his tax situation. Mediums don't like the subject of money on the table. Obviously, he didn't like us much. He didn't know it yet, but he was going to like us a whole lot less. Stanley was about to grace the middle-page spread of our next issue, as the subject of our monthly 'Take-Down' section.

'Ah, yes,' Sarah said. 'I remember.'

'We can't give this to the fucking charity shop, can we?' Rob shouted. 'Someone might buy it.'

I heard him ruffle through the pages.

'I wonder if we can burn it.'

'Just . . . hang on.'

'It's okay.' Sarah gave me a smile. 'I'll make a start on the pantry.'

I took a last glance into Owen's room, then pulled the door closed again.

'You're a star,' I told her, and meant it.

*

I found Rob kneeling down in the middle of the front room, surrounded by piles of books and open boxes, flicking through the one in his hands. He looked up as I came in, then tossed the book to one side.

'Close the door.'

I did. He was looking at me intently.

'What?' I said.

'Are you okay?'

'Yeah, I'm fine. What do you mean?'

'Nothing.' He leaned on his knees then climbed to his feet. 'Just checking. I wanted to make sure you were all right. With this place, and everything.'

'Thanks. How are you doing in here?'

He kicked a pile of books with his feet. 'Not too bad. There's such a lot of shite here.'

'I know.'

'How are you getting on in the kitchen?'

'We're making some progress.'

'Not with the cleaning, you idiot. I mean with Sarah.'

'Oh. Yeah, it's okay.'

'She seems very nice. I like this one.'

'That's good. I'm glad.'

Actually, it was high praise from Rob. In the manner of incredulous best friends everywhere, he'd given nicknames to most of the girls I'd been out with over the years, and the majority of them hadn't been nice. Tori was 'the mad one'. Emma, 'the miserable one'. Julie, God help him, had been 'the slut'.

Thankfully, he hadn't referred to her as that in the office yesterday when I told him what had happened. He had given me a lecture, though.

After I'd explained about the interview, he'd gone out to get us both lunch, leaving me alone with the newspaper I'd bought on the way in. The photograph on the front page was the one Julie had used on her profile at the dating website. I think it must originally have been taken for the notice board in the department: a posed, professional shot that made her look almost innocent. But there was a slight glint in her eyes that hinted at the playful sexuality I associated with her.

When he'd got back, he'd thrown the sandwich on the middle of the paper and ordered me to stop reading it. Every time I protested, he told me again. Eventually, he'd taken it off me altogether. *Stop dwelling.*

'How are you holding up?' he said now.

'This place? It's not been as bad as I expected.'

'No. About Julie.'

'I'm okay, I think.'

It was partly true. The evening after the interview, all I'd really done was sit on the settee, staring through the television set while I palmed a coin, over and over. I couldn't help thinking about her.

I remembered how small and toned she was. The definition of her back muscles and her thighs. Julie had weighed only a shade over seven stone, but she was deceptively strong: even though I was nearly twice as heavy, she could often overpower me. On our third date, we play-fought and ended up exhausted, face to face on her living room floor, her on top of me, pinning my arms down to either side, our faces deliciously close. We'd stayed there, give or take, for most of the evening.

Why didn't you keep in contact with her?

The coin had slipped and hit the carpet, quiet as a blink.

I hadn't seen or thought much about her in a year – but I still found it hard to believe she was dead, and that the strong, vibrant person smiling down at me in my memory was gone.

When the police had knocked on my front door, I'd been scared they were there because of Eddie. Now, if it meant that Julie might still be alive – even if I never saw or thought of her again – I wished it had been.

'You can't lie to me,' Rob said. 'I know you too well. I can tell you're feeling guilty.'

'I am absolutely not feeling guilty.'

'Yes, you are. Your face twitches when you lie.'

'Don't be so fucking stupid.'

'It just did it again.'

I frowned. 'Maybe I'm feeling a little guilty.'

'And why?'

'Because of what happened to her. Jesus, Rob. She was left to die on her own. Nobody came looking to check she was okay.'

'Yeah, that bothers me too. I should have done something.'

'You didn't even know her.'

'And neither did you. That's the point, Dave. She cheated on you, and instead of hating her like any decent person would, you're actually feeling *responsible* because something bad happened to her a year down the line.'

I rubbed my forehead with my palm. 'You're as bad as that fucking cop.'

Rob said nothing for a moment.

Then: 'Did you tell Sarah?'

'No.'

He almost looked relieved. 'That's probably for the best. Like I said, she seems nice.'

'She is nice.'

'Right. So don't allow your personality to fuck this up.'

'Thank you.'

'Seriously, I mean it. You're my friend, and I'm not going to sit back while you mess your life up. I know how you get sometimes.'

I wanted to be annoyed with him, but he had such an earnest expression on his face that I couldn't bring myself to feel it. And deep down, he was right. Something awful had happened, but it had nothing to do with me. It wasn't my fault. There was nothing I could or should have done to stop it.

'I'm getting there,' I said. 'Honestly.'

He continued to stare at me, then nodded. He picked up Thom Stanley's book and held it out to me. I took it, noticing the two tickets protruding from the top edge.

'What are these?' I said.

'For tomorrow night. I want you to take Sarah.'

'What? But you've been looking forward to it.'

'Yeah, but I really shouldn't go.' He looked unhappy. 'His people might recognise me.'

Rob had shared a TV spot with Thom Stanley last year at the time of our revelations, and I believe the polite way of describing it would be 'an incident live on air'. There had also been accusations of nuisance phone calls afterwards, although Rob strenuously denied any involvement – just as he denied the existence of a friend at the phone company who might supply him with such details as private home phone numbers and addresses.

'We talked about that before,' I said. 'It's unlikely.'

'Yet possible. Jesus Christ, Dave, do you want the fucking ticket or not? I think it might be good for you. You can see a bit more of each other. Christ knows I'm fed up of seeing you.'

I gave up, and folded the tickets into my pocket.

'Okay. Thanks, Rob.'

'No problem.' He took the book off me, then tapped the cover expectantly and raised his eyebrows. 'Can we burn this now?'

I was about to say no, but then thought about it some more, remembering my father and his bonfires. Why not?

'Outside.' I smiled. 'Second garden down.'

Chapter Twelve
Thursday 1st September

Did it work like this with anything terrible, Mary wondered – with everything you were frightened of? You anticipated it, building it up in your head until it reached huge proportions, only to end up surprised by how mundane it turned out to be. How incredibly ordinary.

It was just before noon, and she was sitting in her car at the base of a tower block, feeling almost absurdly calm. What she was doing at this moment had been the subject of nightmares for the last twelve years, but there was something anti-climactic about it now that it was actually happening.

Seeing her father, in the flesh.

He'd assumed such mythical power in her mind that it was almost shocking to see him outside the context of her memories.

He's just a man, she told herself.

And yet she was shaking, and having to fight back the urge to drive off, which every instinct she had told her she must do *right now*. It was horribly fascinating to see him, in the same way it might be fascinating to look down and see your guts in your lap.

No, she told herself. *You mustn't run away.*

You have to deal with him eventually.

She sipped hot soup from the flask she'd brought, and forced herself to watch him. Practice – that was all this was. She was preparing for the day he finally came to take her. Because Mary understood now that it would happen. It was inevitable. After Currie's visit, she'd been left feeling desolate and hopeless – but it had always been stupid to believe anyone might help her. There were only two possibilities now. Either her father would turn up and she'd collapse into the little girl she'd once been, or else he would arrive to find a strong, grown woman who was ready for him. That he would turn up wasn't in doubt. So she needed to get herself used to him.

He's over a hundred metres away; this is perfectly safe.

Over the years, she'd worked hard at risk analysis, and the process was second nature to her now. If her father looked down the hill towards the tower, it was possible he might see her car, but there were several others parked around her, and no reason for him to pick out hers in particular. If he did, he wouldn't be able to recognise her from this distance; she would just be a silhouette: not even a woman, never mind a daughter. And if he approached, either by accident or design, she would drive away before he got anywhere near. That made at least three safety gates between them, which meant she was fine.

As though logic was any defence against monsters.

But in the ten minutes she'd been here, he hadn't so much as glanced in this direction. He was standing in his pathetic little garden, his back to her, working slowly. A sky-blue bucket sat on the step beside him, and he kept dipping a sponge into it, then lifting it slowly and wiping the front door, ineffectually rubbing at whatever obscenity had been scrawled there. It was little more than a white spiral now: some kind of smeared mandala that her father's attentions couldn't erase, but rendered more and more obscure.

His house adjoined the one next door, and his neighbour was in his own garden. The man was overweight – his face and neck a landslide of flesh, his bottom lip pouting out like a ledge – and he was standing very still, holding a hose like a bright-green riding crop, openly inspecting her father at work. As Mary watched, the man spoke – some muttered abuse that made his face work like a belch. Her father paused, and Mary realised she was holding her breath, expecting . . . but then he just bent down slowly, awkwardly, and dipped the sponge in the bucket again.

What had Detective Currie described him as? A broken man. Now that she'd seen him, Mary understood what he meant.

I've seen the picture of him when he was arrested, and he's changed a great deal.

Twelve years ago, when she'd last laid eyes on him, her father had been a big, powerful man. He'd seemed to fill whole rooms with his body and his presence, and people who didn't know better often mistook him for fat. The reality was entirely different. Her father had spent long hours, for years on end, performing exercises she barely knew the names of – if they even had names at all. Modified squats and dead lifts. He curled punishingly heavy barbells in short sets, and swung dumbbells around in his huge fists. Every weight he lifted was training him to heft a person around. He never cared about looks; he only cared about power. If anything, he liked that the layer of fat covering his muscles often gave him an element of surprise.

The intervening years appeared to have trimmed all that excess away, and taken a good deal of the muscle with it as well. Her father looked emaciated and weak, and terribly *old*. Some trick of time had made him serve two years within himself for every one without. And he was moving gingerly, a little hunched over, as though a muscle in his back had torn at some point, and then healed into place at a crippling angle.

He isn't the man you remember.

That was true. The father in her memories would have beaten the neighbour's face apart for whatever he'd said.

He can barely cross the room without a walking stick . . .

Except that – no matter what she tried to tell herself – Mary didn't believe a word of it. Not for a second.

There was nothing weak or fragile about her father, and if he appeared it then he was acting that way for a reason. Biding his time, perhaps. Laying low. People always underestimated him. Currie hadn't listened when she'd said that, and now she could appreciate why. He didn't know this man like she did, so he was easily taken in by what he chose to show on the surface.

What about the electronic tag?

Mary peered closer, wondering if she could see it through her father's tracksuit bottoms. She couldn't, but Currie had been sure about that: certain that it put Frank Carroll in the clear. Once again, she was sure that wasn't the case. There had to be ways around those devices, didn't there? And a man like Frank Carroll would know what they were, or he'd know people who did.

So could she face this man? What would happen when she opened her eyes one night to see him standing there in the corner of her bedroom, holding those old leather belts between his fists?

She stared at him now, thinking again about that night in the snow twelve years ago. It had taken every last drop of courage to escape from the house. By then, her father had begun to tie the bindings looser, daring her to break free, confident that her fear would hold her in place – and it almost had. As she'd staggered along in the cold, Mary had been certain there was nothing left inside her anymore. She'd used up the whole store of whatever fortitude and resolve there had ever been: all of it summoned for one last, desperate effort.

Had it ever returned?

Mary drank the last of the soup from the cup, tipping her head back slightly so it could roll thickly out. As she did, she felt her neck start to itch.

She looked down. Very slowly.

And then froze.

Her father was looking right at her. Still standing on his doorstep, but now with his back to the smeared writing. One hand held up over his eyes to shield out the sun. A look of curiosity on his face.

Her hand started trembling.

No reason for him to pick out hers in particular . . .

But she could feel his gaze squirming all over her face.

You could drive away before he got anywhere near.

And yet she didn't seem able to move. The part of her brain that told her body to work had been displaced, knocked out of alignment. Her mind couldn't even remember what movement was, the way a forgotten word would keep slipping from you the more you tried to think of it.

As she stared across the insignificant distance between them, her father moved his hand from above his eyes and waved once. Still she didn't move. She watched him smile, and then he reached down slowly, apparently with difficulty, and patted his lower leg, like it was a dog that had just performed a good trick.

Get out of here.

He stepped down onto his front path.

She came back to her senses, realising only now that her heart was actually *punching* against her chest. *Go.* Her hand found the gear-stick, crunched it once, and then she was reversing around. The tyres screeched. She didn't look in the rear-view mirror as she drove away.

She didn't need to see him to know he was watching her.

In the summer, if she left the windows open, wasps would find their way into the house.

Mary hated them. They always nuzzled hopelessly at the window, then hummed in loops around the room, looking for something to sting. She'd roll up a magazine, wait for the thing to land, and then smack it as hard as she could.

One time, entirely by accident, she hadn't killed one of them outright. And instead of hitting it again, she'd looked down at it, watching it die with horrified fascination.

It had buzzed and fizzed on the kitchen counter, its head and thorax looking like squashed pieces of sweetcorn, the rest of its body convulsing. The dying wasp kept curling up on itself, again and again, and it had taken her a second to work out what it was doing: repeatedly stinging the air. Even when the rest of it had stopped moving, the end continued pulsing slowly: in and out of empty space. It was the last part of its body to go still.

Mary drove along now. Terrified. Trying to stop herself shaking.

That was what Detective Sam Currie didn't get – that was what *nobody* seemed to get. He'd said her father was a broken man, and perhaps he was right. What he didn't understand was that men like Frank Carroll didn't break like normal people. They broke the way that wasps did.

Chapter Thirteen

Thursday 1st September

If I'd had any doubts about the lecture Rob had given me, they'd been well and truly pushed aside by quarter past seven the next evening, when I was sitting with Sarah in the rather plush bar inside the Western Varieties Theatre.

It was filled with wood, folded crimson curtains and wall-mounted lanterns. Sitting in here was a little like being inside the stomach of a sea-monster that had just eaten a pirate's cabin. The bar had been full when we'd arrived, but the performance was due to start in a few minutes and most people had made their way upstairs now. There was no hurry. We'd already had one drink and were lingering over a second.

'Sorry I had to rush off this morning,' Sarah said. 'I tried to say goodbye, but it was like waking the dead.'

'That's okay. It's not like me to sleep late.'

'Must have given you a reason.'

I smiled. 'I do vaguely remember you leaving. To begin with, I thought you might have done a runner.'

'In the middle of the night?'

'When you realised the error of your ways.'

Sarah raised an amused eyebrow, and touched the straw in her drink, absently stirring the ice. She looked great, dressed in thin, dark jeans, an untucked black shirt and a green velvet jacket. Her skin was luminous.

'I liked waking up with you,' she said quietly.

'Well, I'll have to take your word for that, seeing as I was un-conscious at the time.'

She gave me a secret kind of smile.

'I'll wake you up next time.'

'Glad to hear it.'

'With *ice-cold water*.'

'You could do the washing up while you're at the sink.'

She stuck her tongue out and grinned.

I said, 'I'm pleased you've come with me tonight.'

'How could I not?' She abandoned the straw and leaned over conspiratorially. 'I feel like a spy. It's exciting.'

'That's cool. Don't blow your cover, though.'

'No way.' She leaned back, moving her hand in front of her face. 'Absolutely serious. I promise.'

'Impressive.' I finished my drink. 'Okay, let's make a move.'

The theatre itself was built around a central stage, with a semi-circle of seats rising up in tiers. The stage was plain and almost unadorned – just a single microphone stand at the front, and then a table some way back with a jug of water and a chair to one side, presumably in case Thom Stanley's melodramatics got the better of him and he needed to sit down and recover.

'Excuse me. Sorry.'

We entered at the top, and had to squeeze past the resentfully angled legs of the elderly. There were some younger couples in the audience, but the majority was made up of older people: lonely men and women searching for some kind of solace – for their loved ones to be brought back to life, their loss to be annulled. In return for an entrance fee, Thom Stanley supplied that illusion. In this theatre tonight, the end of someone's life was going to be reduced to the equivalent of a cross-country move.

I couldn't blame anyone for wanting that; I wanted it too. But I could blame Thom Stanley for exploiting it. He was a conman: a parasite that fed on grief and weakness. Everything that was bad about someone dying enabled people like him to make a living.

Sarah and I found our seats and sat down to wait. I listened to the mumbled chatter all around us and checked my coat pocket, ready to turn on the digital recorder when the show started. It was a high-end model and the in-built mic would be more than sufficient to catch what happened. Or what Rob and I hoped was going to, anyway.

Sarah whispered: 'Might he know you're here?'

'Of course,' I said. 'He's psychic.'

She nudged me – just as the house lights dimmed. I pressed record quickly, then reached over and took her hand.

A single spotlight shone down on the microphone, and polite applause began to echo around the theatre, catching and building steadily. When Thom Stanley emerged from the wings, it intensified.

So: here he was. The star of the show.

Stanley was one of the new breed of mediums: young and good-looking, with his hair styled impeccably messily. He was tall and slim, and dressed in a fashion shirt untucked from his neat trousers. Whenever I saw him, I always thought that a cheap, late-night game show somewhere was missing a host. One of those ones where they sucker you into calling over and over, and you just get a recorded message saying sorry, better luck next time.

'Good evening everyone.'

He gave a slight bow to each of the tiers. Amplified by the theatre PA, his voice sounded like it was right in my ear. Good news for the recording.

'Thank you – thank you all for coming – and welcome. I hope it's a productive and useful evening for all of you. I always say I can never promise results, but I certainly *can* promise that I'll do my best.'

He circled his hand in front of his face, swallowed once.

'As you know, I'm only able to work with the spirits who choose to come to me. Hopefully, by cultivating the right atmosphere, we can all encourage that to happen. I want to feel positivity. I want to feel love and acceptance. The aim is to create a warm and safe place for the spirits to come.' He frowned. 'Does that make sense?'

There was a murmur of assent, as though it did.

'All right.'

Stanley walked to the table, poured himself a glass of water and took a sip. Then he moved to the microphone again, cupped his hands together and rocked back on one heel slightly. *Okay, let's introduce our first act this evening.*

He looked at the stage to his left, frowning into the space there. Silence settled on the theatre for a few seconds.

Then he broke it, talking quickly.

'This is good. Straight away, I have an older gentleman here. He's quite tall, and he's smiling a lot. A friendly chap.' He smiled back at the spirit. 'And I like him. He's saying William, Will or possibly Bill. Does that mean anything to anyone?'

I figured the odds were fairly good, and William was immediately claimed by a couple sitting a few rows down from us. I could only see the backs of their heads, but it was easy to guess a lot of what Stanley was going to say, and why.

William would most likely be connected to the woman, I thought, because she'd been the one to put her hand up. And from the couple's age, he would probably be her father. I'd go for 'father figure', myself, because it covered more bases. At some point, the spirit would gesture to his chest, indicating that was the way he'd passed. It was a safe bet – people don't die from breaking a leg – and he'd probably also say he'd been ill for a while. Even if his death turned out to have been from a sudden head injury, it was always possible the doctors had missed something. The point is, you can't really argue with a ghost, can you?

Stanley worked through these and more, and had the advantage over me of being able to see the woman's responses as well as hear them. With every confirmation or slight look of confusion, he tailored his comments accordingly, relaying banal and general information the woman had given him right back to her.

What was your old phone number, Will? I wanted to ask.

Your National Insurance number?

None of that mattered, though, because the woman was being told what she wanted to hear. Her father was at peace. He was still with them. Every day, he smiled and was proud of them. He could hear them when they spoke to him.

Harmless lies. I felt myself growing more angry with every word.

My dislike aside, I had to admit he was smooth and professional. As a magician, I was impressed. I noted three solid hits against more than twenty misses, and yet William's daughter would probably go away amazed at how accurate he'd been. And that was all down to his expertise – Thom Stanley was successful because he managed to obscure the fact he got almost everything wrong. He glossed over mistakes so quickly that even I was hardly sure he'd made them. And I was counting.

The evening carried on in a similar vein for half an hour, and the anger became diluted by boredom. Then Thom Stanley pinched his fingers against the bridge of his nose, looked across the stage, and said the words I'd been waiting to hear. Rob and I had been mentally crossing our fingers about this moment for the last two weeks.

'Okay. I have a young man with me now. Very clear. His name is Andrew, and he's pointing over in this direction. I believe it's you, sir, and you, madam.'

We were going to have an article. I clenched Sarah's hand a little. She clenched it back.

'It's Nathan and Nancy, isn't it?'

He was talking to an elderly couple down the front. The woman nodded, and Stanley smiled at her.

'Lovely to see you both here.'

He knew their names already, of course. I knew them too: Nathan and Nancy Phillips, who were regular subscribers to the *Anonymous Skeptic*. They occasionally volunteered their services to help us out with take-downs, and we'd figured they would be ideal for tonight's little adventure.

'It's your son, isn't it?' Stanley said. He turned back to the empty stage. 'His name's Andrew. Brown hair. He's smiling too. And my word, he's a strapping lad!'

The audience laughed; the Phillipses smiled at each other.

'He was, yes,' Nancy said.

Stanley knew their names already because the Phillips were on his client list; they'd booked a private appointment earlier this year, which they'd acted as though they were very pleased with. That's how these things work – there would be strangers in this audience, but I imagined there was also a large contingent that Stanley had already met and talked with in the past. Needless to say, that made it slightly easier for him to guess right. In magic terms, we'd call them stooges – people who are in on the act – but this was slightly different. The sympathetic people in here didn't realise there was a trick to be in on.

To my and Rob's immense delight, Thom Stanley had visited Nathan and Nancy again last week, giving them a free consultation and tickets for tonight's performance. The audience didn't know that, of course, and so he could use their names, along with the details they'd given him, and act as though he was getting this information from the spirit.

'Andrew says he knows it's not easy, but he's asking you not to worry about him.'

'That's such a comfort.'

'He's pointing to his stomach too. That makes sense?'

They nodded again.

'He's such a young man.' Stanley frowned. Then: 'Oh – he's saying "it's gone now, Mum". It was cancer, wasn't it? Yes, he's nodding now.'

'It was cancer, yes.'

'He's saying it's gone now. He wants you to know he's not in any pain.'

Stanley's voice was soothing and full of reassurance, like a therapist. If I hadn't known the truth, it would have been surprisingly easy to imagine there really *was* a young man standing on the stage, invisible to everyone but him.

Unfortunately, Nathan and Nancy had never had any children at all, never mind one who'd died. When Stanley had visited them, almost everything they'd told him about 'Andrew' had been a barefaced lie. The one – noble – exception was his appearance, which Stanley would be basing on the photograph he'd seen on their mantelpiece. A tall guy. Medium-length, sandy-brown hair. Average build: not all that strapping, really, but then parents like that, don't they? A slightly shy smile. To put it another way, a picture of me.

Thom Stanley carried on talking about Andrew for nearly ten minutes, and my distaste for the man grew stronger with every moment. We already had enough to cause him severe embarrassment, but there was one further path he could take, one that would utterly ruin him, and I found myself willing him on.

'Andrew's also telling me something about a necklace?'

Bingo.

He stood up and walked back to the stage, looking confused by the message. 'He's saying it's gold, and he's holding his chest. Is it a heart? A necklace with a heart on it?'

Nancy Phillips nodded quickly. 'Yes, yes.'

'He thinks you've lost it?'

'Yes!'

'Well, Andrew says not to worry. He's been keeping an eye on you, and he says you should check the landing upstairs. A bookcase – does that make any sense? He says it's near a bookcase there.'

You piece of shit, I thought.

Towards the end of Stanley's visit to their house, he'd excused himself and gone upstairs to use the toilet. We'd set up a hidden camera in the bedroom and left the door tantalisingly open. The camera had captured him entering the room and quickly removing a necklace from Nancy's jewellery box. After he'd left, we found it down the back of the small bookcase on the upstairs landing, where he must have casually deposited it on his way to the bathroom.

As we watched the footage afterwards, Rob and I hadn't been able to believe our eyes. It was strangely beautiful. We knew about such methods, of course, but still felt like deep sea divers who'd just captured some rarely-seen jellyfish on film.

Oblivious to what he'd just done, Stanley walked back to the stage. Then he closed his eyes and scratched his forehead, looking troubled. We were meant to think someone else was coming through, but apparently with more difficulty than the others.

You absolute piece of shit.

He opened his eyes and peered across the empty stage.

'Oh.'

Then took a step back.

'I don't like that.'

My first thought was that it was a strange thing to say. The expression on his face was misjudged too. He looked almost horrified – as though whatever spirit he was seeing was unexpectedly frightening.

Where are you going with this? Surely he was smart enough to realise people wouldn't appreciate their dead relatives looking scary?

The audience shuffled, a little unsettled by the performance. He had gone very pale and appeared to be listening intently, wanting to look away from whatever he was seeing but unable to do so.

I had a sudden premonition that he was going to ask about a 'Julie', and I shivered as he turned back to us, all the earlier reassurance and comfort gone from his face.

He cleared his throat.

'Does the name Tori mean anything to anyone?'

Chapter Fourteen

Thursday 1st September

'This is what I called you about,' the tech officer said.

Currie leaned on one side of the desk, Swann on the other, both of them bathed in green light from the monitor. Seated in between them, the techie clicked twice on the mouse. The screen changed to show the list of text messages sent from Julie Sadler's phone over the last three weeks. The four at the end were the messages that followed her death:

You let her die.

The six before that were the same two lines, repeated again and again:

Hey there. Sorry for silence. Am fine, just busy. Hope u r too.
Maybe catch up sometime soon. Julie

It was more or less the same wording as they'd found in the previous murders. The assumption was that the killer had stored the 'I'm okay' message in Julie's phone, and then forwarded it to anyone who contacted her in the meantime.

Currie gestured to the complicated series of numbers at the side of each message, which related to the GPS location of Julie Sadler's mobile phone when the text was sent. 'These have all been traced already,' he said.

'That was what I wanted to see you about.'

The techie double-clicked on one. The new window took a second or two to open. When it did, they were looking at a satellite photo.

'This one is the same as all the others,' he told them. 'He turned the mobile on in a very quiet neighbourhood, sent the text, then switched the phone off again.'

Currie looked at the area laid out on the screen. For each of the sent messages, the tech team had isolated the position of Julie Sadler's mobile phone to within a few metres. They were looking at a stock photograph of the landscape from above. It was mostly fields, with a couple of small streets curling in from the side.

Knowing the exact location the killer had been at certain times generated equal amounts of work and frustration. Because he avoided anywhere with cameras, all they were left with was the small hope that a resident might have seen something. There was little chance they'd remember anything from such a specific date and time – nobody had yet – but they still had to be interviewed, tying up more of the team.

And Currie had actually come to hate these overhead GPS views for another reason. They were infuriating, because he knew the killer had been *right there*. In most murder investigations, all you had was a single scene, the one where the crime had taken place, but this case kept providing them with the killer's exact location at other times. They had access to his whereabouts. It felt unfair that he could still elude them so completely, as though he was showing them his face, but then turning quickly away before they could look. Too damn smart.

'No CCTV nearby,' the techie said.

'No.' Currie was impatient. They had already been through this. 'He's too clever for that.'

'Maybe not as clever as you think.'

'What do you mean?'

The officer didn't reply, but minimised that window and then clicked on the second message from the top. The new window loaded slowly.

'Are you saying we've caught him on film?'

'We have. Although don't get your hopes up just yet.'

Currie wanted to shake the man. *Don't get your hopes up.*

After a second, the new screen appeared: another aerial snapshot.

This one appeared to be a section of the city centre. The middle of the screen was filled with a large grey square.

'The old shopping centre in town,' Currie said. Although that was actually giving the place way too much credit. It was more of a wide, covered walkway, with shops all along to either side. Currie dimly remembered there had been repeated calls for surveillance cameras to be installed throughout, because of skateboarders. It had never happened.

The techie said, 'He sent the text from inside, just after midday on Friday, when he knew the centre would be very busy.'

'There's no CCTV in there,' Currie said. 'Some in the stores, maybe, but none on the concourse itself.'

'No, there isn't. But there are only three entrances.' He zoomed out a little and moved the mouse pointer between the top, bottom and side of the centre. With a single click of a button, several small yellow circles were overlaid on the satellite picture, and then he sat back, proud of himself. 'We have cameras on all three of those streets.'

Currie leaned in, estimating distances in his head. The cameras to the top and bottom were very close. The one to the side looked further away, but it was still possible it would have caught something.

'They cover all the ways in and out?' he said.

'All the standard ways. The ramps and steps.'

Currie thought it over. There were probably a hundred other routes the killer could have taken, in theory – back doors on the shops, perhaps – so none of this would prove anything. But at the same time . . .

'You can pull the footage from all three entrances for, say, an hour either side of the text message?'

'Yeah. Unless he went in earlier and hung around?'

'He wouldn't do that,' Swann said.

Currie nodded. 'Too much chance of being remembered. Plus, it would imply he knew about the cameras. So why not just go somewhere else?'

He caught his partner's eye, and saw the faintest glint there. Conclusive or not, it was likely they had the killer on film. If they took an hour from either side of that text message then three separate cameras gave them six hours of material. They could sit down, watch it, and when it finished they would have seen the killer in the flesh.

They were still holding each other's gaze.

'But why go somewhere with cameras?' Currie said. 'He's always been careful before.'

'Might work there?'

'It's possible. Or maybe there was something he couldn't get out of. He wouldn't have done it from there if he didn't need to.'

Swann smiled, and Currie could read his partner's mind.

Or maybe we got lucky and he finally made a mistake.

He stood up and put his hands in his pockets. Of course, despite the buzz in his chest, there was no way they were going to have time to sit down and watch six hours of footage right now.

Still, there were ways around that.

'Okay, we'll need an hour either side, from each camera.'

The techie nodded. 'Yep. That's easy enough.'

Currie smiled.

'Don't get your hopes up just yet,' he said.

At eight o'clock they left the tech officer to sort the footage. Where it was possible, Currie explained, he wanted stills from the surveillance films, labelled with times and sorted into categories. If he asked to see men with dark hair, for example, he wanted to be able to click through a series of photographs. It would be a tedious and time-consuming task. The techie had looked a little crestfallen.

'Everyone?'

'No, no,' Currie told him. 'Just do the men for now.'

After they were finished there, Swann drove home to catch some sleep, and Currie went back to the incident room. He sat down, absently picked up a pencil and stared through the whiteboard that covered most of the wall. Photos of the four dead girls were tacked along the top, while the rest was filled with details of the murders written neatly in black or red marker pen.

On the surface, he was trying to make sense of what was there; deep down, his thoughts were occupied with other things.

Since his encounter with Mary Carroll last week, the things she'd said, the way she'd reacted – they kept coming back to him. He hadn't expected it to go well, of course: he'd known enough about the case in advance to appreciate there was no 'good news' he could take that would provide any real comfort. But, perhaps stupidly, he *had* wanted to reassure her a little. To let her know that whatever her father had done in the past, and as repulsive a man as he might still be, he was far less of a threat than she obviously imagined.

His visit had only made things worse, and it still bothered him. Even knowing Frank Carroll had been electronically tagged, and that it was impossible for him to have committed the crimes, she'd been adamant that he was responsible. On one level Currie understood it; he'd seen what she'd done to her leg, after all. The abuse she'd suffered might have ended ten years ago, but it was never a finite thing: not a case of stop and start. It was ever-present. And so it was entirely natural for her father still to loom large in her mind. A broken old man casting a huge shadow through a trick of perspective. But . . .

You have no idea what my father is capable of.

That was true.

He tapped the pencil against his teeth a couple of times – then swivelled the chair round to the desk and slid out the details he'd printed from Frank Carroll's online case file. Skipping past the photographs of Mary and Frank, he looked for the contact number for the detective who'd handled the investigation. There it was. Dan Bright. The area code was for Richmond.

He dialled it now, then glanced at his watch as he waited. The chances were slim, but—

'Richmond PD. How may I help?'

'Hi there,' he said. 'I was hoping to speak to Detective Dan Bright. Is he available?'

'No, I'm sorry. Dan's gone home for the day.'

Dan's a lucky man, he thought.

'That's okay. Could you ask him to call me back, please? It's Detective Sam Currie.' He gave her the number. 'It's nothing urgent. Tell him it's in connection with Frank Carroll.'

'Will do.'

So that was that. He didn't know what Mary's father was capable of, but he could find out.

And in the meantime, the one thing you do know is that Frank Carroll has no connection with this case.

That was true as well.

Currie stared at the whiteboard a little longer, until he felt both his eyes and his thoughts begin to blur, and then he stood up and put his coat on.

Currie had lived in the same house for nearly thirty years, and the changes within it mirrored the path his life had taken over the course of that time. At first it was simply his, and then Linda had moved in, bringing her things and mixing them with his own. All the furnishings and belongings that were *theirs* had been slowly added, item by item, as the years passed. Neil was born, and an extension appeared on the side of the building. As their son grew up, he gained possessions of his own, and they mingled with those of his parents. It had become impossible, amongst this mess of life, for Currie to see clearly what had been his.

And then suddenly, it had been revealed again. Linda had taken her things when she left, of course; Neil's had been boxed up and put away in the attic. All that was left now was him, spread in a disordered, random fashion around a house that was too large for him, too full of conspicuous gaps and absences that he was only slowly becoming used to.

Currie turned the lights on in the kitchen and poured himself a glass of wine, but left it on the counter for the moment. Instead, he went upstairs to the landing. He pushed the trapdoor in the ceiling – *click* – then lowered it gently, bringing the old ladder down with it. There was a shriek of metal as he slid it down to the floor.

He didn't have to go up into the loft properly, as the box was at the nearest edge; he just brought the whole thing down and brushed the cobwebs off the top. Sealed with parcel tape. He fumbled for a minute, then gave in and used his house key to slit it open. The cardboard ripped back with a hollow echo.

Neil's old books.

Currie took a few out, smiling at the covers one by one, and then found the one he was looking for.

The Knight Errant. Mary's favourite book. He'd recognised it when he was at her flat, and remembered reading it to Neil when he was a little boy as well.

Currie took it downstairs now and sat in the armchair in the corner of the lounge, beneath the soft glow of the standing lamp. As he flicked through, memories seemed to solidify inside him.

Most of the pages contained large watercolour illustrations of the knights and soldiers and fair maidens that populated the tale, and then a few lines of text that explained what was happening. The first letter of each paragraph was italicised and ornate: swirling gold on a red background, like some kind of medieval heraldry.

The heroine of the tale was a peasant girl called Anastacia. In the first few pages she fell in love with a boy named William, who went off to become a knight and had many adventures. She found it difficult to be away from him, but accounts of his heroism reached as far as her hamlet, and she was proud of his deeds. When he returned to her, revered throughout the land and laden with titles and money, she couldn't have been happier.

After the lovers were reunited, however, an army descended on the land from the east, and word was sent from the king himself for William to join the legions defending the country. Anastacia begged him not to leave her again, and at first he resisted the calls to battle. But they came ever stronger. As the story went on, his titles were revoked, he was mocked in the streets, and people began calling him a coward and decrying his good name. William was torn. Eventually, driven by pride and a sense of duty, he relented and went to fight, leaving Ana with a broken heart – and a sharp dagger with which to defend herself from the invading hoards should he fail to return.

But upon reaching the front line, William realised he was there for all the wrong reasons. Everything he'd done when he was younger had been motivated by his love for Ana, and now he found that she was all he wanted; the glory and acclaim suddenly meant nothing. To universal derision, he turned tail and rode home – where he arrived to find his true love with the knife he'd left poised over her broken heart. He grabbed her hand before she could kill herself . . .

And they lived happily ever after.

Currie sipped his wine as he turned the pages. On a subconscious level, he knew what was going to happen in the story before he got to it. He must have read this to Neil a lot when he was younger, and reading it again now was like rediscovering paths he used to walk down every day in a place he'd forgotten even existed.

The illustration on the last page showed Anastacia and William embracing in their small, thatched cottage, tears rolling down her perfect face in happiness.

I failed my duty, William told her, *because I had to.*

No, she replied, *you have faced the only challenges that mattered, and you came back to save me.*

The End.

At the time, he remembered, he'd thought the moral of the story was simplistic. And it was, of course. Who was fighting that invading army? Because someone had to stand up and protect people, didn't they? There would have to be knights and soldiers manning that front line, and sacrifices made. It was absurdly idealistic to think that love conquered all.

But sitting there now, the cover creaking as he turned the last page and closed the book, he could see the appeal. It was a world where people followed their hearts and did what they thought was right for those they cared about, no matter what the consequences for themselves. A world where the hero always arrived to save the day, and always in time.

Chapter Fifteen

Thursday 1st September

When we'd arrived at the theatre it had been a cold, clear evening; by the time we left, at quarter to nine, it had started to rain. As we emerged down the front steps I felt the first few drops hit me. The change in weather summed up the way I was feeling quite well. Everything had felt so promising two hours ago. Now, it all seemed to be balanced on a knife-edge.

'Fuck.' Sarah grimaced at the sky and pulled at her velvet coat. 'I wouldn't have worn this if I'd known it was going to rain.'

'I'm sorry.'

'Hey, it's not your fault.'

'But we could have stayed to the end,' I said. 'Maybe it would have stopped by then.'

'No point, though. You've got what you came for.'

She put her arm in mine and we walked in the vague direction of the taxi rank. Where before it had felt comfortable to walk like this, now there was a little tension between us. Perhaps that was just my imagination: my emotions were all over the place. One second I felt outright panic, the next, calm, rational anger at myself for how I'd let the performance back there get to me.

Sarah leaned against me.

'So,' she said, 'are you going to tell me who Tori is?'

I tried to smile. 'That obvious, huh?'

'Uh-huh. You practically went green.'

As soon as Thom Stanley had said her name, I'd felt something lurch inside me – a wave of nausea. I'd let go of Sarah's hand as though I was afraid of her.

She's coming through a little strangely, I remembered now. *I don't even know if it's someone who's passed.*

A few people were waiting for taxis, and we joined the queue. There was a drunk-rowdy group of lads in front, huddled up against the weather and complaining. Further down, a taxi pulled out

'Tori,' I said carefully, 'is a friend of mine.'

'Just a friend?'

'We went out briefly, but it was a long time ago.'

'Okay.'

Sarah didn't say anything else, but we both took a step forward. The queue was moving quickly. It wouldn't be long until we were at the front, and I had a feeling I needed to handle this conversation well before we got there. Avoiding it wasn't an option after the way I'd reacted. If Sarah had gone pale after hearing an ex-boyfriend's name, I wouldn't exactly have been overjoyed either.

'It just threw me,' I said. 'Him saying that. I know he's a fake, but at the same time, it's not exactly the most common name in the world.'

'That's true.'

'Which is why he used it.' I'd realised this as we left at the interval, and wanted to kick myself. 'Obviously, nobody wants to think their dead relatives are horrible, and so he picked something unlikely.'

'Why do that at all?'

'So he could put on more of a frightening show, I guess. Add a bit of power and depth. A bit of edge, you know?'

If anyone does know her, I think she might be in trouble.

'And for a second you believed him?'

'Yeah. For a second I did.'

We took another step forward.

'Why, though? You'd just seen what a fake he was.'

An image of Julie flashed into my head and I forced it away.

'The thing with Tori is, sometimes she gets sick. And when he said her name, I suppose it just made me realise I hadn't spoken to her for a while.'

'Okay.'

Don't ask me how long, I thought. It was only a few weeks. Rationally, I knew there was no reason whatsoever to think she might really be in trouble: it was only because of what had happened with Julie. But even so, I kept remembering Tori's phone call from Staunton, and the guilt I'd felt at not being there when she needed me.

I could explain a little of that.

'Something happened a few weeks ago,' I said, 'and she ended up in hospital. I felt pretty bad about the whole thing. Guilty, you know? Like I was a bad friend. And what he said in there just made me think about that. It's only a coincidence, but it pushed the buttons. I'm fine now.'

I couldn't think of any other way to explain it. The drunken group in front of us clambered into a five-seater. We stepped forwards.

'Well . . . why don't you text her, or something?' Sarah said. 'If you're worried.'

'Yeah, that would be the sensible thing to do.' I took a mental sigh of relief. 'I didn't mean to upset you.'

'Why would I be upset?'

'I don't know. I suppose I went a bit strange there.'

'Yeah, but you're going stranger now.' She laughed and tightened her arm in mine. 'It's okay, Dave. Part of what I like about you is that you obviously care about people. I just wanted to make sure it wasn't going to be a problem.'

'It won't.'

'Just don't run off with her, okay? Friends I can deal with. Baggage, of course . . . that might be a different matter. I don't handle that quite so well.'

'You're not a baggage-handler?'

'That's right.'

She smiled, but I got the feeling she was also assessing my words a little more seriously than she was letting on, and I felt annoyed with myself again. Rob had been right. Damn him.

'Honestly,' I said. 'You've nothing to worry about. It was just a stupid show.'

'Well, then, that's okay,' she said. 'Let's go home.'

We spent the taxi ride quietly holding hands, both of us staring out of our respective windows. Simple contact, but important. Even if we were both a little preoccupied, at least we had that connection. For my part, I was just glad she'd been okay about my reaction. I would text Tori at some point, but there was no urgency because nothing was wrong. It was more important to keep myself focused on Sarah.

When we reached my flat, the taxi driver pulled in between parked cars. I rounded up the fee then climbed out after Sarah, while the driver counted up, the engine grumbling to itself.

The rain was spitting down, but it didn't seem to matter so much anymore. I walked over and unlocked the front door.

'Hey hey.'

A car door slammed behind me. I turned, the keys in my hand. Choc and Cardo were walking towards me.

Something inside me collapsed at the sight of them.

They'd been waiting for me.

Choc was smiling, but not in a friendly way. It reminded me of a schoolyard bully sidling up to you like a friend, all okay – then going for you when he gets in close enough.

I pushed the front door open and turned to Sarah.

'Do you want to go on up, get us a drink?'

'Sure.' She frowned, unsure what was going on. 'You okay?'

'Yeah,' I said. 'It's fine. Just old friends.'

Choc stopped directly in front of us and stared at her. Waiting.

'Okay,' she said slowly. 'I'll be upstairs.'

I closed the front door behind her, then turned, angry.

'What do you want?'

Choc looked at me, his expression full of disdain. His body language, refined over years of practice, was designed to unnerve – he was standing too close and looked wired. Full of little movements, as though he might lash out at any second. I understood what he was doing, and I tried not to be intimidated. It didn't quite work.

The taxi was idling at the kerb, but that wouldn't influence Choc in the slightest. If he wanted to kick off, he would. My keys were still in my hand. Very carefully, holding them where he couldn't see them, I moved one between my middle knuckles and found a grip that worked.

'What do you want, Choc?'

And then his whole body relaxed. He sniffed and took a step back. As though his intimidation routine was his mind doing weights, and now it was shaking its muscles out.

'Just need to have a little chat, you know?'

'It's not a good time.'

'It's good for me. Which is good enough.'

He smiled, pleased with himself.

'What?' I said. 'You have to come and fuck up my life like this?'

'Now *that's* what I wanted to see.' He stepped back. 'Some of the balls I thought you had. I'd never have taken you along that day if I didn't think you had some balls hidden somewhere.'

'I shouldn't have gone.'

'Yeah, but you did. And you know what? It shouldn't be anything you feel bad about.'

'I don't.'

He inclined his head one side, then the other. *Ah, I'm not convinced about that.* 'I'm worried you heard something, you see? Maybe got the wrong idea.'

'No.'

'Because nothing happened to Eddie. He just got a little beat and sent on his way.'

I remembered the gunshots I'd heard, and quickly pushed them out of my head.

'Yeah,' I said. 'That's exactly what I figured.'

'So you shouldn't feel bad. I'm a decent guy until you break the only rule I have. Don't fuck with me or my friends. Nobody does that to Tori and gets away with it.'

'I feel the same.' I reached out to the door. 'I said I shouldn't have gone. I didn't say I had a problem with what happened.'

'Well, I'm worried that you do. Stop that.' He frowned, pulling the door closed and holding it shut. 'I'm bothered it's still on your mind.'

I shook my head, confused.

'What the fuck is this about?'

'One of my boys was down the station a couple of days back. He said he saw you.'

So that was it. There had been a few people in the waiting area when I arrived, a few when I left. I hadn't noticed any of Choc's crew there, but that didn't mean anything. They'd probably know me better than I knew them. And I'd had other things on my mind.

Something else to thank Detective Currie for, then.

'Yeah. He told me you were there a long time. It looked like you had a good chat with someone.'

'It wasn't about that,' I said.

'Oh yeah? About what, then?'

'About none of your business.'

That was probably a step too far. His expression fell away. His voice, when it came, was low and full of menace.

'It had better not be my business.'

We stared at each other. I could hear a buzzing sound, like when you stand close to a pylon, and I knew it was in my head.

'We clear?'

'Yeah,' I said. 'We're clear.'

'We're done.'

Choc let go of the door, walked back over to the car and got in. Cardo clambered into the driver's seat. As the engine started, Choc wound the window down and leaned out. He still had his killing face on.

'I let you get away with a bit because of Tori. But if you start to concern me . . . you're gone. You don't fuck with me or my friends. Don't make me worry. Understand?'

'I understand.'

He nodded, then leaned back inside the car and Cardo began to pull out.

Without even thinking what I was doing, I took a step closer.

'Have you heard from her recently?' I said. 'Tori?'

For a second, Choc looked thrown by that. He frowned at me. I had no idea where the comment had come from. Perhaps it was because Sarah was upstairs and Choc was here, trailing those bad memories behind him, and so now it was easier for my concerns to float to the surface.

But whatever he thought, Cardo obviously hadn't heard – he pulled out and started driving off. A moment later, I was on my own again. Staring after them. Then another car drove past, tyres slashing the wet road, and the spell was broken.

And I thought:

Because I think she might be in trouble.

Part Three

Chapter Sixteen
Friday 2nd September

It was bright and sunny on the day my brother died. That's important, not only because of the lesson I took from it – that people can be taken from you in light as easily as darkness – but also because of something that happened, and something that didn't.

I was wearing shorts and a T-shirt, as always in the summer, and my hair was longer back then. Owen and I looked very much alike, except that the two years in age between us were becoming more noticeable as he approached his teens. There'd be pictures of us together, and he'd have the look of a young man, whereas I'd be this little kid standing beside him, my whole body squinting at the camera. I was still awkward in ways he'd started growing out of, and desperate to catch up. I didn't know that he was about to be frozen in time: that I would soon overtake him, leaving him behind for ever.

It was the school holidays, and Mum and Dad were busy with their own work. Me, I felt slightly restless; I was in need of some activity and I went searching for it. I walked into Owen's room that day to find him squatting beside his bed, getting his things together. He looked up as I opened the door.

'Jesus.' He turned round, angry. 'Don't you knock?'

'Sorry.'

'As if you are.'

'I'm just bored.' I peered down. 'What're you doing?'

'Have you got to know everything? I'm going to play in the woods.'

'Can I come too?'

'No, you can't.'

'Please.' I shuffled in the doorway, trying to think of a way to convince him. Then I remembered what my friend Jonny and I had found a couple of weeks earlier: 'I know a good tree we could climb. I worked out how to get close to the top. It would take ages to figure it out on your own.'

'What makes you think I'd want to?'

But he looked at me standing there, and it must have been clear he wasn't going to shake me off. He sighed. *Nothing clings like a little brother.*

'All right.'

So we made our way outside and down towards the woods.

My childhood memories all exist in saturated colours; everything is exaggerated. That day, the world was full of bright greens and deep blues, and it was so sunny that the garden seemed to be shimmering gently. When I breathed in, the grass smelled rich and warm and sweet, and I had to waft away midges as we reached the bottom. The air was so hot it was like clearing steam from a mirror. As I climbed over the fence behind him, I was already sweating.

We walked a little way in. The grass gave way to the parched brown earth of the woods.

And suddenly, everything went dark.

It wasn't because of the trees. The sunlight was still cascading down between the branches, dappling the ground and sparkling around the outline of the leaves above; I remember looking up to check. This darkness was different. It was all on the inside. A feeling that something was *wrong*. And the further we walked, the worse it got, as though my soul was falling into shadow. There was a storm gathering, and I could sense the distant rumble of an enormous cloud unfolding slowly towards me . . .

I stopped. Owen took a second to realise, then turned around.

'What's wrong with you? You've gone all pale.'

'I want to go back.'

'Huh? Five minutes ago you wanted to come.'

I looked amongst the trees. I didn't know what I was frightened of.

'Something's wrong,' I said.

'What? Jesus. Why do you have to be such a baby?'

Taunting me like that would normally have made me angry: turned my hands and face into little fists. That day, I barely even registered it.

'Something bad's going to happen,' I said.

He stared at me for a second, and I could read the expression on his face. *Why am I having to put up with this?*

'Go home if you want,' he said. 'I never asked you to come, did I?'

He turned around and started walking off.

'Owen.'

'Shut up.'

I stood there, watching him move away, and everything inside me was screaming to make him stop, or to go with him and try to prevent whatever was going to happen.

'Owen!'

'Shut up, baby.'

Then I heard something, although not with my ears. It sounded a little like a crack of lightning – except it was a beautiful day and there wasn't a cloud in the sky.

That was what happened. This is what didn't: the noise started me moving, but in the wrong direction. I turned around and ran home as fast as I could. And I never saw him again.

I had plenty of time to think, of course.

Now that I'm older, I understand what happened that day a lot better. I can rationalise and explain it; in fact, it's part of my job to do just that. I can tell you all about confirmation bias and co-incidence. That I only remember it because what happened later made me concentrate on the event and turn it into something bigger and more important than the irrelevant daydream it really was. Tragedy does that; afterwards, everything gathers meaning and weight. In reality, it had probably just been a slight uneasy feeling – one that my subconscious had elaborated and gilded over the years. Maybe it was even the onset of a headache that I've forgotten about since.

The truth is, I'll never know.

One thing I am certain of is that it wasn't a psychic flash. There was nothing I could or should have done because of it. It had no connection to Owen's death, and so there was no need for me to feel guilty, and no need to blame myself for something I had no reason to do.

I know that, but the lesson remains with me.

That's how it happens. The things that are important will slip away if you let them.

'Dave – wake up.'

Someone was shaking me. I opened my eyes and saw that morning light, the colour of butter, was extending in a solid wedge from the skylight. Sarah was crouched down within it, fully clothed, her hand on my shoulder and a look of concern on her face.

'What?' I said.

'You were having a nightmare.'

'Was I?' My mouth was too dry. I made an effort at sitting up, propping myself on my elbow, and picked up the glass of water from the bedside table. I took a swallow. 'I can't remember.'

That wasn't entirely true. The dream had fallen to the floor and smashed into dim pieces, but even as they skittered away from me I could make out the details on a few shards. The warmth of the day. Owen's face. Me turning, running away from him.

Sarah sat back on her heels. 'It looked like it.'

'Thanks for waking me. What time is it?'

'Half eight. So I was going to anyway. I've got to head out now, and I wanted to say goodbye this time.' She stood up and ruffled my hair. 'You look cute when you're sleepy.'

I did my best to smile. 'You look cute when I'm sleepy too.'

'Works for me. Shame I've got to go. I'll see you at seven thirty tonight, then? The Olive Tree?'

It took me a second to place it, and then I remembered.

When I'd finished talking to Choc last night, the first thing I'd done before coming back inside was send a quick text message to Tori's mobile, asking if she was okay. No big deal, I thought; no harm in it. Then, I'd come back upstairs to find Sarah waiting for me in the kitchen with two glasses of wine at the ready; she handed one to me without speaking, and clearly expected an explanation in return. And obviously, the way Choc had dismissed her, she deserved one. I was even more annoyed with him for turning up – and then with myself for ever getting in the position where he would have a reason to.

So I apologised. Profusely. It was difficult to explain who Choc and Cardo were without detail I didn't want to give, so I just told her the basics. They weren't old friends – more like vague acquaintances, but ones you didn't want to get on the wrong side of. They didn't want to talk to me. They were looking for Emma, so I told them she'd moved out.

I wasn't proud of lying. But it was a small lie, told for what I hoped were good reasons. I was doing my best to leave behind the mistake I'd made and move on with my life, and I resented Choc for coming here and dredging it up for me to deal with. I told myself I wouldn't lie to Sarah about anything I did in the present, and I meant it.

Suggesting The Olive Tree for tonight hadn't been part of any effort to placate her. She'd accepted things by then and we were sitting in the front room, drinking our second glass of wine and chatting as normal again. The restaurant had been her idea.

'Yeah, sounds good,' I said now.

'I'll look forward to it.' She leaned over and kissed me on the lips, then walked over to the bedroom door. 'Catch you later, then.'

I smiled. 'You will. Take care.'

After she left, I allowed myself to lie back down for a minute, waiting to hear the front door go. When it did, I blew out slowly, then picked up my phone from the bedside table. I had a message.

I opened it and read:

Hey there. Sorry for silence. Am fine, just busy. Hope u r too. Maybe catch up sometime soon. Tori

I felt almost absurdly relieved. After all that, she was fine. *You fucking idiot. Of course she is.*

I was about to put the phone back down, but then something struck me. When had she sent it, for one thing? It must have come through fairly late on. I clicked back until I found it.

Four in the morning.

That wasn't like her. The whole time we'd been together, she was almost always in bed for half-nine, ten at the latest, and not up again until the last possible moment in time for work. There'd only ever been a handful of times when I'd had texts from her in the early hours, and the explanation had always been the same. She was with a guy.

That had always made me uneasy too, but this morning there was something more to the feeling than plain jealousy. Something else was wrong with the message. I re-read it, trying to work out what it was.

When I did, it became all I could see.

The offices for *Anonymous Skeptic* consisted of one small room on the first floor of a rather plush block in the city centre. Everything in the building was uniform and new, from the wooden fittings in the offices, via the neat carpets and paint jobs in the hallways, all the way to the potted plants and bland, abstract watercolours on the walls. There was secure parking out back, meeting rooms available upstairs, and magazines and water-coolers in the corridors. In the reception downstairs our nameplate rested, a little uneasily, between those of web designers, translation agencies and accountants. Most of them earned more money in a day than we saw in a month. We couldn't really afford it, but it was good to have a base.

It was almost one o'clock when I finally arrived. Rob was on the phone, but he acknowledged my presence with a wave of his pen and a disapproving look at his watch. I was busy sipping coffee from a small plastic cup when he finished the call.

'Good afternoon,' he said loudly. 'Did you enjoy the gig last night? I spoke to Nathan this morning, and he said that it all went according to plan with Andrew and the necklace. Dead on, you might say.'

'Yeah. We got him.'

'Nathan also said you weren't around at the end. You were supposed to meet up, weren't you? Get a few quotes. I thought we agreed?'

'Yeah, we did.' I'd forgotten about that. 'I'm sorry. Something happened.'

'Something? What kind of *something*?'

I glanced over. He had that look on his face: the expression that said he would go on and on until he got the truth out of me, and that he suspected he wouldn't like it much when he did.

'Here,' I said.

The digital recorder was on the desk in front of me. I'd already listened to it again that morning, and I selected the right file now and played it. The sound of Thom Stanley's final performance before the interval filled the office. The recording was pretty good – you could hear every word – and as it played out I kept an eye on Rob to check for his reaction. He held a pen between his hands, using his heels to slowly rotate the chair back and forth. Giving away nothing. Except when Sarah asked if I was okay, at which point he grimaced.

'That's rubbish,' he said at the end. 'I hope you know that.'

'Yeah. But it got to me at the time.'

'I warned you about this.'

'There's something else. I got a strange text from her.'

'From Tori? Like the strange phone calls you get from her?'

'No, not like them.'

I walked across and showed him the message.

'She's never up at that time,' I said. 'Plus, she always signs her texts off in the same way. 'Tor xx'; with a double kiss. In all the time I've known her, every single text, she's finished it like that.'

That was what was wrong with it.

In the early days of the magazine, Rob and I had attended a Ouija-board session that was more convincing than most. We'd attracted a 'spirit' that claimed to be the grandfather of a girl who was present, but she was unconvinced by it and got very frightened. It wasn't that she didn't believe in the spirit; it was that she didn't believe it was her granddad. She thought it was something else, pretending to be him.

Rob had taken the piss out of her in private afterwards, but I couldn't quite bring myself to. I knew it was rubbish, but the idea of it unnerved me. You don't have to believe to find it creepy. What she said had got my mind working: if it wasn't her grandfather, then what was communicating with her? And where was her granddad?

I'd had that same feeling looking at my mobile.

But if so, who was it, and where was Tori?

Rob looked up from the phone and stared at me. Was I kidding him?

'Am I being ridiculous?'

'Yeah, you are.'

He handed the phone back and sighed.

'I don't know what you expect me to say. Have you texted her again?'

'Of course. I left a message asking her to get in touch. I've tried ringing her too, but the phone's switched off. I tried her work. The girl in the office says she's off sick.'

He spread his hands. 'Well, there you go.'

'I called her house and there was no answer.'

'Jesus Christ, Dave. You're a hair's breadth from stalking her, you know? Maybe she's asleep. Or perhaps she's having one of her *episodes*. Have you phoned the hospital?'

'Not yet.' I hadn't thought about that. 'But she wouldn't be allowed her mobile in there.'

'Maybe you should try anyway.'

I walked back over to my desk. 'Maybe I will.'

I found the number for Staunton Hospital online, studiously ignoring Rob as he made ostentatious head-shaking gestures on the other side of the office. When the hospital answered, I asked to be put through to Ward Eight.

A woman answered. 'Reception. How may I help?'

'Could I speak to Tori Edmonds, please?'

'Just a moment. Is she a patient here?'

'I think so, yes.'

I heard her sorting through paperwork. Then she picked the phone back up.

'I'm sorry. We don't have anyone here by that name. Are you sure you've come through to the right department?'

I hung up.

'Should we call the police?' Rob asked himself.

I ignored him, wondering what to do next. On the way over here, I'd decided I had to do something. My mind kept returning to that phone call I'd had when she was in hospital. At the beginning of all the mistakes I made, the first was very clear: I'd promised to be there for her, and I hadn't been. No matter what I told myself now, that feeling – that urge – wasn't going to go away on its own.

I gathered my things together and stood up.

'I need to get some fresh air.'

'What? You only just fucking got here.'

I shrugged my coat on.

'Dave—'

'I need to be sure, Rob. Okay?'

He looked at me for a second, as though unable to believe I was putting us both through this, then dropped his pen loudly on the desk. Dismissing me.

I closed the door and headed downstairs.

I've just got to be sure.

Chapter Seventeen
Friday 2nd September

At half past one, for the second time in as many weeks, Currie and Swann drove up the hill into the Grindlea estate.

'This is going to be interesting,' Swann said.

Currie nodded. When they'd come here to interview Frank Carroll, he'd thought about how volatile the neighbourhood was – that if the residents wanted, they could barricade the bottom of the hill and keep the police out. The fact that Charlie Drake and his crew all lived here.

One fewer now, if reports were to be believed.

One of the locals had called the incident in a little over an hour earlier. The man had heard a disturbance during the night, but thought little of it until later on this morning, when he was leaving for work and noticed his neighbour's door was ajar. Out of concern – he claimed; Currie had his doubts – he'd gone inside, where he'd found the occupier dead in the living room.

Alex Cardall.

There was a time – not even very long ago – when Sam Currie would have exchanged his career, possibly even his life, for five minutes alone with Charlie Drake or Alex Cardall. After Neil had died and Linda had moved out, when he was left with that sagging house full of spaces, it eventually reached the point where it was all he could think about.

The drug dealers who'd supplied his son.

The people who were responsible.

One night, he'd driven into the Grindlea Estate and parked

halfway up the hill. He'd been drinking – but only a little, and his head was sharp and focused. He kept his thoughts clear, free from the emotions boiling below the surface. Although he hadn't articulated to himself what he was going to do, he'd allowed his body to follow its course and come here, fooled his mind into believing this was something happening to him rather than an action he was carrying out. He'd sat in his car a little way down from Charlie Drake's home, teetering on a precipice. And finally, after a period of time that could have been minutes or hours, and hadn't really felt like time at all, he'd started the engine and driven home again, unable to go through with whatever he'd been considering.

At first, he'd felt like a coward – that his inability to act was yet another example of failing his son – but in later months he looked back and saw the event in a different light. Currie understood violence very well, along with the motives behind it. People hurt others for many reasons, but the most common one by far was because of weakness and feelings of inadequacy. Violence was often about stamping your authority on the world: about being unable to land a punch on the shadows inside you and so hitting outwards instead. The man who starts a fight in a bar probably doesn't know the person he beats up, and doesn't care about them at all, and each angry punch is directed at something far more nebulous than the person in front of him. Currie understood that, just as he would understand, months later, when he met Mary Carroll, that the wounds on her leg were something similar.

And he knew his failure to kill Charlie Drake – the half-thought he hadn't allowed himself to consider – had come down to that recognition. Currie did not want to be that kind of man. He refused to turn away from his own failings, his own guilt, and strike out at others. Instead, he would take responsibility: admit his mistakes and learn from them. He wouldn't blame others for the things that went missing from his house over the years.

Right now, though, he didn't know what to feel. He was glad to have moved on a little from that hate, towards himself and others, because those emotions weren't ones he wanted to associate himself with. But as they drove up the hill, he was aware this was going to feel different from other crime scenes. He wasn't thinking of this as a tragedy. At the moment, in fact, his mind was occupied with more practical issues, such as containment.

They approached the base of the nearest tower block in the Plug. When the portable had phoned it in, the scene had already been receiving attention. Currie had immediately requested a back-up team to the flats to contain it as far as possible until they got there. And from first appearances now, they had their work cut out for them. There were four police vans here, with several officers distributed around the entrances to the tower. Others were standing with bunches of angry, gesturing residents, talking calmly, trying to placate them and keep them under control. Most of them probably thought it was a raid.

They got out of the car into the ice-cold air and did the ritual.

'Gum?' Swann offered.

'Thanks.'

'Means you go first, though.'

'Oh yeah?' That bit was new. 'How does that work?'

Swann shrugged. 'I don't know how my TV works either, but it does.'

Currie led the way, moving quickly through the bunches of people, showing his ID to a rather nervous young officer on the main door of the tower. Then they made their way under the tape and up to the fifth floor, their footfalls echoing around the skeletal stairwell. There were officers guarding the corridor, and when they arrived at Cardall's flat, two more waited by the door.

Currie glanced between them. 'Helliwell?'

One of them nodded: 'That's me, sir.'

'Nobody else has been in? Is that right?'

'Yes, sir. I cleared the other rooms, and then I've been standing out here since.'

'Good job.'

He turned to Swann. *We ready?*

His partner nodded.

Since Helliwell said he'd checked the other rooms to ensure nobody else was present, they limited themselves to the front room. Later, the entire flat would be picked to pieces, and a number of officers would be very interested in the findings. Currie was one of them, but for now he reminded himself . . . *priorities.*

'Jesus,' Swann said.

They found Cardall lying on his back on the far side of the room, arms and legs resting slightly away from his body, like some kind of snow angel. A couple of his fingers had obviously been broken, but most of the damage was from the neck up: his face looked like the features had been beaten off it onto the cheap carpet underneath. As they stepped around the body, Currie saw the white glint of an eye beneath the blood.

'I'm pretty sure it's him,' Currie said.

His partner nodded grimly. 'Someone obviously didn't think very much of him.'

'The line forms to the left.'

'Sam, even you didn't dislike him this much.'

'No,' Currie said. 'Not even me.'

He turned his attention from the body to the front room itself. It was almost bare: old, threadbare furniture; a carpet too small to reach the walls. There was a set of open drawers at an angle to the wall, the clothes from inside strewn on the floor. A tiny television and music centre had both been smashed open.

'Looks like someone tossed the place,' he said.

The smell of marijuana lingered beneath the aroma of blood, and his thoughts turned to Cardall's occupation. It was a possible explanation for what had been done here, but it didn't seem enough.

Swann's phoned buzzed. He picked it out and held it to his ear.

'Yep?' He listened for a few seconds. 'Downstairs? Don't let them anywhere near . . . I don't know. I guess we'll be down when we're down. Do your fucking job.'

He flipped the phone shut.

'Drake?' Currie guessed.

'Outside. With most of his crew.'

'Shit.' It had only been a matter of time, though. 'We need to talk to him anyway.'

'We should get out of here,' Swann said. 'Let's get SOCO on site. Maybe hand it over to someone else, too. We've not got time for this. It's got "war" written all over it. What do you think?'

Currie nodded. Still, he couldn't resist looking back as they left the front room. He wanted to clarify his reaction to what had been done here.

Nobody deserves this.

Currie tried that thought on for size. It wasn't quite right, but it was close enough, and that was something: almost a relief. For a long time, he'd been worried he might never fit inside such ideas again at all.

Out front, things were threatening to get ugly.

He picked out Choc's men straight away. There were only five or six of them, but they were big guys, very handy-looking, and they were spreading themselves around and making their presence felt: two to an officer, arms spread, gesticulating. A pack hunting for the weak spots in the chain. They wanted in. Their friend was dead in there, and this was their territory. Unaccustomed to police involvement, they had no respect or use for it.

No fear, either. Only a sliver of common sense was stopping them barging straight through. Their outrage seemed as much at the imposition as anything else. Who did the fucking police think they were?

We're a minute away from chaos here.

'We need to get this under control,' Swann said.

Currie nodded.

'Call it in. I'll go talk to Drake. See if I can calm this down.'

'You going to be nice to him, I hope?'

'Yeah,' Currie said. 'Maybe.'

He walked across the car park. Charlie Drake wasn't talking to anyone or causing a scene; he was leaning against his car, one foot over the other, chewing at a fingernail. Almost relaxed, but not quite – he was staring too intently at the tower block for that, as though he was concentrating on knocking it down with his thoughts.

Currie had met him a few times before, and always had the same reaction upon seeing him. If you didn't know what Drake did for a living, you'd never have guessed it. He wore old suit trousers and an expensive white shirt, which was untucked and a little dirty. If you blurred your eyes, he might have been a sixth-former, bunking off school. Like the bare interior of Cardall's flat, he belied the image of suited, booted, jewelled-up charisma the public probably associated with people high up the drugs chain.

Currie stopped in front of him, nodded once.

'Charlie.'

Drake looked at him. It was only in his eyes that you caught sight of what had taken him so far in this life – if you could call it that. Right there, you knew he was the kind of man who could kill someone and barely even think about it afterwards. Once someone had that, the rest of it was just supply and shipping.

Currie stared right back.

'I remember you,' Drake said.

'Yeah. You knew my son.'

'Neil.'

'That's right. Good customer of yours.'

Drake looked at him for a few more seconds, then returned his gaze to the block of flats.

'My boy's in there, isn't he?'

'Yes.' He surprised himself. 'I'm sorry.'

Drake tutted. 'You're all fucking dancing over this.'

Currie watched the scene, said nothing.

'Especially you.'

'No, you're wrong about that. This will probably get transferred. If it doesn't, I'll do everything I can to find the person who killed Alex. Nobody deserves what happened to him.'

'Don't worry yourself. It's nothing to do with you.'

'It's a police matter, Charlie. Whether you like it or not. We'll be the ones handling this.'

Drake smiled without humour. *Yeah. We'll see about that.*

'Can you think of anyone who'd want to hurt Alex?'

'Maybe.'

But to Currie, that seemed more like bravado than anything else. Beneath Drake's studied calm, he sensed the same human emotions that anyone would feel. Grief and anger. Confusion, too. As though he'd already scanned through a list of enemies and come up empty for this one. The man was hurt, and doing what a predator always did in those circumstances: hiding it.

'Were you with Alex last night?'

'Yeah. He dropped me home around eleven.'

'Where were you before that?'

Drake didn't reply.

Currie eased away from the car and moved to stand in front of him. Kept his hands in his pockets. Deliberately blocking his view of the flats, but also blocking Drake from the view of everyone else.

'You're going to talk to someone,' he said quietly.

'Is that right?'

'It depends how you want it.' He nodded back towards the tower block. 'We'll go through every single associate, every single property, every drawer and every cupboard.'

Drake glared at him, but Currie shook his head.

'And don't think you intimidate me, Charlie, because you don't. If your boys keep causing trouble back there, you're all going in. Nobody can see you right now, and nobody can hear, so I'm going to ask you again. Where were you last night?'

If looks could kill.

But Drake was a smart man. He might have laughed another officer off, but he remembered Neil. He knew Currie hated him. Even if he didn't know how far Currie had nearly taken that, he would know he'd carry out his threat, no matter what the consequences.

He looked off to one side. 'We were in The Wheatfield.'

Currie almost laughed. Throughout the department, officers who'd ever had dealings with Drake and his crew used 'The Wheatfield' as short-hand for any dubious alibi. It was a small pocket of the city where the usual rules of morality didn't seem to apply – a little like the confessional box in a church: you went in full of sin, then emerged with it miraculously lifted from you. 'He was in The Wheatfield' meant someone had stepped outside of society for a moment, into a place where nothing you did was required to have consequences. Where you could take time out from notions of guilt or responsibility. Currie despised the place.

'All night?' he said. 'Don't lie to me, Charlie. I doubt you've had time to organise that with the landlord, and I'll go through every camera in the city—'

'We left about ten.'

'That's an hour missing.'

'We like to obey the speed limit, officer.'

'Don't fuck with me. Where did you go?'

Drake weighed it up. 'We called in on an acquaintance.'

'Who?'

'Guy named Dave Lewis.'

Currie managed to confine the shock he felt to a single blink. It was a Herculean effort. How the hell did those two know each other?

'Oh yeah? You have stuff to talk about?'

'Just catching up. Chatting about mutual friends. You know how it is.'

'Mutual friends.' Currie thought about it and took a guess. 'Tori Edmonds?'

'Yeah. Tori.'

'I remember her. How's she doing?'

'She's fine. Dave – he was worried about her. Said he hadn't heard from her in a while. Just bothering over nothing.'

Behind him, Currie could hear that the commotion was continuing – raised voices, feet scuffing at the tarmac in frustration – but he tuned it out. Thinking.

Dave Lewis. Tori Edmonds. Julie Sadler.

He hadn't heard from her in a while.

'What about you?' he said. 'Have you heard from her?'

'Yeah. I texted her last night. Got one back.'

'Show me.'

Drake frowned. 'What?'

'Show me your fucking phone.'

'All right, all right.' He muttered to himself, digging into his baggy suit pockets. When he got the mobile out, Currie noticed it was a nice one: a single nod to the lifestyle. Drake clicked through, then held it face out towards him.

'Here. Don't be looking at anything else though.'

'Yeah, like I want to look through your dirt.'

153

Currie peered at the screen, and read the text.

Hey there. Sorry for silence. Am fine, just busy. Hope u r too.
Maybe catch up sometime soon. Tori

The exact same wording as the texts sent from Julie Sadler's phone. And those of the other victims. *Christ.* Everything had just flipped, and it felt like the pieces in his head had scattered accordingly.

He turned his attention back to Drake.

'I'm sorry, Charlie,' he said. 'I think we might need to take a closer look at your dirt, after all.'

Chapter Eighteen

Friday 2nd September

Tori lived in the north of town, and I had to drive out and around to avoid the early-afternoon traffic in the city centre. It was after two when I finally pulled up on her street. The first thing I did after I parked was check my mobile again.

No messages. No missed calls.

I put the phone on the passenger seat, then folded my arms and rested them on the steering wheel.

Tori's house was just up the road from me. It was a tall, cramped back-to-back in one of the cheaper areas of the city. The buildings here all had their stomachs sucked in and shoulders hunched, their belts tightened. They had character, though: all painted differently, in whites and greys, so that no single one seemed to fit with its neighbour. The skyline was like a row of dodgy teeth. Her house had windows that seemed to have been squeezed from the side to fit them in. Right now, all the curtains – hippy-purple in the bedroom, I remembered, dotted with yellow stars and moons – were closed.

A network of pipes ran all the way down from the gutter to a grate beside the steps to the front door. The morning after we broke up, I'd stood at the top of those steps, smoking a cigarette, listening to the roar of the boiler in the kitchen behind me and smelling Tori's shower lotion as it swirled and foamed in the drain below. It was blocked by leaves, so the water filled up and then spilled in fingers across the path.

If you ever need me, I'll be there for you. No matter what.

It was an easy promise to make. But when the landscape of a relationship shifts, you have to forge new paths across it. Rob had a point when he'd talked about stalking. I wasn't her boyfriend anymore, and I had no real right to be here. I'd pestered her with texts and calls all day, phoned her work – even the hospital – and now turned up at her house. All based on . . . nothing. When she answered the door, what was she going to think?

Well, why don't you find out?

I locked the car, walked up the street and knocked on her door.

There was no answer. No sense of movement inside.

I waited a minute, then knocked again.

Nothing.

It was an anti-climax. The frustration built up, and I tried the door handle. Even as I was asking myself what the fuck I thought I was doing, the handle turned and the door swung open into the kitchen, creaking twice on its way to the wall.

I leaned inside. It all felt dark and quiet.

'Tori? It's Dave.'

I stepped into the kitchen and called out again. If she was here – which she had to be – I didn't want there to be any confusion about my intentions. I certainly didn't want to walk in on her in bed with someone.

'Hello?'

Just concerned. There was no answer, and the door was ajar.

I listened carefully, and heard nothing but the full, silent sound of an empty house.

I closed the front door, revealing a small spread of post across the kitchen floor behind it, like you get when you return home after a weekend away. I knelt down and gathered it together, then flicked through the pile. A hand-written envelope, a gas bill and what looked like a bank statement. Not a lot, in other words, but it wasn't like Tori to leave stuff lying around.

I wrinkled my nose. It was stuffy in here too. There was a plate on the side, covered with crumbs and a few dry swirls of what looked like tomato sauce. It looked old.

Perhaps she's gone away, I thought.

And left the front door unlocked?

I moved through to the pitch-black lounge, found the light switch, and the front room came to warm, yellow life. The sight of it brought a flood of memories back. When we'd been together, we'd spent a fair amount of time slouched about in here. There were little differences, but it was still mostly as I remembered: the rich yellow of the walls; the orange throws over the settees; knick-knacks on the shelves. And there were books everywhere. She kept them close, like friends, as though she might need one at any moment and had to have at least a few within reach.

'Tori?'

I went through. The back door was locked, at least, with the key on the inside. At the bottom of the stairs I hesitated, looking at the dark landing above. I could imagine what Rob would say if he saw me now. This was bona-fide, A-grade stalking. But then I thought about Julie, restrained in her home. Nobody coming.

The door was wide open and there was no answer.

Up on the landing, I stood and listened, but everything was quiet. The bedroom door was closed. I tapped gently and got no answer – but even if she'd been asleep, she'd have heard me by now. I reached out and pushed the door, expecting the room to be empty.

And it was.

Immediately, it felt like cold water rushed down from my head to my feet, washing a layer of tension away with it. I leaned against the doorframe and took a deep breath. A part of me had genuinely believed something had happened to her. Something like Julie.

Moron.

Her bed was unmade. The thick, white duvet was twisted like candy, the pillow crumpled with an old indent of her head. The other pillow was full, I noticed. The last time she'd slept here, it had been alone . . .

And then I realised what I was doing, and it just felt wrong.

Above the bed, there was a shelf full of books. Night-time reading. I remembered lying there one night while she was in the bathroom, and I'd taken a book down to flick through. It turned out to be a gift from an old boyfriend; he'd written a note on the title page. I'd replaced it quickly. Seeing it had been like sneaking an illicit glimpse into her private world – a time of her life where I didn't belong. And that was exactly what I was doing right now.

I was about to turn and head downstairs when I noticed it.

A white envelope.

It was tucked slightly beneath the pillow. There was handwriting on the front. Small, neat, black letters.

Dave Lewis.

I walked slowly across to the bed and picked it out, gripping the corner lightly between my finger and thumb. The paper made a scratching sound as I hooked my thumb in and tore it open.

There was a letter inside. I unfolded it, holding it as firmly as possible between my hands. The same neat black handwriting filled half of the single sheet. As I started to read, my eyes skipped over words and lines, and I had to set myself in place, focus hard and concentrate to make sense of what was there.

For Dave Lewis

You think you care but you don't. People pretend to but only when it suits them. You are scared and selfish, whatever you might think, and full of shit and this will be revealed for all to see.

You can take the coward's way, hand this note to the police and explain everything. If you do that, then it is over and you will never hear from me again. She will die and you can go on with your life as though this never happened, which is to say as you do now.

If you wish to rescue her, you must prove you are as worthy as you are stupid enough to believe. You must earn the privilege of rescuing her. We shall see. Have no contact with the police and tell them nothing. This is only the start of what we will do together. She will know of your successes and failures and when you let her die she will know how full of shit and lies you have been.

You will hear from me and I will be watching. I leave you a gift so you know I am serious.

Everything else in the room receded slightly.

I felt disconnected from my body, as though I was watching somebody else from the inside, or listening to something from under water. The light coming through the curtains illuminated motes of dust hanging undisturbed in the air, and for a few moments I might as well have been one of them. I had no idea what to do with myself. It was as though my mind had got lost inside my head.

I checked inside the envelope and found the 'gift' he'd left for me. Tori's necklace: the thin, silver chain curled and coiled around that small crucifix. Her sister's necklace.

The only time she ever took it off was to shower, or sometimes when she was in bed. It was her most treasured possession: the first thing she put on every morning, the last she removed at night. *So you know I am serious.* I held it now between my fingers, allowing the chain to hang down over my hand . . .

Three loud bangs from downstairs, and I was back in my body again, my heart thumping.

The front door.

I put the note and necklace back in the envelope, then made my way back downstairs as slowly and quietly as I could. Across the lounge, I could see the silhouette of what looked like two people standing on the doorstep, rippled in the blue curtain.

The silhouette adjusted itself slightly. *Knock, knock, knock.*

'Nobody home.'

I could hear them through the window, and it took me a second to place the voice. The detective who'd interviewed me. Currie.

'Guess not.'

'Work said she was off sick.'

A silhouette moved closer to the window. I saw someone cup his hands above his eyes and try to see through the curtains.

'The lights are on.'

The letter-box clacked. 'Ms Edmonds?'

Christ. All they'd have to do was turn the handle. I backed away across the living room. What the fuck were they doing here?

Was it because of Julie?

Because of me?

'Ms Edmonds?'

Whatever the reason, I couldn't stay where I was. The note had been clear about one thing. If I talked to the police, Tori would die. Until I'd had the chance to think it through properly, I couldn't allow that decision to be made for me.

I went back through to the stairwell, closing the door to the lounge quietly behind me. Through it, I heard the front door open. *Shit.* But the back door opened directly onto the alleyway behind the house. I turned the key as quietly as I could and pulled it open.

It juddered in the frame, creaking loudly.

'Ms Edmonds?'

They were in the kitchen, moving through.

I stepped outside and glanced right and left. The alley ended sooner to the right – so I ran that way, as hard as I could. All that mattered was reaching the end. I passed four houses, five, six, then rounded the corner, checking behind me as I went. Nobody on the street yet. They hadn't seen me.

But my fingerprints would be everywhere.

I ran up the short road until I reached the corner where it joined Tori's street, then turned right again, slowing to a cautious walk. There was a new car parked up outside her house. Mine was slightly nearer. I moved along, keeping close to the hedges for no sensible reason except that it felt safer. I could have abandoned the vehicle altogether, except that my mobile was in there. I'd left it on the fucking passenger seat.

You will hear from me.

I reached the car and fumbled the keys for a moment, then fell inside. *Get moving.* Started the engine and drove off. Didn't even glance sideways at Tori's house as I passed it.

At the end of the street, I took random turnings by necessity as much as anything else, and didn't feel safe until I hit the ring road, heading further north.

That was when I checked my phone.

[1 Missed Call] it said. [1 New Message]

Chapter Nineteen
Friday 2nd September

Carpe Diem was an underground pub in every sense of the word. From the main street, you went down some innocuous stone steps into a spit and sawdust interior that stayed just the right side of dirty, to mix with a clientele of young punks and old rockers. The wood was faded, like old timber, and the red leather in the booth I was sitting in was hard and cracked. Yellow foam poked out from a hole resembling a shotgun wound. Across the bar, on a small stage, amps and guitar cases were waiting for later.

Rob and I came here a bit. I was sitting across from him now, sipping a beer, still trying to get my thoughts into some kind of order.

The missed call and voicemail when I'd got back to the car had been from Rob. First and foremost, he was wondering where the fuck I'd gone. More importantly, from my point of view, he wanted to let me know that an email from Tori had arrived. We'd arranged to meet here for a drink.

I'd already read the email, which he'd printed out and brought with him. 'Tori' had sent it to our work address.

It was strange to be sitting here attempting to pretend that every-thing was normal when I knew it wasn't. I had to act as though I was okay, even while adrenalin was surging through me and my head was in bits. My hands kept shaking slightly, and my throat was tight.

'I wouldn't have opened it normally,' Rob said, casually sipping his beer. 'Except I knew you were worried.'

'It's okay.'

I read it again.

Dave
I'm sorry I've not replied properly. I've just been busy – you know
how it is. Don't worry about me. I'm fine at the moment. I'm off
work with an infection, and I'm at my parents' house as I was
visiting for the weekend when I got sick. Not feeling great in all
honesty, but battling through.
  I'll probably stay here for a few days and then hopefully head
back after that. Depends how things go, I guess. Might be good to
have a chat, though? I think you said your mobile was out of
commission, so I'll give you a ring at your parents' later on? I know
you were planning to go over there rather than head home.
  Take it easy in the meantime, and hope you're well,
Tori
(P.s. Sorry for cluttering up your work email. You might want to get
rid of this.)

'So,' Rob said. 'Are we happy now?'

'Yeah.'

I smiled, doing my best to make it look convincing. No, I wasn't
happy at all. My mind kept flitting back to that Ouija board spirit,
the one that had been pretending. I knew for sure now that this
wasn't Tori. The text might have come from her mobile and the
email from her account. But someone else had sent them.

The man who'd killed Julie.

I tried to wash away the images that summoned up with a
mouthful of beer. It didn't work.

'What's up with your phone?' Rob said.

Out of commission, I saw on the page before me. It wasn't, but I
understood what the man was telling me. The police had turned up
at Tori's house, and I could only assume that was because of me.
She was missing and my prints were everywhere. They'd be looking
for me soon, assuming they weren't already. I imagined it was
possible for the police to trace a mobile if it was turned on, and
the man was warning me not to let that happen.

I said, 'Battery's dying.'

'Well, that'll be a blessed relief for her.' Rob looked at the stage, uninterested. 'I didn't know you were going to your father's house. Do you need a hand?'

I shook my head. 'Just got to sort some papers I missed.'

'Right.'

'No big deal.'

He turned back to me, unsure. Rob had always been good at reading people, but it would have been obvious to anyone that something was wrong. I was talking in clipped sentences and couldn't meet his eye.

Across the pub, I heard the clack of pool balls, and then a couple of cheers. I glanced over, grateful for the distraction. A skinhead was down over the table, the lights gleaming on his skull. He played a slow shot and another ball went down. That group wasn't paying us much attention, and my gaze moved to the other people in here. The couple in the next booth but one. An older man stood still by a tall table, head tilted up to watch Sky Sports. A student holding a pint at his hip, knees bent to collect the winnings from a fruit machine.

All far enough away for us to have privacy, but . . .

I will be watching.

. . . it was easy to be paranoid. I'd even waited across the street for Rob to arrive, watched him ambling along, hands in pockets, with that familiar swing in his step. But just because a person says something in an anonymous note, it doesn't mean it's true. You could post a note saying 'I will be watching' through a random stranger's door, and they'd be looking over their shoulder whether you followed them around or not. It's too easy to manipulate people when they can't see what you're doing, and if I was going to get through this, I needed to remember that. My skill-set was small, admittedly, but it was specialised.

'Are you all right?' Rob said. 'You're acting really weird.'

'I'm fine.'

'No, you're not. What's on your mind?'

'I've just been a bit of an idiot. That's all.'

'Yeah, but you often are. It doesn't explain why you're acting weirder than usual.'

163

'Maybe I'm pissed off with myself.'

He leaned back. That answer seemed to satisfy him. I felt bad for lying, but it needed to be done. And then thinking about lying made me remember Sarah.

Our date tonight. *Shit.*

Obviously, I wasn't going to be able to get to The Olive Tree. Worse than that, I couldn't even risk turning my phone on to let her know, never mind explain why. So at half past seven, she would be sitting there in the restaurant on her own, wondering where I was. Perhaps it was strange, given what else had happened, but the image filled me with panic.

Put it out of your mind for now. Concentrate.

But it reminded me that the police might be tracing my mobile phone: I needed to leave right now. There was something I'd been mulling over, though, and if I was going to do it then now was the time.

'Rob,' I said. 'Do you remember when we met?'

He frowned, the pint glass at his mouth. 'Yeah.'

'You remember where we were? Don't tell me; just tell me you remember.'

He put the glass down slowly.

'What are you talking about?'

'Just listen to what I'm saying. Do you remember that?'

I was sure he would – the bar in the University Union. He was doing his mentalism routine, and we got talking when he stopped at my table.

'Yeah, I remember. But what's that— '

'Nothing, but I want you to do me a favour. Whatever happens, I want you to keep remembering that. Okay?'

He stared at me.

'Dave – what the fuck is going on?'

'Just do that for me.'

I folded the email, slipped it into my pocket, then stood up.

'You're going again?'

'Yeah,' I said. 'Things to see, people to do.'

'But—'

'I'll see you tomorrow.' I held my hand up, not turning around as

I walked away, thinking: *for Christ's sake, don't follow me.* 'Take care, Rob.'

I left my car in the parking garage beneath the Sphere for now, and made my way through the city centre streets. It was a little after five, and the sky was already dark blue, with the night's first prickling of stars appearing overhead. Illuminated shop windows stood out in the gloom, and people filled the streets.

When I arrived at the top of the cobbled alley where our office was located I stopped and looked down, past the Blue Bar and the deli. Although a few groups of people were cutting through both ways, I couldn't see any police waiting for me. And Rob had only left here half an hour ago. If there'd been any around then, I was fairly certain he'd have mentioned it.

I still didn't understand everything that was happening, but I was sure the police would be looking for me soon. The man had told me to go to my parents' house, which implied they'd go to my flat. If they did that, they'd probably come here to the office as well. Maybe they wouldn't know about my parents' house yet.

I started walking.

Sorry for cluttering up your work email.

You might want to get rid of this.

In the time since finding the note at Tori's I'd calmed down a little and had a chance to think things through. And for the moment, I'd decided, I was going to do what the man told me. Once you settle on a course of action, you've got at least one less thing to worry about. Disregarding the panic, I was now faced with a series of tasks to perform, analysing and evaluating things as I went.

In the short term, that meant evading the police, getting to my parents' house, and seeing what happened. As time went on, I would look for opportunities to prod the gaps. See what could be done while the man wasn't paying attention.

First things first, I had to get rid of that email.

The lights were still on in reception, but I looked in and saw the girl there had gone home for the night. And the front door was locked: another good sign. I used my swipe card to get inside, and the door shut behind me, the magnetic seal ticking as it came to rest.

I listened for a moment.

From somewhere on the higher floors came the *suck* and *bang* of a corridor door. Then nothing.

I took the stairs, telling myself to relax. Keep calm. Breathe steady. There was plenty of time.

Our office was dark and quiet, with just a couple of green standby lights visible on the hard drives, and the slight whirr of electrical equipment in the air. I left the lights off, went over and jogged the mouse to bring my monitor to life. The screen was immediately headache-bright in the dim room. After I entered my username and password, the computer began the long, difficult process of pondering life and wondering what it was all about.

A shrill, nasal blare burst across the office.

Over by the door, the intercom was flashing red. Someone was downstairs, buzzing to get in.

As they leaned on the button, it felt like they were electrocuting me. The sound continued for a few seconds, then cut out, leaving my heart racing.

The computer had gone to desktop now, but the icons spread around the screen were appearing painfully slowly, one at a time. Down on the hard drive, the LED was flashing overtime. *Busy, busy, busy.*

I lifted one of the slats in the blinds a fraction and peered down. Two uniformed policemen out on the street. One of them looked up at the window and I stepped away, the blind clicking back into place.

Keep calm and take it steady.

One thing at a time.

I opened the shared email package and saw the message from Tori at the top of the list. Instead of deleting it, though, I opened an internet browser window and went straight to Yahoo. The accounts there were as anonymous as you needed them to be, and quick to set up.

As I ran through the fields, creating a random ID and inventing details, the intercom blared again. I glanced over, then back at the screen. They'd try another office soon, and someone would buzz them in.

Breathe deeply.

With the account set up, I returned to the email program, selected 'forward' and sent the message from Tori to my new account. Then I deleted it, along with the new version in my 'sent items', and emptied both from the 'trash' folder. If I needed the email, I had a copy.

One last thing to do. Back on the internet, I removed the pages I'd just visited from the browser's history. A technician would still be able to recover them, but it would at least give me a bit of breathing room.

I heard a dull tone from downstairs.

The police had tried another office and got lucky.

I turned the computer off at the plug, then moved back out into the corridor, closing the office door behind me. The corridor formed an 'L', with the stairs just to my right. I could hear the footfalls *chitting* up. I ran in the opposite direction, rounding the corner in time. The fire door was at the end. As I put my hand on the metal bar, I heard someone knocking on a door back down the hall. The sound echoed for a second – and then was cut off by the piercing alarm as I pressed the lever down and pushed through into a drafty, concrete stairwell.

Two flights of stairs: my feet drumming; a grip on the banister spinning me round the bend on each landing. At the bottom there was another levered door, and I fell through it into a dirty court-yard behind the building, full of wheelie bins and drains.

Keep calm.

I pressed the door closed behind me, dragged a large bin in front of it, and ran.

The car park in the Sphere was built on about six different levels, and my car was right in the basement. I came down in the elevator and paid for my exit ticket at the vending machine.

It was quarter to six. Behind me, large colourful panels on the wall advertised films showing in the cinema, and a couple were standing in front, clearly debating what to see. I envied them. I wished I could do anything as simple and straightforward as catching a movie right now.

Back at my car I sat in the dark, listening to the high-pitched squeak of tyres that echoed around the garage from the levels above. Every sound down here was amplified and threatening.

Sarah would be on her way home from the studio by now, if she wasn't back already, and she'd be expecting to see me at The Olive Tree in about an hour and a half.

I was thinking. The police knew I'd been in the city centre. If they were going to trace me, it didn't matter too much if they had this car park down as my last known location. After I left, they couldn't know in which direction I'd gone.

So I turned my mobile back on.

Am sorry, I typed in. *Something's come up and I can't make tonight. Will talk soon, promise. Take care in meantime.*

I stared at the message, which felt incomplete and ridiculous, imagining her reaction when she received it: if it had been a letter instead, she might screw it up and throw it away. Frustration rose up within me, and I pressed 'send' before the feeling could overwhelm me.

Then I turned the phone off again, started the engine and drove out. Halfway up the ramp, a sign reminded me to turn my headlights on, and then the car bumped up into the cold, crisp night, and I headed for home.

Chapter Twenty
Friday 2nd September

You smoke too much, Mary told herself.

But that was okay.

When she'd been a teenager, she'd enjoyed the easy, safe flirtation with death. She felt each intake of poison in a similar way to the thin slice of a razor on her skin. Without having to think about it consciously, smoking had always seemed to keep her on some form of level, as though a part of her was always checking to make sure she was being punished, and slowly killing herself was enough to pacify it most of the time.

A man had come up and talked to her once, outside some bar, and said that only interesting people smoked. He'd told her 'it's about the urge to self-destruction', as though there was something fascinating and even romantic about such a thing, and maybe more people should pursue it. She'd wondered, briefly, how interesting he'd find it if she stubbed it out on her hand.

Mary flicked some ash out of her bedroom window.

She was sitting at one end of the sill, her legs stretched out so that her small feet were resting against each other. It was an old house. The window here was one of those old-fashioned ones that you simply hefted upwards, and then it stayed aloft by magic until you hefted it down again.

On her right-hand side, there was about a metre of cold, night air. Below, a paved back garden full of split rubbish bags. Each house on this street had these little courtyards at the back: all full of crap, because you had to take your bins out front for collection, and most people were lazy. Most people didn't care.

She took one last drag and tossed the cigarette out into the night. But she stayed where she was for a moment. There were no streetlights in the back alley. Everything there was blue or black, except for the dull red dot of her cigarette end.

Mary could imagine her father standing down there right now, hiding in some wedge of darkness and watching her. She was brightly lit up. He would be able to see her very well.

Are you out there? she thought.

It had taken her a long time to calm down after he'd seen her outside his house that day. She'd been frantic because it was clear she couldn't deal with him herself, and yet she had to. If he wasn't down there tonight, he would be tomorrow. And nobody would stop him.

Gradually, though, she'd come to a kind of peace with the idea. It was either that or go insane. In place of the terror her body kept producing at the thought of him, she tried to will some determination into herself instead, and it seemed to have worked. Last time, the sight of him had slipped a key into a lock inside her, opened it, and let everything out. Next time, she would be better prepared. He was just a man.

She kept repeating that to herself: a mantra that would help her through the approaching madness.

Just a man.

Mary hopped down and closed the window. It descended with a screech and a judder, and then she closed the latch. Despite her efforts, the bedroom smelled of smoke. She wasn't sure why she even bothered—

The phone rang.

She held very still, listening to the noise as it blared through the quiet house. There wasn't a single person in the world, as far as she knew, who had any reason to call her.

Suddenly, she didn't feel as sure of herself anymore.

The noise kept coming, insistent and alarming.

You have to do this.

She crossed the hall and went into the front room.

The phone here had Caller ID, but the number on display was unfamiliar . . . and then she placed it. The area code was

Rawnsmouth. Her brother's phone number. She felt a flash of anger, remembering how the police had found her. She didn't need this conversation. But she answered it anyway.

'Hello?'

'Mary?'

She didn't answer. She wasn't sure why. Instead, she shook the curtains across with her free hand, closing herself off from the main street below.

'Are you there?'

'Yes,' she said.

'It's me.'

'I know. Why are you phoning me?'

He paused, sounding unsure of himself.

'The police called me . . .'

'I know that too.' The anger rose up: 'And you told them my number. How could you do that? Did I ever give you permission to tell people my business? Do you remember that happening?'

'No.' His voice was almost whining. 'I'm sorry.'

'You've no idea how hard I've worked to keep my life private. None at all. And with one . . . you've put me at risk.'

'Hang on.' He sounded like he was about to start arguing with her, but then seemed to think better of it. He paused. 'Look: I'm sorry, okay? I didn't realise it would be that big a deal.'

'Well, it is.'

'I said sorry. What else did you expect me to do, though? He wanted to know where to find you, and it didn't sound like he was going to give up very easily.'

Mary closed her eyes and rubbed her forehead, wanting to hang up the phone. Wanting all this to go away. But she couldn't.

Over the years, she'd been through so many emotions. She'd felt anger at the people who did nothing, fear at what her father might do next, and there had even been hope that someone, somewhere, would help them – because that was what good people did. But one thought had remained constant over time. It had filled her mind on that desperate night in the snow, almost the only thing she could still feel. *I must protect him.* Her beautiful little brother. *I must make sure he's safe.*

That urge had been the only thing that kept her moving.

'Mary?'

She opened her eyes and said, 'Is that the only reason you've called? To tell me that the police have been in touch?'

'No.' He hesitated. 'I . . . need some more money.'

She should have expected that. Why else would he call?

'Money,' she said.

'Yeah. Just . . . I just need some.'

Mary pictured her brother in her head. Whatever he said or did, she always remembered him in the same way, and she always would. His eyes, wide and blue, his face so still it wasn't even trembling. Just a little boy who hid away from the terrible things he saw, and sometimes became so lost inside himself that she had to coax him patiently out again, feeling responsible with every soothing word she uttered. No matter what he did, he would always be that little boy, and she would always feel that way.

'Mary?'

She said, 'How much do you need?'

Later, she was sitting in the front room, her legs tucked beneath her on the settee, still thinking about her brother, when the phone went again. She didn't check the ID this time, assuming it would be him again, and just picked it up.

'Hello?'

Nobody replied.

She looked at the display on the phone. Number withheld.

Mary's skin was suddenly alive, tingling. She could feel every hair, every faded white line hidden away on her body

Slowly – as though something dangerous was in the room with her – she uncurled her legs and stood up.

She didn't say anything else, but kept the receiver pressed tightly to the side of her face, listening carefully to the silence on the other end of the line.

There was somebody there.

Someone who was listening right back.

She went through the checklist in her head. This window, that window, the front door – they were all locked. The nearest escape route, if necessary, was the network of pipes outside her bedroom window. This process was second nature: Mary did it every time she heard a creak in the night, or a *thump* from the plumbing upstairs.

She crossed the room, listening to the heavy silence on the phone, turned off the front room light and returned to the window.

Crouched down and edged the curtain aside, just a little.

A car was there. Parked up directly opposite the house.

She stared down, unable to make out much detail at first. The interior was dark, but she could see just enough through the windscreen to be sure there was someone inside. She could see his leg. Tracksuit bottoms.

Oh god, please not now. The panic overwhelmed her. *Not yet.*

She cancelled the call, jabbing at the receiver, her finger trembling so much she had to press the button twice, three times. Then she looked out at the car below, watching it through the sliver-gap her finger dared to make in the curtain.

Nothing.

And then the engine grumbled, the sound muffled through the glass. A second later the headlights came on, and the car pulled out and drove away up the street.

Mary watched it go, then allowed the curtain to fall back into place.

She put the phone down carefully and deliberately on the table. It felt like her mind was starring over and her thoughts disappearing entirely. She sat down on the settee, pulled her knees up to her chin and closed her eyes, searching inside for the determination and fortitude she'd once had, and finding in its place only the sensation of leather round her wrists and a body that refused to move.

Just a man, she told herself, but it wasn't true.

She realised now that she'd been wrong: it wasn't possible for her to deal with this. A phone call had the ability to reduce her to almost nothing. If she saw her father up close and heard his voice . . . it would be impossible. Something inside her would snap in self-defence, break irreparably into pieces that nobody would ever be able to put back together.

After a moment she leaned over, her hand shaking, and picked her book off the coffee table. It had once been a thing of beauty to her, but now it felt almost treacherous to the touch. *You came back to save me.* Her father had delighted in dispelling everything good she saw within it, and yet she'd never given up hope. Faith, even. If it wasn't true then there was nothing left.

So Mary clung to that now: the image of Ana with the knife held high over her breast, saved at the last moment just as all seemed lost. It was all she had left. She couldn't face her father on her own, but she wouldn't need to. Her mantra shifted; it was no longer a cry of defiance.

Someone will come, she told herself.

Over and over, repeating it until the words filled her head.

Someone has to.

Chapter Twenty-one
Friday 2nd September

At half past seven I should have been sitting down for a meal with Sarah. Instead, I was in my parents' kitchen, sitting at the small wooden table by the wall.

My car was parked beside the skip at the bottom of the curling tarmac drive, next to those arched trees I was too big to climb. The first thing I'd done when I arrived was check the house and make sure it was secure. It seemed to be. As far as I could tell, nobody had been inside since Rob, Sarah and I had started cleaning it out.

The next thing I'd done was come into the kitchen and check the drawer under the counter, selecting a knife that would fit in my coat pocket. It was madness to think I'd ever be capable of using the thing, but I did it anyway. I could feel the weight there now, an insistent, surreal question at my side: *what the fuck are you doing?*

The short answer was nothing. I was sipping a glass of water and waiting to see what would happen. There was no phone line here. I'd remembered that on the drive over: it had been cancelled after my father died. A fax machine sat in his old office, and still seemed to work, but the phone on it was dead. No matter what he'd said in the email, Tori's abductor wasn't going to be calling me here.

Which must have meant I was going to be meeting him.

Face to face.

I was trying to subdue the panic at that idea and think. As carefully and rationally as I could.

The only thing I knew for sure was that someone had kidnapped Tori. It was natural to assume it was the same man who'd murdered Julie and the other girls, but that raised a series of uncomfortable questions. Was it a coincidence that he'd taken Julie and then Tori? If so, it was a big one. And where was she? According to the media, the previous victims had all been tied up and left in their homes. Perhaps not, though. Maybe if one of their boyfriends had gone round to her house in time, he'd have found a letter there instead, just like me.

But it was useless to speculate; you had to deal with what you knew. And that was simply the note, the email, and the things he'd made me do so far. Two of my ex-girlfriends were involved, my fingerprints were now at one of the crime scenes, and I'd been forced to run from the police. Was he intending to frame me in some way? He had to realise that wouldn't work.

What the fuck are you doing?

I stood up and went across the hallway to Owen's room, then turned the light on to reveal the grey, forgotten world inside.

The sensible, rational thing to do right now was go to the police. I remembered reading a book about hostage negotiations, and the main rule was always the same: the kidnapper was never allowed to leave, even if it meant that all the hostages died. The situation had to be contained. By acting on my own like this, I was in danger of getting both me and Tori killed, and leaving her abductor free to hurt someone else. If I went to the police, they'd at least have a chance of catching him.

I knew that.

But I couldn't do it.

I walked over and nudged a book on Owen's desk; it scraped out of place, revealing a pale square of polished wood amongst the grey. I ran my finger down the bedpost, collecting an ellipse of dust on the tip.

And remembered something.

It wasn't true that nobody had been in this room. I'd come in here myself, a year or so after Owen died. I'd stood inside, thinking about the gunshot I'd imagined I'd heard, and I'd been full of guilt. Because if the beliefs my parents had started to reassure themselves with were true, then I could have saved him that day, and I hadn't. It wasn't long after that when I started kicking back at them, but the lesson had always been there. He had slipped, and I had let him.

I remembered. I'd sat on the bed and looked around, missing my brother more than I could ever tell anyone. I'd hoped that – if he was still conscious somewhere – he didn't hate for me what I hadn't done that day. And I'd wondered whether my parents would ever love me again.

Time dragged on, and nothing happened.

I began to worry I'd missed something: a creeping fear that I'd messed things up in some way; that I'd been too late or stupid to catch whatever ball he'd thrown. Or that the man's plans had been interrupted. He might not have realised there wasn't a phone in my parents' house. I had no idea what was going on in his head.

Gradually, the fear was supplemented by frustration and anger. I hadn't missed anything; he was just giving me a chance to stew, and it was working. However much I tried to keep calm and push my feelings aside, they stayed close. The police were going to show up; I was going to walk into the next room and he would simply be *there*, standing in the middle; Tori was dying right now . . .

Isolated in my parents' house, my emotions bred like bacteria, and by eleven o'clock I was practically climbing the walls – wired for fight or flight, but with no one to confront and nowhere to run. I was aimlessly pacing the living room when I heard it.

A phone was ringing.

For a moment I stood very still, shocked by the noise. Then moved out into the hallway.

Where was it coming from? The sound was muffled, so I started off towards the far end of the house, but the ringing grew quieter that way, so I stopped and turned back again.

The front door. The noise was coming from there.

I walked down and peered through the spy hole. There was nothing to see. But it was so dark outside I could hardly even make out the garden.

Do it.

I took out the knife and held it down by my side. With my other hand I undid the chain – then stepped back and pulled the door open.

The cold night breeze rushed in past me.

A sprinkling of rain. Nothing else.

The phone lay on its back on the doorstep, the screen glowing softly. Rather than picking it up, I stepped out into the rain and looked around. The garden was full of shadow: intricate shapes that were barely distinguishable from the darkness around them; the trees just grey skeletons standing shivering against a black background. Despite the rain, the breeze was almost gentle. It rushed and rustled in the distance.

I put the knife back in my pocket and picked up the mobile.

[Number withheld].

I answered it and held it to my ear, scanning the night. If he was nearby, I should have been able to see the illumination from his own phone. There was nothing.

'Hello?' I said.

There was no immediate response from the other end, but I could tell someone was there. I could hear a sound like wind on the line.

'Be quicker next time,' he said.

The voice was harsh and impatient, and it didn't seem to be disguised. Had I ever heard this man before? I couldn't be sure, but I didn't recognise him.

'Where is she?' I said.

'Nowhere.'

'I want to speak to her.'

He laughed. It sounded very far away. 'No.'

'How am I supposed to know she's not dead?'

'Because I'm not a killer.' He spat the words at me in contempt. 'She's only been gone a day and a half. Don't you know how long it takes someone to die of thirst?'

I remembered a mantra from some survival programme on television: something about the rule of threes. Three minutes without air, hours without shelter, days without water, weeks without food. But the body started breaking down long before that, the damage becoming more and more serious. Irreversible. Not to mention the pain.

I put the image of Tori out of my head and didn't reply.

'All you need to know is that she's alone and suffering, and that it's going to stay that way until you help her. But you won't.'

'Why are you doing this?'

'I'm not doing anything. Just like you.'

'I don't understand.'

'Try harder. This is about whether you choose to stop her dying. That's all. It's not *complicated*, Dave. If you choose not to, you'll never hear from me again.'

'Until they find you.'

'Even if they caught me in time, I'd never tell them where she is. So you'd have killed her, wouldn't you? This is the only chance she'll ever have to stay alive. You'll have to work out what's important.'

'I'm not hanging up,' I said.

'Not yet.'

His words hung in the air for a moment, and I sensed a hundred others were being held back. There was such hatred in his voice – such anger at me. I could even feel the venom coiling in the silence.

'What do you want?' I said.

'Have you got the note?'

I nodded, wondering if he could see me.

There was no reply.

'Yes,' I said.

'And the email?'

'I deleted it.'

'I know that. But your fat friend printed it out.'

How did he know *that*? I tried to remember some of the people I'd seen in Carpe Diem, or walking near the office, but their faces were lost to me now. I just knew that nobody had caught my attention.

'I've got that too,' I said.

'Then the first thing you're going to do is leave the house and go to your car. Close the front door, but don't bother locking it. The police will only have to kick it in.'

'Okay.'

The rain swiped at me as I made my way up the path, conscious of that long, dark spread of garden behind me. I glanced back, but the blackness down there was implacable. As my shoes tapped on the stone steps, I half-expected someone to jump down at me from the arched trees above, but there was nobody there – just the rain softly coming down against the leaves.

My car was still parked up at the bottom of the drive, but there was something else there now.

Someone had left a cardboard box beside the back wheel.

I forced myself to walk across. The lid was closed but not taped up: the four flaps folded one under the other, the way you need to bend one back to do properly. It was slick from the rain. Water was creeping up the sides from where the base touched the driveway.

'What's this?'

'Don't open it yet.'

Frustrated, I rotated on my heels, looking in different directions. Everywhere was dark. No glow from a mobile.

'So what *do* you want me to do then?'

'Put the box on the passenger seat, then get in and start the engine. At the top of the drive, turn left. Carry along the street for about twenty metres, then stop.'

I took out my keys. The central locking *click-clacked* open.

'I need two hands for the box.'

He hung up on me.

The box was about the size of the five-ream paper boxes we ordered in at the office, but whatever was inside, it wasn't paper. The box was too light for that. I put it on the passenger seat, then started the car. The gears hitched as I reversed around in a loop, then I drove up the steep slope to the road.

At the top I turned left, then pulled in against the kerb a little further on. The wipers squeaked across the glass.

I glanced in the rear-view mirror.

My parents' house was on a quiet street in a residential area, and the road was deathly quiet at this time of night. But a single car was back there, parked just beyond my parents' driveway. The head-lights were on but dimmed; the wipers sweeping steadily, silently, back and forth.

I could make out the dark shape of a man behind the wheel.

I watched him in the mirror, wondering what would happen if I got out and ran at him. *Or reverse quickly*, I thought – *smash into him*. But even if I got to him in time, what exactly was I going to do? I had a knife, but I expected he did too. Even if I did manage to get him, what if he wouldn't tell me where Tori—

The mobile rang.

I accepted the call, watching the car behind me. A small pinprick of green light was visible in his windscreen.

'The note and the email,' he said. 'Screw them up and throw them out of your window.'

'I'll have to put the phone down.'

I took the silence for consent, so rested the mobile on the passenger seat, then scrunched the two sheets together into a ball and threw it out. It skittered over to the far gutter.

'That okay?'

'Lucky for her it didn't go down the fucking drain. Be more careful next time.'

'What now?'

The lights on the car behind me went to full beam.

'Drive on a little. About twenty metres. Then pull up again.'

I released the handbrake and eased the car forwards. As I did, his own vehicle began crawling along, neither gaining nor losing ground.

When it reached the bunched paper, he pulled over slightly and came to a stop, and then the driver's-side door opened. I struggled to catch a glimpse of him, but I couldn't see anything behind the shield of those headlights, just a sense of movement, like birds fluttering in a column of light. The door closed and I saw him back behind the wheel again.

'Now what?' I said.

'Wait.'

In the mirror, the green light disappeared. He'd put the phone down. It took me a moment to realise that he was checking the paper to make sure I hadn't tricked him. The contempt and anger in his voice were in stark contrast to the care and precision he was taking with his actions. He'd planned this carefully and knew exactly what he was doing.

'Now,' he said, 'we're going for a drive.'

Chapter Twenty-two
Friday 2nd September

Half past eleven at night, and the incident room was teeming with activity. People were taking calls, typing, carrying bundles of paper between desks – all of them working a little quicker than usual. The door seemed to be constantly opening and closing, with officers either bringing in fresh information or taking actions away. There was a buzz to the place, a feeling of energy. The team was pulling harder now, because they all knew that in the last few hours everything had changed.

Currie glanced around and thought:

It should feel like we're closing in.

Normally it would have, but despite the activity around him, he was frustrated. Itching to move.

He and Swann were sitting across from each other at the far end of the room, beneath the whiteboard. Currie had spent the last twenty minutes making his own notes in the A3 pad he kept on his desk, but the only thing he seemed to have created was a mess.

He put his pen down and looked at the information on the wall.

Swann raised his eyes from the screen. 'You okay?'

'It feels like we should be doing more.'

'Doesn't it always feel like that?'

A rhetorical question.

Currie said, 'Found anything interesting so far?'

His partner only grunted in reply – *what do you think?* – and continued to work at the computer. Earlier on, the IT tech had provided them with a CD full of stills from outside the shopping centre where Julie Sadler's phone had been used. Swann was now clicking through them, one photo at a time. Not looking for anything in particular, but looking regardless, because it had to be done.

That task summed up the whole investigation. They'd always been left chasing witness statements, opinions, conjecture: following up every possible lead, no matter how insignificant. Currie had contented himself with that before, because a methodical approach would eventually yield results. If they checked everything, the killer would only have to make one mistake, and they'd catch him off the back of it. Now, it felt like they should be more active.

'But we're doing everything we can,' Swann said.

Currie nodded, but he wasn't convinced.

There were two new names on the board. The first was TORI EDMONDS. Several people in the room were attempting to trace her whereabouts – all of them, so far, without success. There might still be an innocent explanation for her disappearance, of course, but he was sure something had happened to her, and it was this conviction, more than anything, that made Currie *need* to be moving. Negotiations were in place to access her mobile phone records, but the time involved in arranging that was as frustrating as every other aspect of the case.

The other new name on the board – the one that bothered him equally, in its own way – was DAVE LEWIS.

When they'd interviewed Lewis for Julie Sadler's murder, Currie had been convinced he'd heard the name before, but couldn't remember where. This afternoon, he'd dug it out. When Alison Wilcox has been killed, they'd thrown the Eddie Berries abduction to another team. *Priorities.* That team had briefly looked into it, then thrown it to the bottom of the pile. Currie had scanned the details in a spare moment the week after, and been pleased to see they'd at least *spoken* to Drake and Cardall. Both had visited Tori Edmonds at Staunton Hospital the afternoon of Eddie's disappearance, and then gone – where else – to The Wheatfield. A photocopy of the log-in book from the hospital was included in the file to corroborate their story. Dave Lewis had been there too: his name appeared directly under theirs, and he'd left at the same time.

So he was connected to that investigation, and now he was doubly connected to the murders.

The person who fled from Tori Edmonds's house when he and Swann arrived had not yet been identified, but Currie would bet money it had been Lewis. Since then, he hadn't returned to his flat and his phone was switched off. Someone had been at his office too – and run when officers showed up. No signs of forced entry. They'd soon have a green light on searching the premises, but that didn't concern him so much as where Lewis and Edmonds were right now.

'How are you doing over there?' Swann said. 'Made any breakthroughs?'

'Ha.'

On the sheet on his desk, Currie had written Lewis's name in the middle. Lines then spiralled out to other names, the vast majority accompanied by question marks and scribbled queries. Some crossed, others went nowhere.

'Okay,' Swann said. 'The usual. Talk me through what we know.'

'We know Dave Lewis dated one of the murdered girls.'

'Julie Sadler.'

'He also dated Tori Edmonds, who now appears to have been abducted by our murderer.'

'Agreed. And where is Lewis now?'

'We don't know. But we know he's run from us at least once, probably twice, and isn't showing up in any of the places he should. What we don't know is why.'

Swann clicked the mouse. 'Bingo.'

'And then there's the fact that, aside from Charlie Drake, Lewis was the last person to see Alex Cardall alive last night. Which brings us to Eddie Berries.'

'Sam, you're not listening to me. I said "Bingo".'

Swann's face was pale blue from the light of the monitor in front of him, and he'd stopped clicking the mouse. He wasn't even blinking.

Currie walked around and leaned on his partner's desk – then froze as he saw the image that was on the computer screen. Dave

Lewis, in black and white, was turned slightly towards the camera. There was just enough of his face showing to be sure it was him.

'Entered the shopping centre at 11.57. Left again at 12.09.'

You're wasting time with me when you should be out there finding the man who did it.

'We had him,' Currie said. He realised it was precisely this fact that had bothered him the most when they'd written Lewis's name on the whiteboard.

'Yep.' Swann folded his arms, breathing out heavily. 'And we'll get him again.'

The department didn't have anything as grand as a canteen on this floor. Instead they had a small room, which Currie recalled had been a toilet in a previous life. They'd ripped out most of the fittings and stuck a fridge, counter and cupboards beside the sink, and a coffee machine and water-cooler against the far wall.

Currie clicked through on the machine: black, no sugar. It hissed and spat, the liquid rattling down into the small plastic cup.

There was no way he could have known, of course, but still: he was furious with himself. Full of anger and frustration. They'd had Lewis right there in front of them, and they'd let him go. As simple as that. And now Tori Edmonds was missing. Currie kept going back over what had happened, and it all seemed so obvious to him.

If they dug back far enough, he was sure, they'd find something connecting Lewis to the other victims. As it was, they hadn't picked up on him until Julie Sadler. During the interview, Currie had mistaken the shock he'd seen on Lewis's face for surprise that Julie was dead, but now he could see very clearly what it had really been – that Lewis was beginning to panic. He'd thought they were closing in on him. When they'd released him, he'd figured there might not be too much time left, and so he'd started to accelerate.

He moved the first cup out of the way and added another.

Click, *whirr*.

Of course, it was always easier to blame yourself in hindsight, wasn't it? But Tori Edmonds was still missing. If she died, it would be because of them. Because of what they hadn't done. Yes, hindsight made things easier, but it didn't mean the repercussions would be any less devastating, or the mistakes that led to them any more excusable. That kind of reasoning didn't change a thing. Never had, never would.

As he took the two cups of coffee back along the corridor, the only questions still remaining hung over Eddie Berries and Alex Cardall. He couldn't see how they fitted into this. It was possible they were unconnected, but Currie didn't think so. Lewis had been there the day Drake and Cardall abducted Eddie, and Cardall had met up with Lewis just before he was killed. It couldn't be a coincidence, but he had no idea how those strands came together.

They'd know more when they had Lewis in custody.

And Tori Edmonds home. Safe and sound.

He pulled the office door open with his foot and put Swann's coffee down on the table beside him. His partner was resting his elbows on the desk, his face in his hands. Currie knew Swann must be annoyed with himself as well, because his fingers were messing up his hair and he didn't seem to have noticed.

'Coffee,' he said.

Swann looked up slowly.

Currie frowned. 'What's wrong?'

'Pete Dwyer just called. His team's finished itemising the contents of Alex Cardall's flat.'

Currie blew on his coffee. 'And?'

'They found a stash of heroin and money hidden beneath loose floorboards in the bedroom. And guess what else?'

'Dave Lewis?'

Swann shook his head. Almost laughed.

'Even better than that,' he said. 'Alison Wilcox's mobile phone.'

Chapter Twenty-three

Friday 2nd September

The man stayed on the phone for the whole journey, giving simple directions whenever we approached a junction, staying silent the rest of the time. As we made our way towards the main roads he hung back a little, keeping that same cautious distance between us, and when we joined the ring road he ordered me to hold a steady pace, then allowed his own car to drop even further behind. Even though the other traffic was relatively sparse, I soon lost his vehicle amongst it.

At least it gave me the chance to think. Despite the hum of danger in the air, I was trying to be rational. Everything I knew about him, I was filing away.

I knew he was male, that he could drive, that he either owned or had stolen a car. He understood technology: computers and mobile phones. He had thought all this through, and was being scrupulously careful as he carried it out. At the same time, beneath that precision, he was full of rage – contempt and hatred for me. The way he spoke, it was as though I was responsible for all this. Just like the note he'd left me at Tori's, in fact – the way the neat handwriting contrasted with the jumbled, barely-controlled grammar, as though his temper kept slipping from his grip.

So far it was just small details and impressions. But I was used to working from those during my routines. If you got enough then eventually they added up to a larger picture.

'Right at the next lights.'

'Okay.'

We left the ring road and began to wind our way into the edges of an estate. A row of local shops on the left was shuttered up, the ridges stained with graffiti. The houses were all squat and flat: boring buildings that looked like they'd been patted on the head once too often and would bite the next thing that touched them. A moment later, I saw that his car had reappeared in the rear-view mirror, the same maddening distance away. He'd measured and timed all this perfectly.

'Round to the left,' he told me. 'Park up underneath the second streetlight, then turn off your engine.'

I took the corner, slowing the car slightly as I passed the first, then coming to a halt directly beneath the second. Amber light fell in through the windscreen. I killed the engine and heard the sudden, startling tapping of rain on the roof. The windscreen began to speckle with water, distorting into yellow spider webs.

Behind me, the man parked up just round the turning, allowing more space between us this time.

I glanced either side out of the windows. I had no idea where we were. There were residential houses on the left, with hard, grey faces. On the other side of the road, tarmac lots sloped off behind spiked metal fences, stretching away to single-storey warehouses. A phone box, its glass smashed in, stood back-to-back with a post box on the sodden grass verge.

'Why this place?'

'You'll find out.'

I peered in the mirror and saw it. A CCTV camera on the first lamppost, pointing my way. He'd parked up just short of it.

'So what happens now?'

'Now, you open the box.'

'Okay.'

Nervous as to what I might find, I pulled at the flaps and they sprang open easily. At first glance, the box seemed empty. It was only when I tilted it towards me that something rattled, and then I saw a few strange shapes inside. The contents resolved themselves, and I pushed the box back across the passenger seat.

Clothes.

'The police take an inventory,' the man said. 'Someone close to the victim is asked to say whether anything's missing.'

I tried to suppress the horror I was feeling.

'But who's going to notice a pair of jeans?' he said. 'Or a top? Especially someone who cared so little.'

'Why did you keep them?'

'Because they were precious to me. Take out the phone.'

'What?'

'The fucking mobile. It's on top.'

I reached in and found it. As I lifted it out, the backs of my fingers brushed something soft, and I recoiled. *Only clothes.* But they were tainted by the circumstances in which they'd ended up here. He'd taken them while a girl was lying emaciated and dead in the room beside him. Julie . . .

'Turn it on.'

It was an old Nokia model: you had to stick a fingernail in the top to activate it. I pressed the button, then waited as the mobile powered up, an image swirling on the screen.

'Go to sent messages. There's only one. Open it.'

I clicked through and selected it. The message appeared.

Hey there. Sorry for silence. Am fine, just busy. Hope u r too. Maybe catch up sometime soon. Tori

Oh God.

'This is her phone?'

He ignored me. 'Press forward, then go into contacts. You'll see a girl called Valerie in there. Send her the message.'

I'd been right earlier on: the man was trying to set me up. But you couldn't just transfer guilt from person to person like that. The police would know. Surely he didn't believe this was going to achieve anything.

He might if he's crazy.

'But—'

'Do it now. Hold the phones close together so I can hear the tone.'

I scrolled down until I found Valerie's name, glancing in the mirror at the CCTV again. That was why I was here – to implicate myself on camera. The police would trace where the message had been sent from, check the CCTV and see my car.

I scrolled up through Tori's contacts list and highlighted my own name instead.

That would work. The man would hear the tone and believe I'd sent the message. And if the police were looking at me as a suspect and tracking my mobile, this would throw up a massive question mark for them.

My thumb touched the Select key.

Then paused as something awful occurred to me.

How careful is he being?

'What's taking so fucking long?'

'I'm not used to this phone,' I said. 'I'm sorry.'

I hit Cancel, then Menu, then Contacts.

Scrolled down. *Valerie, Valerie,* Valerie . . .

Select.

'If you don't send that text,' the man said, 'I hang up and drive away. In the next five seconds, you're going to kill her.'

The screen changed to tell me I was dialling Valerie's number. I could dimly hear the ring tone from Tori's mobile and immediately cancelled the call. For a moment, I'd had the awful suspicion that there *was* no Valerie – that Valerie's phone was the one in the man's hand, thirty metres behind me – and that he was just testing me. I'd had to make sure.

'Okay.'

Sweating now, I clicked quickly back through, and forwarded it to myself.

The phone beeped.

'Did you hear that?'

'Yeah. I heard it. Turn her mobile off.'

'Now what?'

'Get out of the car,' he told me, 'and walk down the road. Number twenty-six is about five along from where you are now. The front door's open. Go inside.'

'*What?*'

'Just do as you're fucking told. Don't look back, and keep the phone out of sight.'

He hung up.

I stepped out of the car and was immediately hit by the rain; it picked at me as I walked down the road, passing the houses one by one. Scared now. Why did he want me inside somewhere? Was he coming after me? But I didn't want to disobey him by looking behind. I was glad I had the knife with me. I just hoped I'd get the chance to use it.

What the fuck are you doing?

Number twenty-six.

It was a small, drab semi with a metal gate separating a patch of concrete garden from the street. The gate creaked badly, scraping across the ground as I opened it, then clattering down when I let go. At the front door I looked up. No lights on. No noise from within. The place was empty and silent, just like Tori's house had been.

Deep breaths.

The door was unlocked. I turned the handle and stepped into a thin hallway. The wind followed me, tinkling a wind chime suspended beside the door. A staircase led up on the right, while straight ahead was a dark, moonlit kitchen. Two doors off the hall to the left, both shut.

I closed the front door – he hadn't told me not to – and took the knife out with one hand, the mobile with the other, and waited for him to call back. Seconds passed, and nothing happened. The phone stayed as dark and still as the house around me.

Then I heard it, and glanced up the stairs.

A dull, whining noise coming from above me.

Tori. I didn't even hesitate.

Upstairs, the whirr of flies in the air was louder, and the smell hit me. It was like ascending into a black cloud: a revolting haze in the air, which my throat objected to on a primal level. It reminded me of the last time I'd visited my father in the hospice, when his skin had been yellow and he'd looked like he was sweating death. There was that same sickly sweet aroma of disease here. The air felt damp with it.

I held my sleeve up to my face and pushed the bedroom door open.

The curtains were open. They allowed a wedge of light to come in and fall like a blanket across the girl lying on the bed. Flies cut through it in tiny black flashes.

Oh God.

I nearly fell down.

It didn't even look like a real person. She was too still: an object rather than a human being; a waxwork dummy lying naked, spread-eagled, on the bed. I noticed the thick coils of leather tying her wrists to the bed-posts, beneath the horrible, splayed fingers. Rope was wrapped around her head, cutting into her mouth.

One of her eyes was shut. The other was open just a sliver, showing a crescent of white.

All completely motionless.

I took a stupid step towards the bed, needing to get a better look at her face and make sure . . . and then stumbled backwards, my heart tumbling down into my gut. Emma.

The mobile went.

My hand shook as I held it up to my ear. For a few seconds I heard nothing but the whine of flies in the air. When his voice finally came, it was as cold and callous as anything I'd ever heard.

'You let her die.'

It wasn't true, but the violence in his words pierced through any of the rational things I could tell myself. Emma, who'd been lying here all this time, forgotten and uncared for. Whom I'd barely thought about since she left. Not even a person anymore. Just a thing, left there on the bed.

'Why?' I said quietly.

'You thought you were a better person.' And as hard as his voice remained, I could tell that he was taking some pleasure from this. 'But you see now you're no better than anyone else. That you don't care at all about people when it's hard for you.'

'Why are you doing this?'

'You should have asked yourself that. Every second you did nothing.'

I closed my eyes. Even though Emma was out of sight, I could smell the decay. And sense something on a deeper level, as well, hanging in the air. I felt like a sinner, standing alone in the quiet, echoing dignity of a cathedral.

'What do you want from me?' I said.

'Nothing.'

'What?'

'Nothing. You've already abandoned her once. Now you just have to do it again. Walk out of here, get back in your car and drive away.'

'What – I'm supposed to leave her here?'

'Just like you did before.'

I opened my eyes and forced myself to look at her, and deliberately tried to put the girl I'd known out of my head. It wasn't Emma. There was nothing I could do for her now.

'Or can you not bring yourself to care enough about Tori?'

I'm sorry, Emma.

'All right.'

I turned around and walked out of the bedroom. Headed back downstairs. The front door was still closed.

'I come out now?' I said. 'Then what?'

For a few seconds, the man didn't reply.

'We're done for tonight,' he said. 'We'll have more fun tomorrow. I don't care where you go in the meantime, but the police will be looking for you. If you contact them, you'll never hear from me again. I'll be watching.'

'Right.'

'Remember that, Dave,' he said quickly. 'Really try hard. Because you might think you're *so fucking clever*, but you're not. You have no idea what I can do.'

I opened the front door and stepped out. Was it worth wiping my fingerprints away? I didn't know whether that would make me look less guilty or more. Better to do nothing.

'I understand,' I said.

He laughed at me. Mocking the idea.

And then the line went dead.

I stepped back out into the night. The immediate tapping of the rain startled me, and I shivered. One last glance up at the profound silence of the house – *I'm so sorry* – and then I walked back to my car, facing the CCTV camera the whole way.

The street beyond was already empty; the man had gone. And yet I felt his eyes on me every step of the way.

Part Four

Chapter Twenty-four

Saturday 3rd September

After I got back to the car, I didn't know what to do next. Where could I go? All the places I had a key for weren't safe. At the same time, I couldn't fill up on petrol and keep driving: the police would be looking out for the car, and possibly even monitoring my bank account. I had a quarter of a tank in the car, about ten pounds in my wallet, and no easy way of replenishing either. But I set off anyway, without thinking, because the one place I did need to be was somewhere else.

I was driving fairly aimlessly, my head in pieces, when I thought about something. My hands tightened on the wheel.

You have no idea what I can do.

I didn't know how or why, but the killer had clearly singled me out for some reason. And if he knew about Julie and Emma, maybe he knew about Sarah as well.

Immediately, I indicated and took the next turning. But then, when I was nearly there, I began to question what I was doing. What if he didn't know about her at all? If I called round to her house – if I even phoned her – I might be placing her in danger.

I didn't know what to do.

I just wanted to park up and collapse. Let someone else deal with all this.

In the end, I drove down her street and kept my eye out – intending to sweep past and see if anything looked suspicious or out of place. But then I had a bit of luck: there was a car park a little way down from her house. It was far enough away that, if the killer was watching me, he wouldn't be able to tell why I was there, but close enough to catch an angled view of the front of her building, including the door. I pulled in. In the context of everything that had happened, this felt like winning the fucking lottery.

I sat there, feeling blank but determined. There was no point in trying to sleep, and I had nowhere else to go. So I would sit here, instead – wait out the night, and as far as possible make sure Sarah was okay.

The rain sounded almost peaceful now. I started thinking about what had happened, trying to piece what I'd learned together into a bigger picture.

The killer had laughed when I said I understood, but it was obvious I was in a lot of trouble. Maybe he couldn't frame me in a way that would stand up to scrutiny in the long term. Then again, maybe I'd underestimated just how convincing and full an illusion it was possible to create. A handful of small details. Not so hard.

But why me?

You might think you're so fucking clever, but you're not.

He was wrong about that. I didn't feel clever at all. In fact, sitting there, I felt like the stupidest person in the world. I knew I should go to the police – turn myself in, try to explain – and every time I closed my eyes, I pictured Emma's emaciated body. Her face demanding to know why I'd forgotten about her, and how I could bring myself to leave her again now.

But the memory also made me think about Tori. If I didn't carry on, someone would find her like that. As long as I believed she was still alive, I had to keep going. I wouldn't be able to live with myself if I didn't try.

So I spent the night slumped in the car with all those thoughts, hiding in plain view. At some point the rain stopped, and everything became silent apart from the wind. Eventually, I could hear birds, and realised that the top sliver of the sun had appeared at the horizon. It rose slowly, a nimbus of yellow and orange spreading upwards, revealing the remnants of last night's storm overhead: tattered clouds like bruises on the sky.

Just after seven o'clock, a light came on in Sarah's house. I watched, and another one appeared beside it.

She was all right.

Shivering a little, I started the car and drove away.

At half past eight, I was sitting in a large cafe about six miles out of the city centre. It was the definition of greasy-spoon, and the dirt and fat seemed ingrained in every surface. There were bottles of scab-topped brown sauce and ketchup resting on the Formica tables. Samples of each had been helpfully crusted to the laminated menus.

The cafe was a few miles up the main road from my parents' house. I remembered it from school bus journeys home, because it always seemed to be full of truckers, and sometimes the braver sixth-formers would venture inside for kudos. Back then, the place had possessed a strange and almost exotic danger. This was the first time I'd ever been inside, and it turned out to be just a cafe. At this time of day, there were only a few weathered-looking delivery drivers at the far end by the counter, barking loudly at their own jokes and occasionally bantering with the waitress. From beyond the counter, I could hear bacon sizzling and pans being scraped out, and a coffee machine that sounded as though it was rasping up phlegm.

As I'd driven past, my body had made the snap decision to stop for some food. It was only as I'd parked up next to the post box outside that I'd realised how hungry I was.

I sipped a black coffee. The remains of my breakfast were on the table in front of me, along with three mobiles – my own, Tori's and the one the killer had left for me. The coffee was hot, bitter and strong. Every time I tasted it, the flavours stuck to the inside of my mouth like a layer of paint.

If nothing else, it gave me a way to occupy myself, because apart from waiting for the killer's phone call, I had no idea what I was going to do with the delightful day ahead. I warmed my hands around the ebbing heat of the mug as the waitress made her way over.

'Finished with your meal?'

'Yes. It was fine, thanks.'

She smiled and started clearing things up. If she thought it was at all strange that I had three mobile phones on the table, she was kind enough not to mention it.

When she was done, I picked up my phone and stared at the blank screen. I'd been completely disconnected from my old life; the me that existed a week ago was like something on the other side of a mirror. The coffee had snapped me out of the dreamlike state I'd been in during the night, and I felt glimpses of the panic below the surface. Sadness welled up. More than anything else in the world, I wanted a flash of . . . I just wanted something normal back.

I turned my mobile on. I'd be leaving here soon, anyway.

The time the phone took to power up and find the network was painful. It looked like it wasn't doing anything. I waited, feeling a ridiculous thrill – an itch in the heart.

Bleep.

Two new messages.

I gave it a couple more seconds, but that appeared to be it.

The first was the one I'd sent from Tori's phone last night. The other was from Sarah. She'd sent it about seven o'clock yesterday evening, when I'd been sitting in my parents' kitchen, my mobile already switched off.

hi u. be good to chat when ur free. A bit worried. things felt really good n am now a bit confused 2 b honest! Are we ok? talk soon babe. take care xSx

Absurdly, I felt tears prick at my eyes, and had to blink rapidly a few times to clear them. *Pull yourself together.*

The phone vibrated.

[Withheld number]

I glanced around. The other customers had all been in here when I arrived, and they were far enough away to not be able to hear. But I still turned away slightly as I accepted the call.

'Hello?'

'Dave Lewis?'

I recognised him. *Fuck.*

'Detective Sam Currie here. We spoke a few days ago.' He sounded inquisitive. Almost friendly. 'Whereabouts are you, Dave?'

There was no point in lying. He'd know soon anyway.

'I'm in a cafe.'

'Which one? We really need to talk to you. Tell us where you are, and we'll come by and pick you up.'

'No,' I said. 'I can't do that.'

'Dave. We have a warrant for your arrest. You're going to make it hard for yourself if you don't tell me where you are. We can come and get you and get all this sorted out. What do you say?'

I didn't say anything; there was nothing *to* say. He was right, but that didn't matter. And I couldn't explain why.

'Okay,' he said, changing tack. 'How about you tell me where *she* is, instead?'

'Who?'

'You know who.' A pause. 'Tori Edmonds. Why don't the two of you come in together? We can end all this now. You don't want to hurt her, do you?'

I said, 'No.'

'We know you were at her house yesterday.'

I didn't say anything.

'Why were you there, Dave? Help me out. I want to understand.'

'I can't explain anything right now.'

'Why not?'

I opened my mouth to say something – I didn't know what – but then immediately closed it again. His previous question suddenly bothered me.

Why had I been at Tori's house?

With everything that had taken place, I'd been too busy analysing events as they happened; I'd not spent enough time thinking about the situation as a whole. It had been nearly a month since I'd last seen Tori. Before that, forgetting Staunton, it had been going on half a year. The killer's note could have sat there for ever if I hadn't called round. So why had I?

'Dave,' Currie said. 'For the last time. Tell me where—'

I cancelled the call.

How could I not have thought of it before? I had to get moving. Instead of having nowhere to go, there was somewhere I should have been hours ago. The first fucking place I should have gone.

I gathered up the phones and put them in my coat pocket, then made my way out to the car.

The post box and cafe swung round in the rear-view, then disappeared behind, as I pulled out and drove away. Still cursing how dumb I'd been, I shifted up a gear and headed for the city.

Chapter Twenty-five

Saturday 3rd September

Sam Currie sipped the coffee and tried to keep his thoughts together.

Not easy. He and Swann had been working through the night, and he'd passed through the point of being exhausted some time during the early hours; now he felt like he was sleep-walking, and could hardly concentrate on anything. Too much was happening, and every time he attempted to grasp any single part of the investigation, the others seemed to slip through his fingers.

The one thought he'd been able to keep track of was:

We had him. And we let him go.

That was the only one that mattered, wasn't it?

He walked across the office of *Anonymous Skeptic* magazine and gazed out of the window, down at the street below. The people there seemed to be forming patterns as they moved past; if he stared long enough, his eyes blurred and they all disintegrated into shapes and colours.

Christ.

'Sir?'

He turned around. One of the officers was gesturing at a stack of hard drives by the wall.

'You want all of these?'

He nodded. 'Everything.'

At the other side of the room, Lewis's work colleague, Rob Harvey, was leaning back in his chair and looking unhappy about the activity going on around him. But then, four policemen were currently removing most of the hardware and documentation from the office, and – as Harvey had repeatedly mentioned – they had a tight deadline on the next issue. Currie explained that was tough fucking luck and he really didn't care all that much. Harvey had simply glared at him. Currie had briefly wondered whether the man might have Asperger's Syndrome.

He'd felt bad afterwards. Following his initial annoyance, Currie had explained how important it was that they found Dave Lewis – for his own sake, as much as anyone else's – and Harvey had relented a little. He'd agreed to spend some time here on the off-chance Lewis attempted to make contact. If he did, Harvey would answer the phone, pretend everything was normal, and try to keep Lewis on the line long enough for the call to be traced.

And at least they'd get a starting location from the conversation he'd just had with Lewis himself.

I can't explain anything right now.

What the hell was that supposed to mean? He knew he should sit down, listen to the recording of that call, and try to analyse Lewis's manner – see if they could work out what was going on in his head and how they might persuade him to come in. But it had been a trying night. The investigation had reached boiling point, and developments were bubbling up faster than he could handle. In fact, it felt like he was being slowly cooked.

A search team had started processing Dave Lewis's flat just after he had been identified on the CCTV footage. They'd taken his laptop away for analysis and were now involved in a painstaking search of the property. So far, nothing.

Other officers were revisiting the older cases, searching for a connection. So far, again, nothing.

But the night had also brought new developments. To start with, there was the text Lewis had sent from Tori Edmonds's phone. Under normal circumstances, he would have been overjoyed at such a development, because as well as catching Lewis on film sending the text, the camera had recorded him going into that house. But there was nothing to be overjoyed about in what they'd found inside.

They'd confirmed Emma Harris's identity, and knew that she'd also been involved with Dave Lewis. Her friends had received the familiar texts. Lewis seemed to be moving faster and faster, hardly caring anymore about the mistakes he made as he went. It implied meltdown. Currie didn't know where the man was heading, but he was sure it wouldn't be good for Tori Edmonds when he got there.

You had him. You fucking had him.

Currie's phone buzzed, jarring him. He put his coffee down on the desk, then stepped out into the corridor to answer it.

'Sam? It's James. How's it going there?'

Swann was at the office, co-ordinating the various scenes.

'In progress.' Currie rubbed his eyes, pinching the bridge of his nose. 'What about with you?'

'A few prints at Emma Harris's house. Obviously, we won't know if they belong to Lewis until we can print the bastard.'

'We know he was there.'

'Yes. And obviously, we're in the same situation with the prints at Cardall's flat.'

Currie nodded. They still weren't sure how Alison Wilcox's phone had made its way beneath the floorboards there. The only working scenario they had was that Lewis had trailed them back there after they called round at his, killed Cardall and planted it there. But they had no idea why.

It sat alongside one of the other questions that had occurred to him over the course of the night. If Lewis had abducted Tori Edmonds, why had he told Charlie Drake he was worried about her? He supposed one answer was obvious – that Lewis liked to taunt people. That was what he'd done during the previous murders, wasn't it?

But still. Something about it didn't *feel* right.

'Any sign of Charlie Drake?'

'Vanished without a trace,' Swann said. 'He's not even in The Wheatfield, drowning his sorrows.'

'Shit.'

'We've had a report from the team at Lewis's parents' house, though.'

'Anything?'

'Nobody there, although it looks like he's been packing stuff up.

Some of the lights were on too. It seems a good bet he spent at least part of last night there.'

They'd only found out earlier that morning, while attempting to trace his family, that Lewis owned the property. Another opportunity they'd missed.

'The team's still on site. They're going through everything, but not found anything obvious so far.'

'That's becoming depressingly familiar.'

'Hang on.' Swann paused, then said: 'Looks like we've got a break on his mobile, though.'

Currie perked up a little at that. 'What?'

'Yeah, he's left it switched on. They're tracking it live now. He's in a car.' He broke off again. Currie couldn't hear what his partner was saying but he was talking to someone in the office. A few seconds later, he came back on the line. 'We've got a team en route. They should pick him up shortly.'

'That's good news.'

But what will they find when they get there?

'There's something else,' Swann said. 'This is strange, though. We know he sent a text from Tori Edmonds's account last night, when we got him on CCTV.'

'Go on.'

'We traced the number. You know where he sent that text? His own phone.'

Currie thought about it. Frowned. Why would he have done that?

'That is strange.'

'Strange and unusual. Hopefully we can ask him why shortly.'

'I'll look forward to it.'

Swann hesitated. 'You okay, Sam? You sound tired.'

'I'm not. Look – let me know when they catch up with Lewis. And they might need armed response. Or a negotiator.'

'I'm on it. What about you?'

'I'm going to finish up here then head back over to you.'

'Okay. See you soon.'

'Take care.'

Currie hung up. *I'm not tired*, he'd just said, when nothing could be further from the truth. But even if he'd had the opportunity to lie down and try to sleep right now, it wouldn't have worked. His mind was too full of Tori Edmonds, and what might be happening to her, or might already have. And he knew what this feeling reminded him of, as well – the window of opportunity when he hadn't gone round to visit his son. In his head, Tori Edmonds had become like Neil. Every obstacle in the way of finding her, alive or dead, reminded him of his own procrastination. Each confusing development was winding him tighter inside.

Back in the office, his coffee was still steaming, so he picked it up and took a mouthful. Caffeine was supposed to wake you up, but he was sure that was just a myth. It never had that effect on him. All it seemed to do was build up a bad taste in his mouth that he could concentrate on.

He carried it across to Rob Harvey. 'Sorry for all this.'

Harvey shrugged, then smiled a little awkwardly.

'It's okay. Obviously, I'm just worried. He's my friend, you know?'

'Yeah. I get that. But you're doing the right thing.'

Of course, after Swann's news about the mobile, they probably didn't need Harvey now.

'Get out of here if you need to,' Currie said.

'I'm okay for now.'

'Right—'

His phone went again. *Fuck.*

'I've got to take this, sorry.'

He went back out into the corridor to answer it, hoping it was going to be news about the pursuit. *Good news.* But he didn't recognise the voice on the other end of the line.

'Sam Currie?'

'Speaking.'

'Sorry to interrupt you. It's Dan Bright here. You left a message for me to phone you?'

'Oh, yeah,' Currie said. The cop who'd handled Frank Carroll's case twelve years ago. His phone call to Richmond seemed like a long time ago, and he didn't need this right now. 'Thanks for calling back.'

'Actually, I did one better. I'm standing in your incident room right now. Detective . . . Swann? He gave me your number.'

'Right.'

There was a brief pause, as though Bright was looking at something – checking his facts for the third or fourth time before he committed himself.

'I'm looking at your white board right now,' he said. 'And I think we really need to talk.'

Chapter Twenty-six
Saturday 3rd September

An hour later I was standing on Park Row in the city centre, facing an innocuous, unmarked door. Most of the looming buildings here were taken up by banks and major offices, but a few blocks had been converted to flats, cashing in on the recent boom in the inner-city property market. This thin, ten-storey building was a prestigious recent development in the heart of the city. Offers on the cheapest flat inside had started around half a million.

Thom Stanley could afford it. Over the past few years he'd amassed a small fortune from his public appearances, the two books he'd written, and a rather nauseating television special. For some reason, however, he didn't like that fact publicised, as though the money he earned was a slightly dirty and unfortunate by-product of a job he was really doing out of the goodness of his heart.

I leaned on the unlabelled buzzer for flat twelve, then waited. Behind me, businesspeople were hurrying past. The day had turned out nice. I looked towards the far end of the street and saw the strip of blue sky visible between high-rises; car windows glinted, as though a camera flash was recording each one as it passed. Where I was standing, the sun couldn't quite make it down to ground level. The two heaving lanes of buses and cars were in shadow, and everything from the road to the suits to the pavement was a monotone grey.

When there'd been no answer after a minute, I repeatedly pressed the buzzer again, in what I hoped would be an annoying pattern.

It was likely Stanley was home. The first proper night of his nationwide tour was tomorrow in Albany, and a subtle enquiry to his publicist had revealed he wasn't travelling until later on this afternoon. She'd stressed that he would be strictly out of contact with the media today while preparing for his trip, and I'd said, *Yes, of course*, as though we hadn't already obtained his address and phone number quite some time ago, from the friend in the phone company that Rob didn't have.

The intercom crackled into life. 'What is it?'

'Mr Stanley? I was wondering if you could spare a few minutes to talk to me.'

'Who is this?'

'My name's Dave Lewis. I publish a magazine called *Anonymous Skeptic*. You've probably heard of us.'

Nothing for a second.

Then: 'How did you get this address?'

'Your agent gave it to me.'

'That's funny.'

'I was hoping to talk to you about your performance at the Western on Thursday night. Get a quote for our article?'

He paused again. 'We've got nothing to say to each other.'

'It would be in your best interests. We've got some pretty damaging footage.'

Another silence. But Stanley was a smart man. I expected the word 'footage' had caught his attention. I could imagine him up there now, in his nice flat, stood next to the intercom with a blank expression on his face.

Working back through the things he'd said and done.

'It won't take long,' I lied.

'All right.'

The intercom cut dead. A second later, the door in front hummed to itself, like a struck tuning fork, and then clicked ajar. I went inside.

The floor in the reception area was polished wood, with locked, glass-fronted mailboxes mounted on the pale-cream walls. Beside them, there was a half-empty rack of neatly folded newspapers. I took a gold and mirrored lift to the fourth floor, emerging onto a corridor where a cleaning woman was running a slow, silent vacuum cleaner along the skirting boards. It was a sad state of affairs, really. Rob could probably have done a more convincing cold reading act than Thom Stanley, and we'd often joked about using our powers for evil. Walking into this place, it didn't seem like such a bad idea.

Stanley's door was closed when I reached it, so I knocked and then stood back a little nervously.

I was taking a chance being here, on a number of levels. Depending on what media coverage there'd been, Stanley might know the police were looking for me. He could be calling them right now.

The other risk was more immediate, and the anxiety was fluttering inside me. I'd started worrying about Tori after he'd used her name in his performance in that very specific way, and I didn't believe that was a coincidence. Since I also didn't buy him being psychic, that meant he knew something. I couldn't see him as a killer – drumming up business, maybe – but he'd come out with her name for a reason, and it certainly wasn't because of any fucking spirits.

Again, I was glad I had the knife.

He opened the door.

I was slightly taken aback by his appearance. His hair was messy, his skin a little blotchy and his eyes ringed and bagged, as though he'd not had much sleep last night. Perhaps it was just the shock of seeing him in a dressing-gown, rather than the smart shirt and jeans. Whatever the explanation, the consummate actor persona had clearly been left on the hanger this morning. I was faced by someone who looked ill, like a regular guy off work with a cold.

'You'd better come in, hadn't you?'

He turned his back on me and walked away. I followed him inside, casually putting my hands in my pockets so that the knife was within easy reach.

But Stanley was just walking off, heading for the kitchen.

The flat was open-plan and uniformly lovely. Up here, at least, the sun could reach, and it shone through a glass front that ran the length of the flat, brightening each piece of furniture: the plush settees, the clean, buzz-cut carpets, the mahogany of the fittings. It was like standing inside an Ikea catalogue. Everything I looked at in

Stanley's flat, you could probably have filmed a commercial for it right there and then.

The kitchen was large, spot-lit and full of stainless steel cooking equipment. He moved around to the opposite side of a central unit, and we faced each other across the counter. Which suited me just fine.

'I hope you don't expect a drink.'

'I'm okay, thanks.'

He folded his arms. 'Well, then. What's this about footage?'

On the way over I'd been thinking, and I'd decided not to leap straight into talking about Tori. I wanted to play it straight to begin with – judge his reactions a little. It was possible I might even bait him into telling me the truth with the promise of cancelling the article we'd planned.

'Do you remember a couple you spoke to on Thursday?' I said. 'Nathan and Nancy Phillips.'

He frowned. 'No.'

'You spoke to them in the first half about their son, Andrew.'

The frown deepened. He began to tap his index finger against his elbow. I guessed his mind was working quickly, trying to put together where this was going before we got there.

'Oh, yes,' he said. 'Andrew.'

'Who we made up.'

The finger stopped tapping. Just for a second.

'We've got your performance on tape,' I said.

He didn't reply.

'We also have footage of you hiding the necklace when you went to their house. Any comment on that?'

Nothing but the frown. He was beginning to unnerve me.

'No? Maybe you're calculating the damage this will do to your career,' I said. 'From where I'm standing, the maths look pretty straightforward.'

He shook his head. 'As though it matters.'

'So you admit you fabricated the whole episode?'

'Of course.' He snorted it. 'We're both professionals. We know how it works, don't we?'

'I know you're a conman.'

'Jesus Christ.' He leaned on the counter and stared down between his hands, gathering himself together. When he looked up at me, his face was full of revulsion. 'Do you think I care what someone like *you* thinks? I'm not like you. What I do doesn't hurt anybody. All I've ever done is provide some comfort.'

'You exploit people.'

'*I* do?' He almost laughed. 'You disgust me. Get out.'

His face was contorted with hate, but I could see deeper emotions there too.

Suddenly, I realised I had no idea what was happening here right now. He hadn't expected the news about Nathan and Nancy, but he was acting as though it was irrelevant.

My hand was still close to the knife. I moved it round to grip the handle. Just in case.

'Mr Stanley— '

'No,' he said. 'No. We both know the real reason you're here. You're very clever, aren't you? But it will make you look just as bad in the end. I'll see to that. Just get out now.'

'What are you talking about?'

'You're scum.'

'I don't—'

'You know exactly what I'm talking about,' he said. '*Her.*'

'Tori?'

Immediately, he looked back down at the table.

I took a step back. 'I really don't know what you're talking about.'

'You tricked me into saying her name. Don't pretend you didn't. And then I saw her on the news last night. A nasty, cheap little trick. But very clever.'

Cogs began turning in my head. Things clicking into place.

'It wasn't me that tricked you,' I said.

'Oh right. Who, then?'

After a few seconds, when I didn't answer, he looked up at me. And I recognised at least one of the emotions hiding behind the anger. It was fear.

I said, 'I think you'd better talk to me, Thom.'

*

It started with a plain white envelope. It had been delivered by hand last Thursday and been waiting for Stanley in his pigeonhole downstairs in reception. There was no stamp and no clue as to the identity of the sender, just his name written on the front.

'What was in it?' I said.

'There was money. A lot of money. Five thousand pounds.'

But that was all there was – no note of explanation – and he told me he was bewildered by the delivery. He had no idea who had sent it or what it was for, and no obvious way of finding out. Since his address wasn't public knowledge, he assumed it must have been something from his agent – some overdue payment he'd forgotten about – but she knew nothing about it when he phoned her.

'And then I got a call.'

It came through on his home number, and the caller wouldn't give his name. The caller told Stanley he was a businessman with a business proposition, nothing more, and that there'd be another five thousand pounds delivered to him if he carried out a small favour on his behalf. No questions asked.

'He told me his daughter was going to be in the audience that night, that she was a big believer in what I did,' Stanley said. He laughed, but without humour. 'The way he said it, it was clear that *he* wasn't. But then, I was listening to him, wasn't I? So I suppose he was justified.'

I didn't comment on that, although the cognitive dissonance in what he'd just said was astonishing.

'What did he want you to do?'

'He said Tori was the name of his wife. His daughter had become estranged over the past year, and his wife was inconsolable. He thought this might be a way of bringing the two of them back together – encouraging his daughter to get back in touch. He said she would believe it, and it was the last thing he could think of. He said he was desperate.'

'I bet that tugged at your fucking heartstrings.'

'Yes. It did.'

'But the money tugged more.'

He ignored me. 'It seemed like such an easy thing to do to help

213

someone. I had a short routine set out for if his daughter put her hand up, but of course, nobody did.'

'And then?'

'The money was supposed to come yesterday.'

'It didn't, though.'

'No. And then I saw her on the news. It's such an unusual name that I noticed it straight away.'

'And you thought we'd tricked you.'

'Yes. Obviously.'

His appearance when I'd arrived – the obvious lack of sleep – made more sense now. Stanley thought he'd been stung into using a name that was already in the public domain. If someone in the audience that night had recognised it and made the connection, it would have looked in very bad taste. Even now, there was a danger someone might recall it. He would either have to explain he'd taken money to fake his performance, or else continue with it and risk the exposé being even worse. When I'd rung the buzzer and mentioned 'footage', he must have thought I was coming to confront him about that.

'You didn't think to contact the police?' I said.

'Why would I do that?'

He looked at me with a mixture of horror and self-pity. The power of denial. Maybe he expected sympathy for the dire situation he'd so innocently found himself in.

'You didn't think who else it could have been?'

'No.'

But he said it too quickly, and I knew the thought had at least crossed his mind. How could it not have done? Even if he couldn't possibly have understood *why* he'd been made to say that name.

The fear wasn't simply of being exposed as a fraud. He was scared because he knew he might have touched the edges of real darkness for the first time in his life.

'Have you still got the envelope the money came in?'

He nodded. 'In here.'

We went back through the living room and he picked it up off the window ledge and held it out to me.

Fingerprints.

'I don't want to touch it. I just want to see the front.'

He showed me. Small, neat, black letters.

The same handwriting.

'What about the phone call?' I said. 'Did you ID it?'

'It was a withheld number.'

'Okay then. What time did the call come through?'

'I don't know. About eleven o'clock, I think.'

After his initial reticence, he now seemed eager to tell me everything. Funny that. As though, by handing me this information, he could hand me responsibility for it too. It was pathetic, but I thought I could use that weakness.

'You know you're in over your head?' I said. 'Don't you?'

He looked miserable. 'I've spent the last twenty-four hours wishing I could take it back. Pretend it never happened.'

'Yeah, but life doesn't work like that, Thom.'

I stared him out. He was silhouetted against the window. It was harsh and bright behind him, but he still looked away first.

I said, 'I'm going to use your phone now.'

Chapter Twenty-seven
Saturday 3rd September

What happened to your hands?

In her more lucid moments, Tori knew she was lying on her left side in an agonisingly small space. It was so compact that her legs were bent double, her knees against her chest, and yet her head and feet were still touching the edges. Everything was numb. Something was tied around her mouth.

Where was she? What—

What happened to your hands?

She didn't know what it meant, but it scared her. What *had* happened to her hands? They seemed to be trapped behind her back, and she wasn't able to separate them; and when she moved her fingers, they brushed something hard covered with rough fabric. Neither of which was good, but it didn't account for the terror she felt when that question drifted into her mind.

Where was she?

She knew, but she couldn't remember. The air in here was musty and horribly warm, though. A series of small holes in front of her were letting in cigarettes of daylight, but she was unable to move her head and get close to them: just enough so that a hint of fresh air wafted past her nose, brushing against it and moving on.

She was going to die in here.

Tori began to cry – and her body immediately came alive, like a burglar alarm responding to a smashed window. Every nerve ending screamed out in pain. Muscles spasmed, either locking and bolting themselves, or else tutting at her with agonising pinches. Her abdomen burned. She heard herself trying to shout, but her tongue was so swollen and dry that it stuck to the inside of her mouth and she gagged instead, then couldn't swallow because her throat was full of sand and shavings of dry metal.

Breathe . . .

Slow and shallow.

Then everything began shaking and juddering. She heard a *whumph* and a roar, then a ticking, rolling noise. Petrol fumes slunk in through the air holes, forming silky, purple ribbons in the darkness. She could see them there. No . . . smell them.

The boot of a car. She remembered now.

There was a shrill whining noise, then she lurched back, and the pain intensified.

She was in a car, and it felt like she'd been here for ever. Countless black hours stretched behind her. What day was it now? Not Thursday anymore. That was the last thing she could remember—

The vehicle rocked heavily, hitting a speed bump, and Tori passed out, remembering exactly that.

The traffic was so bad.

Her small car was inching along the ring road, and the vehicles around it made her feel defensive, even slightly nervous. Everybody was so impatient. Horns kept blaring up ahead, followed by answering calls. Cars angling to push in. People shoving and worming their way through, shouting and waving their fists. Important, important. Now, now, now.

She turned the radio on and pressed the cassette in, hearing it lock into place with a reassuringly chunky click. Some time soon, she'd have to upgrade for a CD player. You couldn't even buy tapes anymore, could you? But she'd always put it off. She liked her old compilation cassettes, despite the deficiencies of the medium, or maybe because of them. The hiss on the tape was as reassuring as the songs; the familiar, faded blue writing on the inlay reminded her of her shared history with the music. She even liked the methodical mending – a pen through the spool when the tape came loose, reeling it back into the case. One day, they'd break and stop working altogether. She could replace the songs themselves, but somehow it wouldn't be the same.

Tori relaxed slightly as *The Heart Asks Pleasure First* drowned out the abrasive world around her. Thinking briefly about Dave, and how she'd lied about not remembering him visiting her in the hospital, without being sure why. She pulled up another car length, the red brake lights ahead harsh in the orange glare of the underpass, remembering her day at work, and thought:

Valerie doesn't trust you anymore.

She wished her hospitalisation three weeks ago had been the result of a broken bone, or a car accident, or at least something physical. Maybe even a good, old-fashioned, debilitating disease. When you damaged your body, people related to that and understood it. Even if they'd never suffered the same thing themselves, it made sense to them. When you went back to work after a broken wrist, you didn't have to put up with your colleagues stealing sideways glances at it all the time, as though it might suddenly flail out of control at any moment and scatter the coffee cups.

In Valerie's averted eyes and hastily mumbled departures, Tori had sensed a feeling of betrayal. It felt like Tori hadn't told her about some criminal past, and now she was in danger of being done as an accomplice. In fact, all of them had excluded her today. They'd even checked her work when they thought she wasn't looking. Damaged goods: she was tainted in their eyes now, not even a proper person anymore. You break your wrist and people can see it heal. You break a less visible part of you and people assume it's always broken and always has been.

It was just so hard sometimes.

Breathe . . .

Slow and shallow.

Later, after drawing the curtains against the world and lighting the house up in warm, bright colours, Tori ate a meagre dinner of beans on toast. When she was done, she scraped the crumbs into the kitchen bin – and then stopped. There had been a noise upstairs.

She stood still, cocking her head slightly.

The floorboards had creaked.

But the sound didn't return, so she finished with the plate and put it down on the counter.

She was about to turn around and put some hot water in the sink when she heard it again. It sounded like it had come from the spare room, which was directly above her, and even though the noise didn't repeat itself, she kept her eye on the hairline fracture in the plaster.

Everything creaked here, of course. The wood was old and the walls were thin. Occasionally, she'd even heard the couple next door making love, and felt a twinge of envy. Not for the sex so much as for the quiet moments afterwards, when she could imagine them cuddling. That would be nice. Someone to hold her.

Creak.

It was nothing. The floorboards flexed and shrank continually as the day went on. But something drew her out of the kitchen anyway, back into the lounge and, from there, to the stairwell by the back door. She listened again, and heard nothing. The landing above was very quiet and still.

She went upstairs.

The door to the spare room was hanging wide open. Tori could see all the way inside, and of course, there was nobody there.

God, she needed to do something with this room, though. She stepped inside and clicked on the light, hit by the sight of bare floorboards, and the wardrobe against the far wall that needed the doors adjusting. A single bare bulb hung down from the ceiling, and beyond that, the purple curtains didn't quite cover the window. She glanced over and saw herself reflected in the sliver of glass visible at the edge, and the reflection of the man standing behind the door.

He kicked it into her – very hard – and the next thing she knew, she'd hit the wardrobe and rebounded onto the floor.

She woke up in panic and fear – and then realised she'd been dreaming. The car rocked beneath her, reminding her where she was. *Oh God.* Still in the boot. What did he want? Where was he taking her? It had got to the point where she almost wanted to die, because at least then this agony would be finished. Her muscles, already on fire, flared up with each jolt of the suspension. It was unbearable, and she was being forced to bear it.

Breathe.

Ignoring the agony running through her body, she tried to move her head closer to the air holes again, straining her cramped neck and stretching as far as she could. All that happened was the petrol smell grew stronger, and her vision became full of the purple stench of it. That was wrong; her senses were confused. She was going to pass out again.

But then the car slowed down, and came to a stop, and she heard the *crick* of the handbrake. They'd pulled up somewhere. She listened carefully, trying to hear if anybody was nearby, and couldn't hear anything. She lashed out anyway: kicked down at the side of the car as hard as she was able.

But her legs didn't even move. She wanted to—

Voices.

Tori pulled herself together and listened. It was definitely people. Or one person, anyway. Half a conversation. It was a moment before she realised it was the man who was driving the car, talking on a mobile phone, but the sound was muffled by the seats behind her. She tried to hear what he was saying, but couldn't quite make it out. The words kept drifting past, the way the fresh air from the drill-holes did – forming blurry impressions of language inside her head that she couldn't decipher.

And then she heard it and thought:

What happened to your hands?

Oh God, she remembered what it meant now.

Tori began to scream silently, not caring about the dry metal and dust in her throat, until the pain bloomed and the darkness took her away again.

Chapter Twenty-eight
Saturday 3rd September

There's one good principle to use when analysing a magic trick. You start with the final effect – the thing you can't explain – and then you move backwards, working through the things you know for sure and looking for clues in the spaces between. That's the way you find the secret. Set the parameters of the trick in stone and then work out how it could be achieved within them.

If a ring appears in a flowerpot by the door then someone must have put it there. If only one person has been near that door, then it must have been him. If there's only one time he could have got hold of that ring, it must have been then. By going over the facts you can see, you work out the ones you can't.

That principle holds true for everything else, as well. If I could figure out how the killer had achieved what he had, I'd learn things about him.

It was obvious he knew a great deal about me, and he hadn't conjured that information out of thin air. So how? He knew three of my ex-girlfriends. It was possible that either Julie or Emma could have told him about Tori, because my relationship with her had come first, and both of them had met her. But they didn't know each other. He couldn't have abducted Julie and learned about Emma, or vice versa. And so he must have learned about them by some other means. The most likely explanation was that I was his starting point, and for some reason he was targeting me. If I'd gone out with different people, he would have taken them instead.

He knew about my ex-girlfriends, going back at least two years. He knew where my parents' house was. And he'd bribed Thom

Stanley to give me a message in the theatre on Thursday night, so he'd known I was going to be there.

From the effect to the secret. As much as I didn't want it to be true, I could think of only one person in the world who could possibly have known all that.

On a Saturday lunchtime, the university campus was almost deserted. I was sitting on a concrete wall a little way up from the main building, watching the entrance. The road swelled out in front, forming an eye with a circular patch of flowers for an iris; the Union building was the brow, while the road thinned out and split to either side, like laughter lines.

A few students meandered past every so often, checking their mobiles, or adjusting their headphones, but there was hardly anyone around. The tarmac and grass were both strewn with fliers: fallout from the various events last night. Sheets of sodden paper had been rain-pressed to the ground, then dried tight to it like stickers. One storey above the main door, an arched window was open. A couple of large speakers were balanced on the sill, entirely silent.

When I'd called Rob from Thom Stanley's flat, I hadn't told him where to meet me. I was hoping he'd still be thinking about what I'd said last night in Carpe Diem. *Do you remember when we met?* If the police were listening, they would have seen someone calling from Thom Stanley's number and heard nothing more than an innocuous conversation about a pre-arranged business meeting over lunch.

If they arrived here now, it meant they'd either followed Rob, or else he'd turned me in. If I was right, there was no way he would do that. And despite the fact I hadn't recognised the man's voice last night, I couldn't think of any other explanation. Because nobody apart from Rob knew all those things about me.

He arrived about five minutes later. I watched him approach down the long road to the left, moving in that familiar stalking shuffle he had, as though he was expecting somebody to laugh at him and intended to be above and beyond it when they did. Nobody else, as far as I could tell.

I hopped down off the wall as he reached the Union.

'Rob.'

He glanced about, confused, then saw me.

I nodded at him. 'Over here.'

As he walked across, I stared at his face and wondered if what I was thinking could possibly be true. I didn't want it to be, and could barely imagine it. He'd been my best friend for nearly ten years: always there for me, watching my back. It seemed absurd to believe he had any connection to this, but the facts stood as they were.

I tried to keep my expression blank.

'Dave,' he said. 'Christ, how are you doing?'

I shook my head.

'Not here.'

'Where, then?'

'Follow me.'

St John's Field was a large area of grassland nestled between the university campus and the main road. It was peaceful and quiet on a weekday. Right now, as far as I could tell, we were the only people in sight.

It was also a remarkably eerie place, even in daylight. In the centre, there was the Garratty Extension, an ominous stone building surrounded by benches and old, judgemental statues. From there, a spider web of paths spread out, some leading to the various passages down to the university, others into small groves of trees that took you out to the streets. The paths themselves were made of arched gravestones. When the oldest part of the city cemetery had been renovated, the stones had been brought here and laid flat, interlaced like teeth.

Fifteen names and dates were chiselled into each, many of them barely legible anymore, and most of them infants and children. In the space of the exposed, windswept journey from one end of the field to the other, you walked across an entire community of forgotten people

'You must have been planning this last night,' Rob said. 'The thing about remembering where we met.'

We were moving slowly, like we had nowhere in particular to go. It was what we'd done before, back when we were students. I narrowed my eyes against the insistent breeze; it was so open here. Instead of looking ahead, I watched the stones beneath my feet.

'Not exactly,' I told him. 'But I was thinking ahead.'

'Do I need to tell you how much trouble you're in?'

'I don't know for sure. So why don't you tell me?'

The animosity slipped into my voice, but Rob didn't seem to notice. He sounded unhappy, though.

'They've been in the office.'

'I guessed that.'

'They were there when you called. They've taken a lot of stuff away with them. I'd say it's pretty serious.'

I nodded. 'They think I killed those girls.'

'And kidnapped Tori, as well. I saw her on the news last night. She's missing.'

'I know. I didn't do it.'

'Yeah, I figured that. So what's going on, Dave?'

'Here.'

I took a piece of paper out of my pocket, unfolded it and passed it over. We kept walking as he read it, but I watched his face. Everything about his expression said that he hadn't seen it before. I wanted to believe that was true, but how could it be?

'Jesus Christ, Dave. What the fuck is this?'

'Exactly what it looks like,' I said. 'The man who abducted Tori left this at her house for me to find. He's playing games with me; I don't know why. He also sent that email you brought to Carpe Diem for me.'

Rob was reading it again. 'Christ.'

He looked shocked, but was it by the contents of the note? If he really had been the man in the car last night, or if he'd known anything about his plans, then surely he would have been more surprised that I still had a copy of it? He'd been very careful about getting it back off me, after all. Just not before I'd had the chance to run it through my father's old fax machine a couple of times.

'He killed Julie,' I said. 'Kidnapped Tori.'

The slut, I thought. *The mad one.*

We were approaching the far edge of the field now. Ahead of us, the path wound its way between two thick bunches of trees. There were more elaborate graves in here, standing by the side of the path like silent, weather-worn sentries. It grew dark as we entered.

Rob gave me the note back.

'Why, though? Why is he doing this to you?'

I stopped. 'I don't know. I was hoping you could tell me.'

'But – what?' He stared at me. Suddenly nervous.

I didn't say anything.

'You're looking at me funny, Dave. What's going on?'

'Like I said, Rob. You tell me.'

'What . . . you think this is something to do with me?' He shook his head. 'Fuck you. After I've just *lied to the police*, and come out here to meet you? What the hell is wrong with you?'

'Thom Stanley,' I said.

'What?'

'I've spoken to him.'

'And what?'

'Someone called him on Thursday morning,' I said. 'A man. He gave him money – bribed him to use Tori's name in his show.'

'Well, it wasn't fucking me.'

'Who was it, then? Who else knew about Julie and Emma, or how I felt about Tori? And that I was going to be there in the theatre that night?'

'I don't know, but it wasn't me.' The indignation seemed to fall away from him. He looked wounded. Betrayed. 'Why would I do that?'

I didn't reply. I was searching his expression for any sign that this was an act, and I couldn't see a single one.

He shook his head: 'We've been best friends for ten fucking years. We've always looked out for each other. Why would I do . . . *this* to you?'

'I don't know.'

It wasn't Rob.

How could I ever have believed it was?

Despair bloomed inside. Suddenly, everything caught up with me, and it was all too much. Without thinking about it, I found myself crouching, then leaning back and sitting down on the ground. I put my face in my hands and couldn't look at him.

'I'm sorry. I'm so sorry. I just couldn't think of any other explanation.'

He didn't say anything.

'I just want all this to go away.'

The silence panned out for a moment. Then I felt his hand on my shoulder. I opened my eyes to see that he'd crouched down beside me. His voice was gentle.

'You have to go to the police.'

'I can't, can I?'

'Because of the note? Jesus Christ. Don't you think he's going to kill her anyway? Whatever you do?'

'I don't know.'

'You've *got* to, Dave.'

'No.' I was adamant, needing him to understand. 'It doesn't matter what he does. It only matters what I do.'

'But—'

'I couldn't handle it if I could have saved her.'

Rob was silent for a moment, studying me, then he sighed and sat back a little. After a few more seconds, he opened his mouth, about to say something.

And then a mobile started ringing.

It was the one the killer had given me last night. The noise seemed to bring me together again – it slapped me out of my self-pity. I looked at Rob and held my finger up to my lips, then got to my feet and picked the phone out of my pocket.

'Yeah?' I said.

'Do you want to save her?' the man said.

'Yes.'

'Then you just have to do what I tell you.'

'Which is?'

I could hear him breathing: a heavy sound, as though he could barely contain the anger he felt towards me. When he spoke next, his voice was full of the same contempt as last night.

'What you're *used to doing*,' he said. 'Nothing. I've made it easy for you, you see? All you have to do is nothing, and she'll live. Say thank you.'

'I don't understand.'

'*Say thank you*,' he shouted.

'Thank you.'

There was a second or two of silence as he contained himself. Then, speaking very deliberately, he said: 'In a few minutes, I'll be visiting Sarah's house. To save Tori, all you have to do is nothing at all.'

A flash of panic. 'Sarah?' I said. 'Wait—'

And then he hung up.

I took off so quickly – without a word – that there was no chance of Rob keeping up with me. My teeth clenched hard enough to make my jaw ache, and stars were gathering in my vision. Everything was going. My brain felt like it was about to crash and shut down.

And when I got to my car, I let it all go. I started pounding my fists against the steering wheel. Over and over. It was like I was pushed out of my body by the force of the emotions. This was what it must feel like to be possessed. The noise I could hear sounded like someone trying to scream through gritted teeth, and even though I knew it was me I had no control over it whatsoever.

Calm down.

Think rationally.

Rationally? What was the fucking use in that?

But I stopped punching the steering wheel, at least – I rested my elbows on it instead, and tried to think of a way through this. I had no idea what I was going to do. If I didn't stop it happening, this man was going after Sarah; if I did – even if I stopped him – he might not tell anyone where Tori was until it was too late.

He might not anyway.

I paused for a moment. If I did nothing, they both might die. If I went to Sarah's, I had a chance of saving her. Maybe I could stop this man. And maybe he would tell the police where Tori was. But whatever the result, I couldn't let Sarah, or anyone, get hurt. Leaving Emma lying there was one thing, but this was something I could actually prevent.

Do it.

I pulled out the phone again. My first instinct was to call her – but then I realised I didn't know her number. It was stored in my mobile, and God only knew where that was by now.

With the police, hopefully.

So call them instead. Then head over there.

But before I could do anything else, a shadow fell over me. I looked up and around, and then suddenly the driver's door was being pulled open. My mind had time to think *police* – before I was dragged out of the car, two huge fists gripping my coat. My arm was rammed into the doorframe and the mobile tumbled out of my hand and fell into the gutter.

For a second, I was face to face with someone, then I was whirled around and a thick arm caught me in a chokehold.

'We've got some talking to do, Dave.'

Shit.

The world tilted and I felt myself being marched back down the street in a headlock so tight I could hardly breathe. I saw the mobile in the road, disappearing away behind me . . . and everything was properly starring over now, not just with anger this time. I stumbled, got dragged—

'Choc, wait—'

'Too late for that.'

I managed to wrench myself out of the grip, and threw a wild punch that landed and did nothing. Whoever had been holding me was the size of a small mountain; my fist glanced off, and then the side of my face exploded like a flashbulb. A second later my thigh muscle exploded too, and I realised my face was against the pavement. How had that happened?

'Much too fucking late.'

And then they were on me properly.

Chapter Twenty-nine
Saturday 3rd September

'Where are we going?' I said.

'Shut up.'

I was sandwiched in the back of a car between the two burliest members of Choc's crew. They were taking me somewhere; I had no idea where. The scenery outside was flashing past: a tree, a building. All I knew was that with each second, any choice or decision I'd been able to make was disappearing behind me. I seemed to have left half my head back there, too. It was only slowly catching up and reattaching itself.

'Need to go back.'

'Shut the fuck up.'

We'd been in the car and driving for a minute before I'd recovered enough to realise what was happening. Even now, I couldn't remember everything; there were the punches and kicks at the road-side – fists and feet coming in at me from all angles – and then I was just . . . here. I'd genuinely thought they were going to kill me right there on the street, but they'd only been softening me up: knocking the argument out of me.

The pain had begun to settle in properly now. Aches in my arms and ribs. My mouth was swollen and bleeding. The side of my face was numb.

'You've got to listen—'

'I'm warning you: shut your fucking mouth now.'

I thought about it for a second, then lashed out, whipping my elbow up and back into the face of the guy to my right.

It hit, but I was obviously a lot slower than the guys he was used to handling, and he managed to deflect the blow a little. The next thing I knew, my face was pressed straight in my knees, and a hand like a steel pincer was holding the back of my neck. Then a huge, heavy fist slammed into my side, so hard I couldn't breathe properly, never mind argue or fight back. The flash of agony burned bright and intense, and then ripples of pain spread out through my body, as though the punch had been a rock dropped into water. I couldn't even move to curl up. Every time I tried, his fingers closed around the back of my neck and pinned me even harder.

Someone must have seen them dragging you into the car.

Whatever happened, they couldn't kill me.

But then, Eddie Berries had probably told himself that.

I deliberately tried not to think of anything, and just listened to the car instead: the whirr and hum of the tyres moving quickly over smooth tarmac; the occasional jolt of the suspension. And then the whine and squeak as the driver turned the windscreen wipers on. It had started to rain again.

'Choc, please—'

'Shut up. You can talk in a minute. And you will.'

We drove a little bit further, and then I felt the car slowing down, and then a bump as we went up some kind of ramp. The car swung around and came to a halt, and then I heard the *crick* of a handbrake.

'Nobody around?'

'Shouldn't be. Can't see anyone.'

'Okay. Get him out.'

The grip on my neck was released and the doors crunched open to either side. Someone grabbed fistfuls of the back of my coat and half-carried, half-threw me out onto the ground. I landed on my hands and knees, rain spitting down around me, and then was hoisted to my feet.

We were parked in a small, deserted area at the top of some kind of recycling centre. Below me, beyond flaky railings, there was a row of enormous skips filled with debris: bin bags and old chairs and broken bits of wood. To one side, several large bottle banks were clustered together. I heard something rattle across the tarmac below, and felt the rain on me, the wind pushing.

Choc was standing directly in front, nodding to himself. The energy I could sense inside him was frightening. It wasn't even like when I'd seen him with Eddie. There was anger then, but it had felt slightly manufactured, whereas now he looked like he hadn't slept or eaten in days. Like the anger was something he'd cultivated and was using to sustain himself. His eyes were hollow and empty.

'Choc—'

He reached into his jacket and produced a gun. I wanted to flinch, but his guys were holding me too tight, and so my heart just flipped inside me. Again and again.

The words came out so quickly they fell over each other: 'I don't know what you're thinking – whatever it is, it's a mistake.'

He ignored me, staring straight into my eyes. 'Tell me what the fuck is going on.'

'I don't know—'

He pointed the gun straight at my face.

Out of instinct, I squinted and tried to turn away. His guys gripped me harder, holding me in place. The barrel gestured to one side, then back again.

'Move him over to the barrier,' Choc said.

I fought against them but had no chance. *You don't fuck with me or my friends*, I remembered. *Don't make me worry.* Was this about Eddie?

'I never told anyone,' I said. 'I'm not fucking stupid. I'd never have—'

'Lean him.'

I felt the railings against the small of my back, as they held me off balance. Choc closed one eye and pointed the gun at my head. His finger moved to the trigger. I screwed my eyes shut.

'One chance only,' he said. 'Where is she?'

Tori.

'I don't know! I swear to fucking God. It's not me.'

I ran out of things to say, and so I stopped and waited, expecting the shot at any second. Would I even have time to feel it, or would everything just stop? It didn't make sense to imagine it, like trying to remember what you were thinking before you were born. I would just stop—

'All right,' Choc said. 'Open your eyes.'

After a second, I did. He was holding the gun loosely down by his side now, looking off into the distance. The guys that were holding me pulled me forward away from the railings, and then let go of me. It took me a second to appreciate the fact I wasn't dead. My heart was beating so fast I thought it might trip up – maybe stop altogether, and I'd just die of fucking fright.

'I believe you,' he said.

I bent down and leaned on my knees.

'Deep breaths.' He patted me on the back.

'She's been kidnapped,' I said. 'By that guy on the news.'

'Yeah, I know.' He rolled his shoulders. 'Come on, man. Stand the fuck up.'

I took another couple of breaths, then risked it.

It seemed more or less okay.

'I got a text from her,' Choc said. 'The police were there and they were interested in that. Too fucking interested. And then later on, she was all over the TV.'

'I know.'

'We've been keeping a watch on your office all day. We followed that fat guy you work with.'

'Rob.'

'Yeah, we followed that guy. The police are at your house and your office, and there's one of them who was keen on you yesterday morning when they showed up. Obvious conclusion is, they think it's you.'

I nodded. 'It isn't, though.'

'Yeah. I believe you now. If I didn't, you'd be in the skip. So the question is, why aren't the police as smart as me right now? Aside from the usual reasons.'

'I got a text from her too, and I went round to check she was okay. I found a note. The guy who's taken her has been making me do things. He said if I told the police, he'd kill Tori. He's been making it look as though it was me.' I thought about Emma again. 'Some of the things he's made me do . . .'

Choc tilted his head and looked at me. Re-evaluating me slightly, perhaps.

'Yeah, but why? And who is this guy?'

'I don't know,' I said. 'But he's got Tori, and he's going round to my girlfriend's house. Probably right now. We've got to call the police.'

Choc turned around and shook his head.

'Not as easy as that.'

'What? You said you believed me—'

'Alex is dead.'

He said it quietly, expecting it to silence me. It did. I tried to piece it together in my head, but I couldn't. The only thing it explained was why Choc was so angry. Beneath it, I could now sense the grief inside him. He was standing with his back to me, utterly motionless.

'What happened?' I said.

'Someone called round on him. Nothing got stolen, but he was beaten up pretty badly, as though someone wanted to get something out of him.'

'What?'

'That, I don't know. But in our line of work it pays to have a few sources. The police have found something at his place. Whatever it is, it connects him to this, somehow. Either the guy wanted it, or the guy left it.'

Why would the killer have attacked Cardo?

It didn't make any sense.

'Maybe he was watching me,' I said. It was the only thing I could think of. 'He might have followed you guys from my flat that evening you called round. But I don't know why.'

Choc nodded once, but not as though he believed it. Then he turned back to me. I expected there to be something in his face, even if it was just hatred or rage, but there was nothing. In fact, he looked completely calm, as though he'd just finished storing away the emotions I'd seen, until he was ready to use them properly.

'You say he's going to your girlfriend's?'

I nodded. 'We need to call the police.'

'No,' he said. 'We're going ourselves.'

He stared at me, as though daring me to disagree. I wanted to. But then I thought about it. If the killer was there when the police arrived, he might be true to his word and not tell them where Tori was. I glanced at the skip behind me. Choc would probably have a bit more success in getting him to talk.

'Come on, then,' I said.

Chapter Thirty

Saturday 3rd September

Back in the incident room, sitting at his desk, Sam Currie was trying hard to soak up the fact that three of his officers had just spent the best part of an hour tracking Dave Lewis's phone to a post office van on its way south of the city. The bastard must have stuck his mobile in an envelope and posted it.

His resources were stretched thin enough as it was. He wearily addressed the officer who had called him.

'You're going to have to stay with the vehicle,' he said. 'And sort through the mail until you find the envelope it's in.'

'Okay, sir. There are about fifteen full bags in the back.'

Jesus wept.

He took his own mobile out and typed Dave Lewis's number into it. Dialled. Waited.

'Is one of the bags ringing, officer?'

'Yes, sir.'

'Then it's in that one.'

He hung up, then closed his eyes and massaged them gently. His head was beginning to pound. An hour ago, despite the remaining questions, everything had been so much simpler. Lewis had seemed a dead lock for the killings, and they'd been closing in on him. Now they had no idea where he was or what was going on, and Currie no longer knew what to think.

'Interfering with the post counts as treason,' Swann offered. 'Doesn't that still carry the death penalty?'

Currie raised his eyebrows but said nothing.

Come on, Sam.

He opened his eyes and picked up his coffee. The three of them – himself, Swann and Dan Bright – were sitting at a round table in the main incident room, slightly apart from the other officers.

Bright was in his fifties, but had the good tan and tight skin of a man determined to wage war on the ageing process by any means necessary, including cosmetic. His grey hair was cut short and spiky, and he seemed trim and fit, dressed in an expensive-looking suit. Currie was annoyed to find himself feeling old in comparison – much as he did whenever Swann hit the gym, or had his hair styled. At least he could console himself that his partner had another ten years to stop caring.

Bright had a case file in front of him, and was clearly waiting patiently for Currie to get his wits together. He still wasn't sure why the man was here, or why they were going to listen to him – more than ever, Currie felt that urge to *be moving* – but at the moment there was nowhere else for them to go. The various scenes were ticking over slowly, and that was all they had.

'Okay, Dan.' He took a sip of coffee and tried to shrug away the tiredness. 'Thanks for coming over.'

'It's my pleasure,' he said. 'If you can call it that. And when I put your phone call together with what I'd seen on the news, it was also my responsibility.'

Currie glanced at the whiteboard. 'I should tell you that I was only wanting some background when I phoned. Carroll's name came up in the course of our investigation, but we don't think he's responsible. In fact, we know he isn't.'

Bright looked at him for a second, and his face reminded Currie of Mary. *You have no idea what my father is capable of.*

'Perhaps it would help if I told you a little more about him?'

Currie relented. 'Okay. Give us some context on him. He was a colleague of yours, is that right? A detective.'

Bright nodded.

'We do things a little differently down there, though. In the city, I guess you cover a lot of different ground, but Richmond is small, and in those days, we more or less handled our own patches. Everything from community support upwards. Frank was Officer in

Charge of the Carnegie estate. It's a pretty scrappy area. A lot of it was dockland and industrial. A few streets of council houses.'

'A bad area,' Currie said.

'A lot of crime on a lot of levels. Frank didn't turn the area around by any means, but the people knew him and liked him. He had a big effect on quality of life without bringing down any majors: came down hard on the gangs when they bothered normal people, left them be when they kept to themselves. So he had a lot of respect. People in the community knew they could go to him if they needed help. And the criminal elements always knew where they stood.'

'I can sense a "but" coming.'

'Frank was dirty as hell.'

Currie nodded to himself, remembering.

That's not in the file. It might say he was a policeman, but it won't say he was a criminal, too. That he ran the whole neighbourhood.

'Taking money to look the other way?'

'No, he was more involved than that. Far happier in the driving seat than waving the car through. Over the years, Carnegie became his own little kingdom.'

'And nobody knew about this?'

'Nobody he didn't know enough about in return. There were rumours, of course.'

'What kind of rumours are we talking about here?'

'People disappearing. Or worse.'

He shot one of them in the kitchen. That man was already dead when I saw him. The other, my father just knocked him down. And then he turned on the stove.

'But I have to stress, they were only rumours.' Bright leaned forward, resting his elbows on the table. He looked a little awkward. 'And as an officer . . . well, you waver slightly, don't you? Frank was very careful about what he did, and in his own way he appeared to be a good cop. So the question is, do you pursue something like that?'

Currie didn't say anything. The answer seemed fairly obvious to him, and he thought it was to Bright as well. But then, hindsight made everything easier.

'Anyway, nobody wanted to talk. They were either too in awe of him, or else too afraid. Frank was a very charismatic man. He exercised a great deal of power and control over everyone he met.'

'Power and control,' Swann said. 'That's interesting.'

Bright glanced at the whiteboard. From his expression, it made far more sense to him than it did to Currie.

'Power was always his real motivation,' he said. 'Frank enjoyed being head of the pack. Liked to feel he was above and beyond the people he dealt with. They were just a "herd" to him. I remember him saying that in the locker room once.'

'But none of this ever stuck?'

'No. When he was arrested, he wouldn't say a word. I'm sure he could have taken a large number of people down with him if he'd wanted, but he chose to keep his mouth shut instead. As a result, it was touch and go whether we'd even make it through with what we had.'

Maybe he's still got friends in the police.

Someone faking it for him.

'And what you had was Mary,' Currie said.

Bright nodded.

'I still remember it. I received a call from an elderly woman outside the Carnegie estate. It was just after midnight. Frank's daughter had knocked on her door. After we brought them to the station, Mary told me she'd been wandering the streets for over an hour in the snow. Her and her little brother. She'd knocked at this lady's house because she'd looked in the window and seen all the books.'

'Books?'

'Yes. She didn't think someone who had shelves full of books would hurt her.'

'So she . . . escaped?'

'Yes. We learned all this later, that her father had been abusing her for years. Both of them, but she always took the brunt of it. One of his favourite pastimes was to tie her to her bed and leave her for the weekend. Sometimes even longer.'

'That's what interested us to begin with,' Swann said.

'No food, no water,' Bright said. 'Hard to imagine, isn't it?'

'Why would he do something like that?'

'Power and control,' Bright repeated. 'To break her spirit and teach her the truth as he saw it. That nobody would come to help her.'

Currie thought: *It was my favourite book when I was a little girl.*

A story where the hero put aside all his other responsibilities and came to do what he knew in his heart was right. If what Bright was telling them was true, he could imagine how much a man like Frank Carroll would have delighted in taking such a pure and idealistic belief and ripping it to pieces. Prove it wrong.

'And nobody did,' he said.

'We didn't realise.'

Again, that almost pained look, as though he knew deep down he hadn't done enough. As though it haunted him.

'Even his neighbours convinced themselves Mary was fine, although they must have suspected. But anyone close enough . . . they either refused to believe it or were too frightened to say anything. And I'm sure that made it all the more enjoyable for him.'

Currie struggled to accept it. Someone like Charlie Drake . . . he could understand the silence there. Even if he despised it, he could see it made sense. Selling smack to other dealers was one thing. But this was a little girl.

'People kept out of his affairs, Sam,' Bright said. 'It isn't that strange.'

'Yes, it is.'

Bright didn't say anything, but his expression changed slightly. Looking at him now, Currie could see the old man behind the façade. And he realised that was precisely what it was. The tan, the hairstyle, the good suit – all just armour to protect the brittle emotions inside.

'So she rescued herself, basically?'

Bright nodded. 'Her brother, too. I can't imagine the courage it must have taken. It was her testimony that got us the conviction.'

Currie leaned back. He could understand now why Mary had been so afraid of her father, so insistent he would want to find her.

Not only had she escaped from the web of power he'd constructed – the control he'd been so obsessed with – she'd taken every scrap of it away from him. It was only natural to assume he'd want revenge for that.

In his head, I'm all that matters.

'And this,' Bright nodded at the whiteboard, 'fits in perfectly with the way Frank would behave. He was always an arch manipulator of people. And he always loved rubbing their faces in their own weaknesses.'

Currie shook his head. They needed to keep a sense of perspective here.

'But we know it's not him. He's tagged. His movements are on record.'

Bright said nothing.

After a moment of silence, Swann stood up. 'I'll check his where-abouts. Bring him in.'

Currie watched his partner head across the office, and remembered the conversation he'd had with Dave Lewis earlier. *I can't explain anything right now.* And Lewis had sent that text to his own phone. Was he trying to tell them something? If so, why not just come out and do it?

He turned back to Bright. 'How would Dave Lewis fit into this, assuming you're right? Let's say Frank Carroll is manipulating him somehow. Why him?'

'There doesn't have to be a reason,' Bright said. 'Their paths will have crossed at some point, and Frank will have decided to play with him. It could be as straightforward as that.'

Over on the other side of the room, Swann was on the phone. One hand on his hip, the fingers tapping impatiently.

'I've met him, though,' Currie said. 'Frank Carroll. He seems very different now from the man you're describing. Beaten down. Broken.'

'You sound like you're trying to convince yourself, Sam.'

Look who's talking. 'No.'

'People always see what they want to see. Or what they expect to. Frank was always very good at helping them do that.'

Swann jogged back across. 'Gone.'

'What?'

'IT got an alarm through half an hour ago. He's cut the device off. They don't know where he is.'

Currie grabbed the phone. A pit had opened beneath him.

'We need to get someone to her house.'

Swann was already putting his coat on.

As the number dialled, Currie remembered *he'd follow you for a* year *if he thought it would help him find me,* and prayed they weren't too late. For Mary Carroll, and for himself.

Chapter Thirty-one
Saturday 3rd September

'Thanks, mate,' Rob said. 'I owe you one.'

He ended the call, then folded the piece of paper up and slipped it into his jacket pocket. Then he took a deep breath and wondered what the fuck to do next.

Nothing – apparently – was the answer.

He sat in his car a little way down the road from Sarah Crowther's house and watched the rain gradually obscuring his view. The car was quiet: he'd turned the engine off to make the phone call, because he'd never been able to concentrate on more than one noise at a time. If he had the television on when he made a call, he had to mute it, or else the words all got jumbled together and he ended up replying to some vapid actress rather than the person on the other end of the line.

Something similar was occurring in his thoughts right now. What he wanted to do was call the police and tell them everything. After what Dave had told him earlier, he was sure it was the right course of action, and he'd nearly dialled them several times already. Each time, he'd stopped himself. Common sense was trounced by instincts he couldn't properly explain, but which he knew were stupid.

I couldn't handle it if I could have saved her.

Rob put the phone down on the passenger seat and turned the key in the ignition. The car grumbled and the radio flared into life mid-shit-song. A second later the wipers squawked across the windscreen, blurring the glass, then swept back the other way and cleared it. Immediately, more drops pattered the window and rolled down like tears.

The truth was that Rob felt more loyalty to Dave than he would ever have been able to articulate or explain. He'd never really had many friends; most people didn't get past the first hurdle with him, even if they made the effort. It was fairly obvious that Sarah didn't particularly like him, but that was okay. Most of Dave's other girlfriends hadn't liked him all that much, either. He could live with it. Because he knew that, without a single exception, he'd always had his best friend's interests at heart, and he always would.

That was why he was here – waiting outside the house of a girl he barely knew – when there were so many better places he could be. Dave had said her name back at the field when the man had phoned him, and then taken off like the devil. Which meant something was wrong here. And Dave didn't want him to call the police, so what else could he do? Sarah was important to his best friend, so whatever she thought of him, Rob intended to look out for her and make sure she was okay.

The windscreen wipers squawked across and back again. One, two.

You should phone the police, he told himself again.

Because having his friend's best interests at heart didn't mean simply doing what he asked him to, did it? He glanced down at the phone.

Another *squawk* of the wipers.

Rob looked back up. Through the clear glass, he saw a man standing at Sarah's door. He turned the handle and went inside.

It happened so quickly, he might never have been there at all.

Rob blinked. His mind had taken a snapshot of the man. He'd been tall and thin, with grey, receding hair, and was wearing a black coat and dark blue tracksuit bottoms. He was in his fifties, at least, probably older. And he'd just walked in as though he owned the place.

Call the police.

He went to pick up the phone, but then hesitated – because, actually, he had no idea who the man was. For all he knew, the man *might* own the place. Or be a friend of Sarah's.

His fingers twitched. What to do?

Check on her, then. He'd wanted to keep his distance and not let her know he was here, simply because it would lead to questions he wouldn't be able to answer. But at heart, he'd come to make sure she was okay. She might not like him being there, but that wasn't the point. The man had looked old – frail, even – but it didn't mean he wasn't a danger to her.

Rob thought about it for a second longer, then turned off the engine and got out of the car, taking his phone with him.

Jesus, it was properly pissing down. He grimaced, then ran awkwardly up the pavement until he reached Sarah's house. The door was shut, and he wasn't quite sure what to do. Knock? It was the polite thing to do, obviously, but if she really was in trouble in there . . .

He knocked twice, hard, then turned the handle, stepped into a kitchen, and shouted as loud as he could.

'Sarah?'

Nothing for a second – and then he heard someone upstairs. The pipes were churning and the air was warm. Maybe she was in the bathroom.

So where was the old man? He'd come in less than a minute ago.

Unless you saw him at a different house, you fucking idiot.

Which was possible. The windscreen wipers could have obscured his view, and he'd not exactly been concentrating.

He crossed the kitchen and went into the hallway, glancing around. There was another small room to the left, and then stairs went up to the first floor. He shouted up them.

'Sarah?'

Immediately: 'Hang on.'

Fucking hell, he was relieved. Of course, now he had to explain himself. He heard a door up there open, and then her feet came pounding down the stairs.

'Dave, I'm so glad . . . oh.'

She stopped halfway down, frowned, then continued the rest of the way a little more cautiously.

'Rob?'

'Yeah.' He ran his hands through his hair. 'Sorry. Listen—'

And then the old man stepped out of the room to his left and punched him in the stomach.

It was fast and hard and created a jumble of sensations. The sight of the man – mouth twisted up in anger, eyes wide – and then the wall of the hallway as his back smacked into it. The pain in his gut was just wrong; it felt like the punch had gone halfway through him and knocked everything loose. His legs were faint, then gone. Rob slid down the wall, his vision sparkling. The man stared at him. One of his eyes was out of place.

It was only when Rob noticed the knife in his hand, covered in blood, that he glanced down at his stomach and understood what had just happened. As he did, the man reached down and wiped Rob's blood onto his shoulder; the knife went *slick, slick* against the leather.

And then he turned and walked towards Sarah. She was just standing on the stairs. Frozen in place.

'Hello, Mary,' the man said. 'Your brother's been busy, hasn't he? I think we should go and see him now.'

Chapter Thirty-two

Saturday 3rd September

'This is her place?'

I was still squashed up in the middle in the back of the car, but at least I hadn't had my face pinned to my knees for this journey. I leaned forward between the seats and peered out through the rain-specked windscreen.

Number thirty-two.

'Yeah.'

My stomach felt tight.

Looking at it, I saw the same building I had that morning – just another anonymous, terraced property in a reasonably bad part of town: two storeys, a muddy front garden. But it was different, somehow. Below the surface, the house now seemed darker and more malevolent than the ones around it. There was no obvious reason it should stand out from its neighbours, but it did. Rain lashed down in front, and every brick of it was pale and grey. Sitting there behind the wet dirt of the garden, it looked like something dead on a riverbank.

There was no way I could know it – I told myself that – but I felt it anyway.

We're too late.

'Park up outside,' Choc told the driver.

I felt the windows impassively staring at me.

'She's not there,' I said.

'We'll see.' Choc threw something over his shoulder. 'Put these on.'

I picked them up. 'Gloves?'

'Yeah – gloves. I don't want you fucking things up for me any more than you already have.'

I put them on. Outside the car, the rain felt heavier than before, flicking and pestering me. To one side, water was flowing out of the guttering on the roof of someone's garage, spattering down and cracking against the concrete. The air was full of the soft hiss of it.

'Come on.'

Choc headed up the front path. I started to follow him, then looked behind me. His guys were staying in the car.

'Just us?' I said.

Choc squinted back at me. The rain on his face looked like tears, and his expression was unsteady. He hadn't quite let the emotions rise up, not yet, but they were close. And it looked like the rage he had inside him could take out half the house.

You don't fuck with me or my friends.

I said, 'Remember he might not have Tori with him.'

'Don't worry about me. Worry about yourself.'

I nodded.

We reached the front door to find it closed and locked. I was about to hammer on it and call out her name, but Choc grabbed my hand without thinking. Then he looked around the street, gauging how much the neighbours might be able to see or hear, or perhaps simply care. Not much, apparently: he took the gun out of his pocket, holding it down by his side.

'We do this in one go,' he said quietly. 'And you follow me in. Quick. Right?'

I nodded.

Before I'd had a chance to think about what he was going to do, he planted a kick at the edge of the front door. I had a snapshot image of him standing there, his whole body tensed, a massive *bang* – and then the next thing I knew he was over the threshold, gun held up in front with one hand, his other holding the door open against the kitchen counter.

One explosion, immediately controlled. Then silence.

He glared back at me: *what the fuck are you waiting for?*

I followed him in, and he used his free hand to close the door behind us. A strip of wood on the lock-side was hanging off, but it still fitted into the frame. If anyone outside had heard the noise, they'd look out of the window a few seconds from now and have no idea where it had come from.

Choc moved across the kitchen, holding the gun with both hands. He looked as professional as a cop, and I was suddenly incredibly glad he was here. As he moved towards the hallway I held back a little, listening. Sarah's house was absolutely silent. Either nobody was here, or else they were keeping very still.

The memory of finding Emma's body flashed into my head.

Please no.

'Dave?' Choc said. 'Here.'

He'd paused in the doorway. I moved over.

Then I saw what was there—

'Oh, Jesus. Rob.'

—and pushed past Choc without a thought, kneeling down beside my friend. His body was sitting propped up against the wall, legs splayed out across the corridor, head tilted away from me and resting on his shoulder. Motionless. There was blood all over him.

We've been best friends for ten fucking years.

'Rob?'

We've always looked out for each other.

'Rob—'

His head moved slightly. My heart leapt.

'Can you hear me?'

He turned to face me – very slowly, but that didn't matter because at least *he wasn't dead*. He was pale, though, and his eyes were closed. I glanced down at his chest. He was breathing, but it was fluttering, uneven.

'What are you doing here?' I said.

'He took her. Sorry.'

Jesus. He'd heard me say her name in St John's Field and come here to make sure she was okay.

'Have they gone?'

Rob tried to speak, but couldn't manage it. He nodded his head slightly.

'Okay, don't. I'm going to get you an ambulance.'

I stood up, looking around the hallway. There. I stepped over Rob and ran down to the table by the back door. There was an old phone balanced on several dusty old phonebooks. I picked up the receiver, heard the tone, and dialled 999.

Choc was standing in the doorway to the kitchen.

'We need to go, man.'

'We're not going anywhere yet.' I glared at him. 'I'd have been here in time if it wasn't for you. Do you know any fucking first aid?'

He glared right back, but shook his head.

I looked down and saw that Rob was trying to get something. His hand was moving awkwardly inside his jacket.

'Help him.' I pointed – then turned away as someone came on the line, interrupting them: 'I need an ambulance now. A man's been stabbed. In the chest, I think. He's still alive, but you need to get here as soon as you can.'

I gave them the address, then hung up and ran my hands through my hair. I wanted to collapse against the door and wait for the ambulance and the police to turn up. Rob was badly hurt, maybe dying. Sarah and Tori were both gone. And I'd missed any chance I had to confront the man who'd done this.

'Dave.'

My legs were about to go. And the most pathetic part was that I wanted them to. Because then someone else would have to deal with this.

'Dave.'

'*What?*'

I turned around and saw that Choc was holding a piece of paper, striped and spotted with blood. Rob's hand was resting on his lap now, his head resting forward. His chest was rising gently, almost imperceptibly.

'Hang on, Rob,' I said. 'They're coming.'

'He was trying to get this from his pocket.'

'What is it?'

Choc unfolded it, then frowned at whatever was written there. Cocked his head to one side curiously.

'Thom Stanley contact,' he said. 'And an address.'

Chapter Thirty-three

Saturday 3rd September

Currie clicked the mouse, taking the cycle of images back to the beginning. He was looking through the pictures the IT technician had provided from the shopping centre CCTV footage. Searching for Frank Carroll. They were working on the assumption that Carroll must have been following Dave Lewis that day – trailing him – so he should have appeared on camera close behind the man. In fact, he had to be there.

But he *wasn't* fucking there.

Currie picked up the photograph of Carroll from the file and studied it intently. Then he put the picture back down and started clicking through the images. Perhaps he'd missed him first time round, despite practically having his nose within the screen. Or maybe Carroll had already been inside the shopping centre somehow.

So you'll have to check earlier as well, won't you?

Currie looked at the phone, willing it to ring. Swann should have been there now. He was trying his best not to think about the hundred things it seemed he could have done differently. What had Bright said? *People always see what they want to see. Or what they expect to.*

But he should have been better than that, and now another girl's life might be in danger. One who had begged him to help her, while the whole time he refused to listen . . .

He began clicking through the images again. Anything was better than just waiting.

Two minutes later, Dan Bright walked back into the office and put a coffee on the desk beside him.

'Anything?'

'No.'

Currie pushed the mouse across the desk in disgust, then leaned back in his chair, folded his hands behind his head and stared at the ceiling.

'Let me have a look,' Bright said.

'You've not even seen him recently, Dan.'

'No, but I'd still recognise him, believe me. And anyway – a fresh pair of eyes might help. I'll run the bare footage and see if anything jumps out.'

It couldn't hurt. Currie moved out of the way, took his coffee and stood in front of the whiteboard. Despite everything that had happened, it was no more comprehensible to him now than it had been yesterday morning. Maybe even less so.

What if it's not him?

Which remained entirely possible.

Currie still couldn't see why Carroll would have targeted Dave Lewis in particular – and whatever Bright said, he was sure there must be a reason. And then there was the question of how Carroll had bypassed his tagging. Most of all, though, he couldn't understand how Alex Cardall fitted into the scenario. If Carroll was the killer, it meant that Alison Wilcox's phone must have changed hands between the two of them at some point. So either Carroll had planted it there, or else Alex Cardall had got hold of it somehow and Carroll had wanted it back.

Neither option made any sense. Nothing did.

His phone started ringing.

Currie dodged back round the desk and picked it up.

'Currie.'

'Sam? James. I'm at Mary Carroll's house now.'

'Anything?'

'Nothing good. We've got a man seriously injured here. The ambulance arrived as we did; someone called from the house. Knife wound to the stomach.'

'Any ID on the casualty?'

'Rob Harvey. That's the guy who worked with Lewis, isn't it?'

'Yeah.' Currie paused. 'He was at the office this morning when I was there.'

'Well, he's here now, and not in a good way. He's unconscious and they're treating him on scene. The front door's been kicked open, but there's no sign of anyone else here now.'

'Mary's gone.'

'Yes. And whoever called from here was male.'

Currie sat down on the edge of the desk and rubbed his temples. What the hell was Rob Harvey doing there? Every time he thought they were making progress in this case, something else happened and he lost whatever grip he'd imagined he had.

'Why would Harvey be at Mary Carroll's house?' he said.

'I don't know, Sam. We're just missing something, that's all. But Dave Lewis, Frank Carroll and Charlie Drake – every cop in the city is keeping an eye out for them right now. We'll find them, and we'll get some answers.'

Currie hoped that was true. But would they get them in time to save Tori Edmonds's life? And Mary Carroll's now, too. *In his head, I'm all that matters.*

'Sam?' Dan Bright called over. 'Come here a second.'

'Stay on the line,' Currie told Swann, then moved round. 'Have you found him?'

'Not exactly.'

Bright tapped the screen. It was frozen at 11:57:46, which was about ten seconds after Lewis had entered the shopping centre. When Currie saw the couple in the centre of the frame, he felt his whole body go still. He'd seen a close-up of the man before, and passed him by quickly, but he hadn't looked at any of the women. If he had done, he would have recognised her immediately.

'That's Mary Carroll.'

'Yes.' Bright nodded slowly. 'It is.'

'Who's the guy beside her?'

Bright zoomed in on the picture. The man had been caught in profile. Average face. Long hair, tied back. He didn't recognise him.

'I *think* that's her brother.' Bright squinted at the screen. 'It certainly looks a lot like him.'

'But he's supposed to be living in Rawnsmouth.' Currie frowned. 'In fact, I spoke to him there just a few days before this. John something.'

Bright nodded. 'Yes. John Edward Carroll. He never changed his name the way Mary did. But then, he always just went by "Eddie".'

Chapter Thirty-four

Saturday 3rd September

Eddie sat in his car, watching his father's vehicle approach in the rear-view mirror. His body felt like a hollow shell around a heart crackling with electricity.

Outside, the rain was lashing down, and the windows were running with it, but he could see enough. Frank Carroll was driving steadily, his wipers streaking slowly back and forth. The car went past him, tyres slashing the water, then carried on up the street. Eddie had deliberately parked a short distance back from his home.

He didn't know what had happened at Mary's house. After seeing his father packing his things into the car and leaving, he'd done as Mary told him, phoned Dave Lewis and given him the ultimatum. The plan was that he would then drive immediately back to Rawnsmouth, leaving Tori Edmonds's body somewhere on route, and putting himself as far from the scene as possible. But he hadn't been able to do that. Instead, he'd come here. The fact that his father was here now as well meant that something had gone wrong.

Eddie forced himself to breathe slowly, calmly.

He watched his father pull in a hundred metres ahead. There were other cars between them, so he couldn't see the vehicle all that well, but he had a decent view of the pavement and his own front door. And a moment later, he saw Frank Carroll standing there, misty in the rain, peering this way and that.

He shivered.

His father was looking for him. So where was Mary? Eddie tightened his grip on the steering wheel and then winced in pain.

He kept forgetting what had happened to his hands. He could close his fingers properly now, but he had to do it slowly and carefully.

His father moved back to the car, vanishing from sight, and then reappeared a moment later, dragging a girl across the pavement. She didn't resist him in any way.

Mary.

He was nine years old, and Mary was twelve, and their father was going away for the weekend and leaving them alone. Before he went, he told Eddie that he would be the man of the house for these two days, and he needed to follow his father's instructions if he didn't want to get in trouble.

Eddie had nodded. He knew what *trouble* meant.

There was food in the fridge, and he could stay up as late as he pleased and do whatever he wanted. There was only one rule he had to follow: he must not, under any circumstances, go into Mary's bedroom.

She was in trouble, and he was to have no contact with her.

Not even if the house is on fire? he asked.

Not even then, his father said. *She has to learn a lesson.*

And he'd done as he was told – to begin with, anyway. But a couple of hours after his father had left, Eddie heard a noise from upstairs – some kind of *thump* – and went to investigate.

He pushed open the door to Mary's bedroom, and then stood there as he saw what their father had done.

Mary was fully dressed, and tied to the bed. *Bound and gagged*, he remembered thinking, because he'd seen that phrase in one of the adventure stories he liked to read. Not soppy like that book Mary read every day, the one his father had taken off her. Maybe that was why she was in trouble, although he didn't understand why.

Her eyes were wide, full of panic.

Please help me.

Eddie's hand went helplessly to his face and he watched her struggle against the bonds – two belts, coiled around her wrists. He wanted to help her, but then he remembered what his father had told him. *Not even if the house is on fire.* And then he pictured a flash of *trouble* in his head, which was something so horrible he couldn't look at it straight.

Eddie started crying, hugging himself, because he didn't know what to do. He was practically jumping on the spot and wanting everything he could see and feel to *go away*. Sobbing. And then he started to get lost inside his own head, the way he did sometimes.

He didn't know how long it went on for, but it must have been a while, because when he stopped he saw that Mary was much calmer now. She was watching him, almost smiling, and trying to speak from behind the gag. He couldn't hear what she was saying, but it sounded very soothing, and he understood what she was trying to tell him.

Everything was okay and he didn't have to worry.

Close the door and go back downstairs.

After a few minutes he did, and he didn't go back into Mary's room that weekend. She didn't thump anymore, and he didn't hear her do anything else either.

He woke up very early on the Monday morning to find his father standing by the side of his bed in the darkness with a very serious look on his face. Eddie flinched away out of instinct, realising that his father *knew* he'd gone into his sister's room, and that he was going to be in trouble.

I didn't. I never did it. I didn't go in.

The fear was as big as a monster inside his mind, and he nearly wet the bed. But his father just looked down at him, an expression of disappointment on his face, and then shook his head.

What have you done, Eddie?

He started to protest, but his father put his finger to his lips – *shhh* – and then knelt down beside the bed, looking so sad . . .

The memory had returned to him every day since, and each time it brought with it the same emotions he'd felt as he crouched there that morning, the covers pulled up to his mouth, feeling the lie his father whispered reverberating in his heart.

You let her die.

Then, above the insistent hiss of the rain, he heard it.

Sirens.

254

The noise was drifting in from the distance, but it hadn't been there before. Were they coming here? What had happened? Eddie knew he was panicking, and he forced himself to keep very still, not wanting his father to notice him. The sirens were still some distance away, but the sound was growing louder.

His father could hear it too and was cocking his head, like an animal sniffing the air. He looked bedraggled in the rain, his shirt soaked through and wrapped tight against his thin, powerful frame. Beside him, Mary was utterly still. She had her hands clasped in front of her, and her eyes were fixed on something on the ground.

Eddie watched his father whisper something to her, and then pull her up the steps towards his front door. Her face remained completely blank. Perhaps she was in shock. He couldn't imagine what would be going through her mind right now, or if there would even be anything at all.

And then they were inside.

His father left the door open just a little.

Eddie started to cry. He wanted to hug himself and jump up and down. He wanted to lose himself and make all this go away.

He'd thought he'd moved on from that shameful little boy. He'd found ways to help him understand he was no worse than anyone else, and he didn't despise himself so much anymore, not after he made others realise they were just as bad. That they let people down as well, and that they were just as weak and selfish as he was.

But sitting there in the car, he realised that he'd never moved on. He was still that same boy, standing in that doorway, too terrified to act. Just as Mary was still the same girl, tied to that bed, sacrificing herself to protect him.

It has to be done, Eddie, she'd told him yesterday. *It's the only way.*

But what if he doesn't come?

She'd just smiled sadly at him, then reached out and touched his face. Even in the silence, he'd understood, and relief had flooded through him. *Everything will be okay, and you don't have to worry.*

Sitting there right now, he hated himself more than he'd ever thought possible. He looked out through the rain spattering his windscreen and saw the accusation in the slightly open door his father had left.

You let her die.

And yet he still drove away.

Chapter Thirty-five

Saturday 3rd September

I held the piece of paper in my hands as we drove, staring down at what Rob had written. I knew what had happened. He'd come through for me. Not only had he gone to Sarah's to protect her, he'd also rung his non-existent friend at the phone company. I'd told him about Thom Stanley receiving a call on the Thursday morning, and he'd found out where it had been made.

Please, I thought. Not praying exactly, but close.

Please let him be all right.

In the meantime, I didn't know what we were going to do when we reached our destination. The call had been placed from a phone box on Campdown Road. I didn't see how that was going to help us, but Choc had led me out of the house without saying a word, full of purpose.

Through the gap between the seats, I could see his leg was jittering up and down. The gun was resting on his knee, moving with it. He was psyching himself up to deal with whatever we found at this address. Anticipating it. He hadn't said anything since we'd set off.

'Almost there,' the driver said. 'Two streets away.'

'Hear that, though?' The guy to my right leaned forwards over the wheel and peered out to one side. 'Sirens, man.'

I listened.

He was right: police cars in the distance.

'Could be going anywhere,' the driver said.

'Charlie?'

But Choc said nothing.

We reached the road thirty seconds later. I saw the phone box up ahead.

'Here?'

'A little further.' Choc pointed. 'Up there on the left.'

I frowned. 'What's going on?'

But nobody answered. The driver took us up, then pulled in. We were outside an old, two-storey house that looked indistinguishable from the ones around it. They were all drab and run-down here, bedraggled in the rain. I wasn't sure why he'd picked—

Then I saw the front door was open. Just a little.

I got out of the car first, followed by Choc. The rain was coming down in misty sheets, and I was soaked by the time I reached the other side of the road. I glanced behind me, and Choc was still standing by the car. He'd started to cross, but something had stopped him. Now, he was staring off into the distance.

The sirens. That was it. I glanced back towards the house and saw a light flick on in an upstairs window.

'Choc?'

He looked back the way we'd come, then up the road again. Hedging his bets. I couldn't believe it – for all his fucking bravado, he was worried about the police. When Sarah and Tori were in there *right now*.

I took a step towards him, but he clambered back into the passenger seat and closed the door in one motion. Rolled the window down and glared out at me.

'The Wheatfield,' he told me. 'Don't forget. And stay safe.'

'What?'

But he tapped on the dashboard, and a second later their car was vanishing away up the street.

I stood there on my own for a moment, full of disbelief. How could he have abandoned her like that, just because the police were going to be here soon? After everything he'd said. And what – he expected me to lie for him as well?

I turned around. Looked again at the light on the first floor.

The sirens were close, but not close enough.

You'll have to do this on your own, then.

The door to the house was up a short flight of steps. I stopped at the bottom. I still had the knife, but it wasn't necessarily going to do me much good – Rob had been stabbed, which meant the man who'd taken Sarah had one too. And what else? Nothing but that piece of paper – which I realised was still in my hand, damp from the rain. I folded it up and put it in my pocket. My hand was shaking.

Sarah and Tori are in there right now.

I didn't hear anything then, because there was nothing to hear, and the sky didn't go any darker than it already was. But something happened. Some switch clicked on inside me, and I understood that if I didn't do this, a part of me would stay standing there for ever. For the rest of my life, I'd look back on this moment and hate the person I saw. You can forgive yourself for the mistakes you make. But only when you don't know they're mistakes at the time.

I went up the steps before I'd had a chance to question myself any more.

When I pushed the door, it scuffed against the tatty carpet in the hallway. The stairs were directly in front of me on the right. There was a soft glow up on the landing. *There.* I kept an eye on it as I reached into my pocket for the knife.

I barely had time to see him as he grabbed me. Just caught a glimpse of a tall man in the doorway to the dark living room beside me, a malformed face full of hate, and then the next thing I knew my head collided with a wall, my shoulder with the floor. He'd just thrown me right across the front room.

Sideways on, I saw him close the door, and for a moment the front room was pitch black. Misdirection, I realised. He'd put the light on upstairs, then waited down here.

Then he flicked on the light switch and I saw him properly.

Oh shit.

The man was thin, but there was an air of strength to him too, like he was made entirely of bone and sinew. He had his back to me, and I watched in disbelief as he hefted an old, empty sideboard up from against the far wall as though it weighed nothing, and moved it across to block the door. The muscles contracted in his back, making it look as hard and armoured as a turtle's shell. His knuckles, where he gripped the wood, bulged out like conkers.

The room seemed to shake slightly as he dropped the sideboard in place.

I rolled over and sat up as best I could, and then saw Sarah. She was sitting on a threadbare settee to my left, her legs tucked up to her chin, slim arms wrapped around them. Rocking gently. Smaller than I'd ever seen her before, with tears streaming silently down her face.

'Sarah,' I said.

No response. Her eyes were staring off to one side, and she seemed completely oblivious to everything that was happening. Her lips were moving, I noticed. She was whispering something to herself, but too quietly for me to hear.

The man laughed. I looked across the room at his face. One side of it was sloped and wrong; the eye there was lower than it should have been, and dead. He looked like an old, grizzled predator that had been in too many fights.

'Sarah?' he said. 'Is that what you're calling yourself these days?'

I didn't understand what he meant – my head was pounding from the collision with the wall. I touched it and my fingers came away red with blood. I clambered awkwardly to my feet, but my legs felt so weak that I had to lean against the wall for support.

Blink.

What was that? My vision was going wrong. My mind's eye felt like it had just clenched shut for a second.

The man looked at me.

'You're not my son,' he said. 'Where is he?'

I just stared back at him.

'Run away, has he?' The man looked down at Sarah. 'As brave as he ever was. I'm looking forward to his face when he comes home and sees what I've done to you.'

I tried to contain the fear. I remembered the power in him when he got hold of me. Despite his age, there was no way I could beat this man in a fight – not even if I could stand up properly, never mind right now. The strength was there in his face, too: in the lack of emotion. His expression was utterly pitiless.

He reached into his jacket and produced a knife.

Pointed the tip at me.

'I've waited twelve years for this. And you're not going to get in my way, whoever you are.'

Whoever you are? That didn't make any sense, either.

I stared back, almost hypnotised, then slowly put my hand in my pocket and pulled out the knife I'd taken from my father's kitchen. His expression changed. He thought I was funny, but there was something else there, too. That I'd dared pull a knife on him. In doing so, I realised I'd just made everything a lot worse for myself. He needed to punish me for even thinking it.

'What are you going to do with that?'

Blink.

'What do you think, Mary? I know what I'm going to do with it. I'm going to cut his face off with it. And you're going to watch it happen, you little bitch.'

Sarah didn't respond. She was staring into space, her lips still moving quickly and repetitively.

'Maybe.' I took a step forward, hoping that my legs would hold. 'Maybe not. I'm pretty good with a knife, you know.'

Come on, man. Get yourself together.

'Is that right?'

He looked at me a second longer, then reached around and put his knife down on the sideboard behind him.

'I've had three fights against men with knives. Real fights, I mean. I used to train it all the time. Got cut once. I know a good ten ways to take a knife off someone.'

I forced myself to take another step forwards. It was hard. Every instinct in my body was telling me to curl up in the corner and wait with my eyes closed.

'And these were guys who'd used knives before. You don't look like that kind of guy.'

'Might as well take my chances,' I said. 'You don't—'

Blink.

I shook my head.

'You don't look too fucking great from where I'm standing, either.'

The smile vanished from his face then. He glanced at Sarah.

'This won't take long.'

I walked towards him, but my legs half went, so he came across to meet me. Everything blurred slightly. I swung the knife up at him—

But he was too fast.

He caught my wrist easily, almost delicately, between his hands, slid his thumbs up the back and leaned over, *pressing* my hand back towards my bicep. My wrist cracked, and something flared in my head that wasn't even pain yet, just damage centres catching fire. I cried out anyway, my knees buckling, and I lost my grip – the folded piece of paper Rob had given me fell from my fingers.

While I could still think, I rammed the real knife as hard as I could into the side of his neck with my other hand. Then stepped away, and fell over.

Blink.

I looked up and saw the man's eyes were wide, his face frozen. Slowly, he put his hand up to where the knife was still sticking out of him, then tried to say something, but it didn't work. It came out as a gargle, and I saw the flash of panic on his face as he realised he couldn't breathe. His eyes clenched shut for a second in pain, then opened and stared at me; his hand reached out, then retracted back. And then again. He fell to his knees. His body seemed to have gone stop-motion.

I looked at him, feeling nothing but horror.

I'd done that. Maybe I would be able to justify it to myself later, but for now, there was only the viscera of what was happening in front of me.

Blink.

The man was resting forwards on his elbows, rattling out blood onto the carpet, and then he fell over to one side, the knife pointing up towards the ceiling. His foot began tapping on the floor, while the blood started to creep across the carpet like ink on tissue paper—

Blink.

My vision kept going for longer and longer. It was as though the room was strobe-lit and time was slowing down. I realised the man had stopped moving, and the thumping wasn't just inside me anymore. Someone was hammering on the door.

'Frank Carroll? Police. Open this—'

Blink.

I glanced up and saw that Sarah was standing now, staring down at the man's body. Her arms were hanging straight down by her side, and her body was very still. She was still talking to herself, ever so quietly. I could only hear the faintest trace of whatever she was saying.

'Carroll?'

'Dead,' I guessed.

'Open the door.'

'I can't.'

Blink.

I shook my head just as something splintered loudly. The door hit the sideboard and someone cursed. Sarah was crouching – blink – and then standing, the knife in her hand. She'd pulled it from his neck.

'Lewis? Is Mary Carroll in there with you?'

'No,' I said.

'Where is she then?'

'What?'

Blink.

Sarah's eyes were closed now, and the intensity of sadness in her face was devastating. I'd never seen anything like it in my life.

Another crash. Behind her, I saw the door judder, the sideboard rocking forward. The man's knife fell off and landed on the floor.

She lifted up the blade she was holding

Blink.

'Sarah?'

But I realised she couldn't even hear me. It was as though she'd retreated entirely into her head. Wherever her mind had gone, I didn't exist there. Nothing in the room did – perhaps nothing at all. And finally, I caught the words she was repeating. The tone of her voice sounded as though every hope she'd ever clung to had been taken from her.

'You did not come back to save me,' she was saying.

And then she plunged the knife into her chest.

Blink.

Chapter Thirty-six

Saturday 3rd September

A dirt path appeared on the right-hand side.

Eddie turned the wheel and took the car off road. The path was slimy and brown from the downpour, little more than wet clay. He had no idea where he was, only that it was some distance away from where anyone could find him in time. That was all he wanted now.

The suspension rocked as the wheels handled the undulations of the track. He followed it up for about twenty metres before it widened out, and then the car emerged into a parking area on the ridge of a large embankment.

There were wooden picnic tables, sodden in the rain, and as he parked up close to the edge he saw that the land stretched away below. The airport was down there. He guessed that people came here to watch planes during the day, and maybe to fuck each other on an evening. But the weather seemed to have put both groups off: there were no other cars here.

Eddie turned off the engine and got out, gripping the door as he almost lost his footing on the slippery ground. When he was steady, he walked round to the boot, opened it, and looked down at Tori Edmonds lying there *bound and gagged* with the rain pattering in on her.

There was a thicket of woods over to the right.

That would do.

When he'd arrived at Mary's house on the evening of Sunday 7th August, Eddie had been almost delirious from the pain. He'd had to wait until nightfall before he dared to leave the woods, and as he'd sat in the undergrowth, breathing heavily, he could already feel the infection setting into his palms. It itched there. He could barely move his fingers, and every time he tried a bolt of agony went straight up his arm and into his neck.

Think you're a musician, don't you?

Drake had put one bullet through each of his hands.

You don't fuck with me or my friends.

Sitting amongst the trees, the stars appearing overhead, Eddie had howled laughter up into the night. Despite the agony, or perhaps because of it, he felt primeval. Powerful. They had no idea what they'd done – especially Dave Lewis. Eddie couldn't forget the way Lewis had looked at him before he punched him, as though he was so fucking special, some kind of gallant protector come to save the day. Nobody looked at him like that. Not anymore.

There had been a time when they had – when those expressions were all he could see – and it became worse after his father was released from prison. From that point on, he'd felt eyes on him everywhere he went. People looking at him, accusing him, their faces full of the knowledge of how much better than him they were. That had changed after he met Vicky Klein. He'd been playing guitar at an open-mic night, and she'd come in on her own: a small, sad girl at the back of the room. She'd been grateful when he talked to her later – and why wouldn't she be? He'd learned all about her busy friends. He'd pictured them in his head, and even without knowing them, he'd felt the weight of their expressions, even though they were just as bad as he was. In time, those people had learned exactly how superior they really were. Just as Sharon Goodall's friends had, and then Alison Wilcox's.

Sitting in the wood, he'd wrapped his hands in his shirt and thought: *I know all about you.* He'd met two of Lewis's girlfriends while he'd been with Tori and he remembered their names. And Tori as well, of course.

You'll be sorry.

I'll show you exactly how much better than me you are.

Later on, he was still laughing as he pressed his hands onto Mary's walls and doors, painting blood-red birds on whatever surface he could find, while she cried and tore at her hair, and didn't seem able to breathe properly.

The days after that had been a blur. Eddie knew he'd slept in a bed in her house, and that she gave him pills of some kind, and dabbed at his forehead. He had memories of her repeatedly bandaging his hands, and smearing cream on them that made the wounds sting. He wanted to know if he could see through them, but she wouldn't let him look. He'd laughed a lot more, and it was only when he thought of Dave Lewis that he stopped.

In some of the earlier memories, Mary wasn't crying anymore. In the later ones, she was. That didn't make any sense at first, but eventually he discovered it was because she'd gone to collect his car, intending to hide it. That was when she found the cardboard box with his collection in it, and understood what he'd done.

But his sister had continued to tend to him and look after him, weeping softly to herself, as though he was an injury of her own that she needed to make better.

'Get out of there,' Eddie said.

She couldn't, of course, and it delighted him, even as he felt repulsed by himself.

'I said, *get out.*'

She screamed through the gag as he grabbed her by the hair – ignoring the pain in his hands – but that didn't work, and he took hold of her blouse instead, folding her over the back of the car, so that her hair trailed down to the ground. Then he lifted her legs, and she tumbled forward into the mud, landing on her shoulder, her legs smacking wetly down a moment later. She lay there crying.

The rain fell down around them, and he thought:

You let her die.

He didn't know if it was directed at himself or Dave Lewis, or everyone in the world. It didn't matter anymore. Every single thought stoked the fire of hatred he felt inside.

Eddie crouched down over her, and prodded at her shoulder to roll her over on her back. It was difficult, with her hands tied behind her, but he managed it. Then he sat on her stomach, his legs to either side, knees pressing in against her shoulders. She was so small. Her eyes were shut tight, and she flinched as he delicately brushed strands of hair from her face.

He would tie her to a tree. Somewhere she'd never be found.

'He let you die,' Eddie told her, and he didn't know or care who that was directed at either.

All the same. Everyone the same.

And then he heard something.

Eddie glanced back towards the dirt path.

Four men were walking towards him through the rain. All of them were black, and three of them were very big indeed. The fourth – Charlie Drake – was a little in front of them, and he was holding a gun. As they approached, Drake raised it and pointed it at Eddie.

'Thought I recognised your car back at the house.'

Eddie stood up quickly and backed away towards the embankment – but his foot slid, and this time he fell, landing on his side, hand splayed out in the cold mud. Pain thudded up.

'Good job I did, isn't it?' Drake said.

He checked something on the gun and then looked back up.

'Not for you, though.'

Instead of walking right the way up to him, Drake stopped a little way short, by Tori, and crouched down beside her. He put his hand gently on her shoulder, inclined his head, and whispered something that Eddie couldn't hear. Then he stood up again, shooting a glance at one of his gang. The three men bent to help her while Drake continued over to where Eddie was lying.

'Stand up.'

He did.

The man moved to one side of him, and Eddie could see that Tori was on her feet now, leaning against one of the men while another cut the rope from her with a knife.

A second later, he felt the gun pressed against his temple.

He was going to die, he realised. Right here and now, standing in this dirty place in the rain. The most surprising thing was that a part of him felt relief at that. It wanted to say 'thank you'.

Drake said, 'Don't watch this, sweetheart.'

And before he could think anything else, Eddie was gone.

Chapter Thirty-seven
Sunday 4th September

It was just after ten o'clock in the morning, and Detectives Sam Currie and Dan Bright were standing on an embankment at the edge of Brimham Woods. Neither of them spoke. The rain hadn't stopped all night, and the body of John Edward Carroll was lying in front of them; it had been here, exposed to the elements, since the previous afternoon. Yellow police tape was threaded across the path behind them, preserving what was left of the scene. The SOCOs had erected a small white tent over the remains, but they could still see the body.

Eddie looked like a dead fish in the mud. His skin was bright white, and his eyes were open wide and staring at nothing, pushed absurdly large by the gun blast that had occurred behind them. His bottom lip protruded. But most of the blood had washed away, and the bits of skull and brain dotted around had been washed bland as litter.

Swann walked up and stood beside him.

'Gum?' Swann offered.

'Thanks.'

'Dan?'

Bright took a piece as well, but didn't say anything. He seemed hypnotised by the body.

'I just got off the phone to Rawnsmouth,' Swann said. 'They've picked up a guy called Jeremy Sumpter. He's the one living in John Carroll's flat down there.'

'What did he have to say for himself?'

'Nothing – for all of about five minutes. Then he started to sweat,

268

if you know what I mean. Said he was a mate of Eddie's, and that he'd been crashing there for as long as he could remember. Eddie started coming up here two years ago. Spent more and more time away.'

'Two years,' Currie said. 'Just after his father got released.'

'Maybe he wanted to be close to his sister. Apparently, she'd go down there sometimes as well. Last visit was a couple of weeks back, but she was on her own that time. Thursday, eleventh of August.'

'Very exact.'

'A red-letter day for Jeremy. She gave him some money.'

Currie thought about it.

'Let me guess. To pretend to be her brother if anyone called?'

Swann nodded. 'Which he did, incidentally, when you spoke to him on the phone. Jeremy is suitably ashamed of himself.'

'Jeremy will be.'

That was the week that Eddie was reported missing. He chewed the gum and nodded to himself, fitting it together in his head.

'My guess is that Choc, Cardall and Lewis went to see Eddie after they'd been to Staunton that Sunday, and they gave him a beating. Shot him through the hands. That must have been when Cardall got hold of Alison Wilcox's mobile. They probably went through his pockets.'

'And afterwards, Eddie went to his sister's house.'

'The only place he felt safe. Because she'd always looked after him. I saw blood on the door handle when I was there. I thought it was from her, but maybe it was his.'

'We can check, if it's still there.'

Currie nodded. But it was just one more mistake he'd made.

'Four days later,' he said, 'she'd found out what he'd done and was down in Rawnsmouth trying to cover up for him.'

'She'd already reported her father by then. Why didn't she turn Eddie in? He was doing to other girls what had been done to her. She should have hated him.'

Bright said, 'Because he was her brother.'

He was still staring at the body. The expression on his face was sad, as though he was seeing the same little boy that Mary must have. Perhaps he was even feeling a similar sense of responsibility. For the things that were done and the things that weren't.

'Looking after Eddie was all that mattered to her,' Bright said. 'I think it was the only reason she ever found the courage to escape in the first place. She was always desperate to protect him from the effects of her father's violence. And that's all she was doing here.'

Currie thought about that and nodded slowly.

'We know from Dave Lewis's computer that she contacted him through the dating site on Tuesday, twenty-third of August. That's the day I went to see her.'

He remembered how desperate Mary had been to convince him her father was the man behind the murders. When he'd told her Frank Carroll was electronically tagged she became frantic, insistent, as though everything was suddenly falling down around her. At the time, he'd thought it was because she was scared of her father. Now, he understood it for what it was.

'She realised her father wasn't going to be arrested,' he said. 'So it would only be a matter of time before we took a closer look at her brother.'

'Yeah, but why Dave Lewis?'

Currie shrugged.

'Maybe she saw Eddie was disintegrating. He was going to take revenge on Dave Lewis for what happened that day. So to make us think it was Frank, she needed to connect herself to him before that happened. Make it look like the killer could be after her, not Lewis.' What had she told him? *You won't believe it until he comes for me.* 'She made herself the target: got involved with Lewis, while her brother went on to attack Julie Sadler, Emma Harris and Tori Edmonds. Eddie must have known what she was doing, but maybe not until it was all underway.'

'Have you heard the tape?' Swann said.

'Oh yes.'

They'd located Dave Lewis's car after they picked him up from the house on Campdown Road. Inside, they'd found a cardboard box full of the dead girls' clothes, and a digital recorder. Lewis had taped everything that happened, from the first phone call Eddie made to him, to the conversation he'd had with Rob Harvey at the university. Taken alongside the phone and photocopies he'd sent through the post yesterday, it was obvious Lewis had been thinking ahead. He had conclusive proof he was being manipulated.

'So Eddie tried to force Lewis round to Mary's house,' he said. 'While she goaded Frank into coming for her.'

'I can't imagine that,' Bright said. 'She was terrified of him.'

'Maybe she was hoping Lewis would save her.' He thought of Mary's small body, and the way it had looked when they found it in the living room of her brother's squat. He said, 'Counting on it, even.'

'Yet she did it anyway.'

They stood quietly for a moment. The rain tapped peacefully on the canvas over Eddie's body.

Currie didn't know how to feel. A part of him remembered standing in the bedrooms of the murdered girls, looking down at their bodies and feeling such sorrow that nobody had come to save them, and he couldn't help but hate the people responsible: Eddie Berries – and Mary by association. But he could also recall her face that day, when she'd begged him to help her. Nobody had ever come to save them, either, including him. That thought was resting in his mind, and he refused to examine it too closely. Not right now. But he felt it there anyway, like a sliver of something radioactive, gently pulsing.

'There's one flaw in this theory,' Swann said.

'Which is?'

'No evidence Lewis ever went near him that day.'

That was true. 'Where is he now?'

'He just got discharged from the hospital. He's back at the department. Minor concussion, but he'll live.'

Currie blurred his eyes slightly and watched the body in front of him dissolve into shapes, until he wasn't even sure what he was seeing anymore. He thought to himself: *priorities*. It was what he'd told himself when Eddie had been abducted – that they had to concentrate on Alison Wilcox's murder instead. So that was something else he could blame himself for, wasn't it? If they hadn't had other priorities, all this might never have happened.

The pulsing feeling intensified.

271

'Let's head back then,' he said.

Swann breathed out heavily, and Currie recognised the weariness in it. 'I hope you remember what the gum means.'

At just after twelve, Currie was sitting across from Dave Lewis, this time in Interview Room One. It was a large room on the first floor, and it had a window.

He glanced at the recorder, the small red light indicating the current silence was being stored away. No answers to his questions, one after another. So far, in fact, Lewis had said nothing other than to confirm his name. His only movement was to pick at his nails, an act that he appeared to be concentrating on now, ignoring Currie completely.

'You're going to have to talk to me eventually, Dave,' he said.

Lewis stopped picking.

'You haven't even told me how she is yet.'

Hallelujah, Currie thought. The man still wasn't looking at him, but at least he'd found a voice.

'You mean Tori Edmonds? She's okay. She's in hospital.'

'What happened?'

Currie opened his mouth to say that *he'd* be the one asking questions here, but stopped as he remembered what Lewis had said on the digital recording.

It doesn't matter what he does. It only matters what I do.

I couldn't handle it if I could have saved her.

He saw the bandages and bruises, and knew that all those had occurred simply because Lewis had tried to save Tori Edmonds. He'd been dropped into a form of hell, and he'd kept going. Whatever else he might have done, which Currie was determined to find out, Lewis at least had a right to know.

'Tori was found wandering along a country road yesterday afternoon,' he said. 'She was in pretty bad shape.'

Which was an understatement. If Edmonds hadn't been in hospital right now, it was likely that she'd need to be sectioned. As a result, she'd yet to be formally interviewed, and it hadn't been until this morning that she'd managed to give them even a disjointed account of what had happened. John Edward Carroll –

known to her as Eddie Berries – had abducted her from her house, and she'd been kept in the boot of his car. She didn't know why, or for how long, only that eventually he'd driven her up to Brimham Woods. Once there, he'd untied her and then shot himself in front of her.

There were two obvious problems with that story. The first was that she'd barely been able to walk when she was found; her legs were cramped from being confined in such a small space for so long. So how had she been able to get as far from the scene as she had? The second was more of an intuitive one. Depending on how you looked at it, her inability to remember the scene until the rain had slurred the ground and made it unreadable was either a complete coincidence or incredibly convenient.

'But she's alive,' Lewis said.

'Yes.'

It hadn't been a question, though – more like an affirmation. Lewis, gazing back at the effort and horror of the last two days, trying to convince himself it hadn't been for nothing.

All this, but at least she's alive.

'I didn't know whether he'd let her go, or not.'

'Well . . . we'll come to that.'

He rubbed his face. 'Is Rob okay?'

'He's in intensive care, but he's stable. Your phone call probably saved his life.' Currie slid a photograph across the table. They'd taken a still from the CCTV footage. 'Do you know these two people?'

Lewis touched it delicately, moving it a little closer.

'Eddie Berries,' he said. 'And Sarah Crowther.'

'John Edward Carroll,' Currie told him. 'Sarah was his sister. Her real name was Mary Carroll.'

Lewis nodded to himself. 'You can be anyone on the internet.'

'What?'

'Nothing. Why did she do that? Stab herself like that?'

Currie thought about the book – about Anastacia, waiting there with a knife poised above her heart. Unable to continue on her own; entirely reliant on the man coming to save her. It was the one thing Mary had loved as a child, and her father had done his best to torture the hope it contained out of her. Why had Mary stabbed herself? They'd probably never know for certain, but Currie guessed it was because, to her, Frank Carroll had been proved right: nobody had come – or at least not until it was too late. She'd been left to confront Carroll on her own, and something inside her had snapped and died when he touched her. From that moment on, there had been nothing remaining.

But Currie didn't say any of that. The truth was that 'why' didn't even feel like a question anymore. It was more a weight to carry.

'From what we've learned,' he said, 'we think Eddie is the man responsible for murdering the girls. His sister found out and tried to stop him from being caught, and that's the reason she got involved with you. He'd already killed three girls before he turned his attention to you. So the only real question we have left is: why did Eddie want to target you?'

Currie left a beat.

'But I think we know the answer to that already, don't we?'

Lewis looked up at him.

'I don't know.'

'You're a bad actor, Dave.'

'I've met Eddie a couple of times. Never liked him much. But I can't imagine why he would want to do . . . this.'

'You're lying. You met up with Charlie Drake and Alex Cardall at Staunton Hospital, and you went with them. Eddie hated you because of what you did to him that day. He wanted to teach you a lesson.'

'No.' He shook his head, but he didn't look sure.

'Why not accept some responsibility, Dave?'

Lewis said nothing, just looked down at the table. But he was conflicted – wrestling with it. Going over what he'd done and realising the implications. Currie could almost see the understanding, the pieces clicking into place. What had happened to Lewis was all his own fault. Everything unfolded from what he'd done. There was no escape from that. And a second later, Currie watched the man collapse inside.

Press him.

'You can't take back what you did,' he said, as gently as he could manage. 'But you can be better than that now, can't you? Otherwise you'll have to live with it inside you for the rest of your life. You don't want to do that, do you?'

'I met them at Staunton that day,' he said.

'That's good, Dave. And?'

'And I went off with them after we'd seen Tori.'

He didn't say anything else for a moment, but he took a deep breath and seemed to be building up the courage to admit what he'd done.

'It's okay, Dave. Just say it. Tell me what you did. You can't lie to yourself about this.'

For a second, there was no reply. Then Lewis lifted his head and looked at him.

But instead of feeling triumph, something inside Currie fell away. Because he recognised the expression. It was the same as when Lewis had looked around Interview Room Five and realised what was happening. Something else – some other understanding – had just clicked into place. The guilt had been pressing down on him, and he'd been on the verge of admitting what he'd done. And then Currie's words had thrown him a lifeline he'd never have found on his own. A way out.

You can't lie to yourself about this.

Lewis spoke slowly and carefully, as though surprised by the words.

'We went to The Wheatfield,' he said.

Epilogue

A month later, I was standing in the front room of my parents' house, looking round at what I'd achieved. It was almost completely empty now. Bare floorboards stretched from wall to wall, and all the old furniture had been taken away in a skip the day before. Every other room in the house looked more or less the same.

I walked through it, checking I hadn't missed anything. I had to turn sideways to get past the boxes lined up waiting in the hallway.

It was ridiculous to think I'd got over what had happened at the beginning of September, but I felt a lot calmer now than I had for a long time.

There were certain images that stuck with me, of course, and I often found myself suddenly awake in the middle of the night, sitting up with my heart pounding, only to see a face receding into the darkness. When it happened, I could never read the expression before it disappeared. Was there an accusation there, or was it guilt? And whose face was it? I could never tell.

But most of the time when I was awake, I kept it hidden away, and I noticed it in the absences more than anything. The way I didn't talk all that much anymore. Or the fact I seemed to move more slowly than I used to, as though I'd been badly bruised somewhere and needed to be careful until I worked out what hurt and what didn't.

Working on this place had helped. The threat of the various charges hanging over me had held me in suspense for a while, but when it became clear that none would be brought, I'd flung myself back here in a bid to keep myself occupied. It proved therapeutic.

The hard work kept me busy, and it felt right emotionally, too. I'd read that one of the main reasons someone self-harms is to give the mental pain they feel a physical dimension – an actual *cut* can be tangibly felt, then cared for and healed in a way that how you feel inside often can't. Clearing my parents' old house reminded me a little of that.

In the kitchen, I'd ripped out the old appliances and taken them to the tip, and the new units had been installed last week. It wasn't all finished. A man with a hang-dog face had pulled the wiring out of the walls like veins from an arm; I still needed to paint over the plaster there. The plumber was coming round tomorrow morning, and the new bathroom was scheduled to be delivered at the week-end. And there were still new carpets to fit.

But my parents' old things were all gone.

I stopped in the doorway to my brother's room. It was just an empty cube now, and had none of the power it used to hold. You learn strange things when you strip a house to the bone, especially one that's so familiar to you. Owen's bedroom had continued to remind me of what had happened that day until the very last moment, when I took the curtains down – and then, with one single removal, it was just a room again. One that could have belonged to someone else entirely, and soon would.

Like I said, I hadn't thought too closely about anything that had happened, but that didn't mean things hadn't occurred to me as I worked. I'd thought a great deal about the mistakes I'd made, and the only real conclusion I'd come to was the same thought I'd had outside Eddie's house on Campdown Road. You can forgive your-self for mistakes. The only ones you're responsible for are the ones you knew were wrong before you made them.

I closed the door to the house's second bedroom.

As I walked back along the hallway, I ran my finger down the edges of the cardboard boxes piled up against the wall. They could stay there for now. I'd wait until the house was properly finished before I started to unpack.

Ten minutes later I was driving slowly along the ring road.

The weather was good: a pale blue sky hanging in front of me, with a few still clouds resting at the horizon. Outside, the air was so cold that my breath formed mist in the air, but the sun managed to leap through that somehow, and it was warm when the breeze died down. Everything looked crystal sharp, from the edges of the buildings to the glint of windows, and the local weather forecast suggested some areas might see snow later.

The traffic was bad, though. I stuck some Nine Inch Nails on the CD player and crawled slowly along until I passed the motorway junction.

I pulled up outside Tori's house a little after three o'clock, parked the car and got out. She'd been discharged from Staunton a week ago, but I hadn't been round to see her yet. For some reason, I was nervous about it. The most obvious thing we had to talk about was something I suspected neither of us wanted to – but then, it would be strange not to mention it at all. It wasn't like we could just sip tea and pretend it had never happened.

She answered the door a second after I knocked. I hadn't arranged to call round – it was just on the off-chance – and she looked surprised for a second. Then she gave me a huge smile followed by one of her hugs.

'Hey you.'

I closed my eyes and rubbed her back.

'Watch the arm,' she said.

'Oh, sorry.'

'No, that's okay where you are.'

We moved apart a moment later.

'How have you been?' she asked.

'Me? I'm okay. It's you I've been worried about. How are you?'

'I'm fine.'

She put the kettle on, and then I followed her through to the lounge, where she settled down on the settee.

'It's good to be home,' she said.

'Good to have you home. I came to see you a couple of times at Staunton.'

'I remember.'

I sat down beside her. She turned to face me, bringing one leg up under the other and resting her elbow on the back of the settee.

'How's Rob?' she said.

'Up and moving about. Still as annoying as ever.'

I'd spoken to him the night before. We'd been forced to put the magazine on hold while he was in hospital, and now he was on his feet again he was keen to get back to it. I hadn't decided whether that was going to happen or not. We had a hell of a scoop on Thom Stanley – bigger than we'd ever expected – but I wasn't convinced that running with it was for the best. For one thing, the *Skeptic* had received a letter from Stanley's lawyers, making it clear that any hint their client might have known about the murders would find us sailing into dangerous waters.

The threat didn't particularly bother me, as I had our conversation on tape. But still, I wasn't sure I wanted to go back into those waters myself. While clearing out my parents' house, I'd realised that I needed to think about where I was in my life, and whether I might prefer to be somewhere else before too long. And after everything that had happened, I thought I might.

'Choc?' I said. 'How's he doing?'

'I've not seen him.'

'Right.'

We talked for a while about what had happened, without mentioning the events themselves. They were the black centre of our conversation, but for now they remained oblique, only glimpsed through the repercussions and consequences. How is this person? What did you do then? What did the police say? She asked if I was okay again; I did the same. The shape of what happened was revealed as we coloured information in around it, but neither of us ventured further.

'Oh, I forgot the kettle.' She got up. 'Coffee okay?'

'Yeah, that'd be great.'

I watched her walk out of the lounge. When she brought the cups back through a minute later, I took mine and put it down on the table, then reached into my coat.

'Just remembered,' I said. 'I've got something for you.'

I held the cross and let the chain dangle over my hand.

Her eyes lit up. 'Oh God. I thought it was lost.'

'No.'

'Put it on for me.'

She turned around on the settee and pulled her hair up in a bunch. I moved a little closer and reached to either side to get the chain around. My wrist nearly brushed the bare skin of her shoulder above the straps on her blouse, but not quite. I fastened the clasp.

'There.'

'I'm so glad.'

She picked up the cross between finger and thumb and turned it around, gazing down at it.

'Thank you,' she said.

'No problem.'

I sipped the coffee and realised I didn't care where this day was going. I wasn't feeling jealous or possessive about her, or pining anymore. I did feel close to her, though, and whatever form it took, that was the important thing. There had been nothing to be nervous about. It was just good to see her again after all this time.

'Hey,' I said. 'While I remember . . .'

I took out my mobile. The police had returned my old phone to me a couple of weeks ago, but I hadn't touched it since. It had seemed sensible to get a new one, and I suspected Tori had done the same.

'I've got a new mobile,' I said.

'Ooh, me too.' She picked her own phone up off the coffee table. 'You'll be wanting my number, then?'

I smiled at her.

'Yeah,' I said. 'I will.'